THE SNAP

THE SNAP

A NOVEL

ELIZABETH STAPLE

DOUBLEDAY NEW YORK

Copyright © 2024 by Elizabeth Staple

All rights reserved. Published in the United States by
Doubleday, a division of Penguin Random House LLC, New York,
and distributed in Canada by Penguin Random House
Canada Limited, Toronto.

doubleday.com

DOUBLEDAY and the portrayal of an anchor with
a dolphin are registered trademarks of Penguin Random House LLC.

Book design by Soonyoung Kwon
Jacket images: (stadium) dlewis33 / Getty Images;
(blood) Mrspopman1985 / Shutterstock; (name tag) Jariya / Adobe Stock
Jacket design by Madeline Partner

Library of Congress Cataloging-in-Publication Data
Names: Staple, Elizabeth, 1984– author.
Title: The snap : a novel / Elizabeth Staple.
Description: First edition. | New York : Doubleday, [2024].
Identifiers: LCCN 2023040435 | ISBN 9780593686171 (hardcover) |
ISBN 9780593686188 (ebook)
Subjects: LCSH: Women sports executives—United States—Fiction. |
Sexual harassment in sports—United States—Fiction. | Football teams—
United States—Fiction. | Murder—Fiction. | Suspense fiction.
Classification: LCC PS3619.T3674 S63 2024 | DDC 813/.6—dc23/eng/20240116
LC record available at https://lccn.loc.gov/2023040435

MANUFACTURED IN THE UNITED STATES OF AMERICA

1 3 5 7 9 10 8 6 4 2

First Edition

For Arthur

PART 1

IN LOVING MEMORY

Red Guillory

SYRACUSE, N.Y.—Beloved Syracuse Bobcats head coach Red Guillory died on September 30 at the age of 51.

Guillory was born in Harrisburg, Penn. He was a star linebacker at Baylor University, where he earned All-American honors in both his junior and senior seasons. A first-round draft pick by Seattle, he helped the team to two conference finals and a Super Bowl before persistent knee injuries ended his playing career.

Guillory pivoted to coaching, beginning as a defensive assistant with Seattle before working his way up to Bobcats head coach at age 36. With two Super Bowl championships, three conference finals and seven division titles, Guillory is the winningest head coach in franchise history.

Guillory was also a giant in the Syracuse community. Known for his philanthropy, he spearheaded the Bundle Up Bobcats winter coat drive in partnership with Wegmans. His annual Red Rover, Red Rover field days raised more than $4 million in charitable contributions to Central New York youth sports programs.

The entire Bobcats organization mourns the passing of Coach Guillory, and extends its deepest condolences to his wife, Lexi, son, Connor, and daughter, Kelsey. We share our grief with all Bobcats, past and present, as well as the whole of Bobcats Nation.

NOW

A frigid October rain beat against my office windows as I read through the team statement again. I was looking for anything that could be given the pull-quote treatment or taken damagingly out of context, but it was as benign as it had been on the last fifteen reviews. Still, I swapped *grief* out for *sadness*. Wouldn't want to sound hysterical.

My cursor hovered over the word *died*. Even as I edited his obituary, it wasn't sinking in that Red Guillory was gone. Over the past fifteen years he'd become such an indelible part of Bobcats football that when he closed his eyes, the stadium should have disappeared in a puff of smoke. Sitting here without him—doing our work, preparing for the next game—was like swapping out the sun for a flashlight and pretending nothing had changed.

An invisible paragraph hovered, full of stomach-twisting details I wouldn't be putting in the release. That Red's death was being treated as suspicious. That he'd bled out over a period of hours. That he'd surely suffered.

"Hi, Poppy." Chloe the Intern walked to my desk without poking her head in or pausing at the doorway. She'd been calling me by my first name since we shook hands at her interview, when I'd had to suck my automatic "Please, call me Poppy" back from midair before it humiliated us both.

She leaned on the edge of the desk, long, elegant fingers splayed. They matched her pale, waiflike body. A curtain of cornsilk hair hung almost to her waist, where the tiniest slip of milk-colored skin flashed whenever she lifted her arms.

"I'm on my way down to the pressroom to set up. Did you want me to change out the background? I could find something black?"

"Why would we do that?"

"Well, you know, the red and the white are kind of bright. Like, for today. With everything."

Back when I'd been in Chloe's seat, I would never have made that suggestion to the director of media relations—which, I reminded myself firmly, was the great thing about this generation. They didn't wait patiently to be asked, they spoke up, and that meant their voices were heard.

Even when they themselves were wearing winter-white pants and an electric teal blouse.

I set my face to a soft neutral, my voice to mentorship warm.

"We want to use the team colors right now because it sets a scene, it visually signals to our fans that we're in this together. This clip is going to be replayed for years and years, so we want something that looks timeless but also brand-forward. But mostly," I smiled, the effort of it making my head pound, "it's what Coach Guillory would have wanted."

*

Less than five minutes after I blasted the statement to our distribution list, the light on my phone blinked.

"It's Bernie," called our admin, Edward, from his desk outside my office.

"Got it." As always, I took a moment to prepare. Let my eyes sweep across the top of the bookcase and its miniature skyline of trophies and awards. Focused on the framed feature from *Inc.* magazine picturing me in a power suit, arms crossed, under a headline screaming IT'S ALL ABOUT MS. BENJAMIN. I slid open my desk drawer to peek at the Post-it note I'd left for myself that read *Slow. Confident. Calm.* Then I smirked as I raised the receiver, because it's scientifically proven that expressions can be heard over the phone. "What's the matter—you found a typo?"

"No, it's not about that. Shit, though—I still can't believe it, Poppy."

"I know."

A dog barked in the background, and the image of Bernie's home office bloomed—a small room with seventies-style wood paneling near the back of the split-level he shared with his wife, Sheila. From his desk, he'd be able to see out to the pool deck where we'd celebrated her Hawaiian-themed sixtieth birthday.

"Fifty-one! That's a kid. He wasn't sick, was he? He always seemed so . . . robust."

"I haven't gotten any details."

It was half true. When our general manager called before dawn, he'd been characteristically direct: *Red's dead—Lexi found him this morning. She's saying it's murder, but since her criminology degree is from fucking Blue's Clues, let's keep a lid on that until the adults get there.*

I knew Asbel well enough to know he wasn't as dismissive of Lexi's theory as he sounded, and he certainly wouldn't waste time having me bury rumors he thought were untrue.

"Listen," Bernie was saying, "I know how petty this is going to sound, and I'm sure you don't want to be dealing with anything extra right now—"

"That's correct."

"—but Twitter picked up the Raj thing, and my editor wants me to write something on it."

"Seriously? Today?"

"You've met Bob. He's like a face tattoo that says MAKE GOOD CHOICES."

"Okay, well, Raj is a full moron—maybe clue Bob in on that."

"That's why he wants me to write it—Raj gives great quotes. And your team's one and three. There hasn't been a lot else to write about. Until today," Bernie allowed, with a note of guilt.

"Is that why you floated the idea of firing Red last week? Nice headline, by the way—IS IT TIME FOR A BOBCATS RED WEDDING?"

"I don't write the headlines, and that was a fair article, Poppy. I'll tell you what, though, I have reflux over it—terrible. The whole thing is terrible."

"Don't be too rough on yourself."

"If you really want to make an old man feel better, what are the odds I can get Raj on the phone?"

"Not great, Bern." I reached for a pile of mail at the corner of my desk and flipped through. Tinged as everything was today with shock and grief, this was my actual job, and it felt good to be doing it rather than figuring out how many buses we'd need to get two hundred employees to a funeral. "I've already talked to Raj, and he's apologized to the school. He's going to sponsor their spring science fair, where the top prize will go to a project that demonstrates the earth is *not* flat. It's a non-issue."

A small envelope slipped out the bottom of the pile. It was handwritten, with a return address somewhere called Truth or Consequences, New Mexico. My brow creased. I didn't know anyone in New Mexico. I checked the postmark, but it was smeared, and as Bernie went on about clicks and podcast streams, I pulled open the envelope. It gave easily, like it hadn't been properly sealed, and a small paper maybe twice the size of a Post-it fluttered to my desk.

The message was only a few words, cryptic little things. Weighed against the more bombastic fan mail—just last week there'd been a three-page rager on our helmet redesign from someone who'd had the prior version tattooed on his head—it was hardly eyebrow raising.

I know what you did.
Tell the truth or pay the consequences.
You have five days.

It was one out of a thousand weird letters and phone calls that came to the stadium every season, but this one came on the same day that Red Guillory was found dead. And in fifteen years, it was the first addressed to me.

"So, anyway," Bernie said, "if you could make some of the position coaches available for us, it would help fill in the gaps until a new head—interim head, whatever—is named. And Mel is going to speak too, right? Do you know when that's going to be yet? Is he releasing an owner's statement, or does the team statement apply to everyone? And what about Asbel? Actually, if I could pick between Mel and Asbel, I'd probably take Mel because he's really starting to lose it and there's a good chance he'll—"

"Bern. I'm going to have that for you soon, but we haven't made any decisions yet. I'm sure you understand this is all a shock and we're figuring it out as we go. But we'll get a schedule out shortly."

As I hung up my work phone, my cell danced across the desktop. Texts to the group chat.

I can't believe it. I'm in meetings all day but call if you need to. That was Annika.

I'm in total shock, wrote Sarah. *Just completely stunned. How are you functioning?*

Are you still going tonight? And would you rather reschedule this weekend?

It was Dayanna's message that snapped me out of it. Of course I was going tonight, and how could she think I would miss the weekend? People were depending on me.

I'm fine. The period at the end of my text did its job, and the group chat fell silent.

I let the note and its envelope flutter into my overflowing trash can, then put my head down on my desk for a slow count to ten. Then I sat up, blinked hard, and turned my attention to the impossible business of navigating Bobcats football without Red Guillory.

CHAPTER TWO

FIFTEEN YEARS AGO

The internship started on a Wednesday.

I had to be there by seven a.m., which explained why I was stumbling around my new apartment—the second floor of the home of Dave and Flossie Anderson, lovers of Camel cigarettes and Precious Moments figurines, respectively—at ten minutes before six. At twenty-two years old, I'd *been* up this early, but never *woken* up this early, and the drowsiness mixed with first-day anxiety left me wobbly. I fumbled with the buttons of my Zara dress, shrugged into my blazer, and added a headband on my way out the door.

There was plenty of signage leading from the highway to Micrans Stadium, and I followed it into an ocean of asphalt parking lots where the stadium rose from the ground like a massive silver spaceship.

This was where I worked.

Now that I was here, pulling into the "staff only" parking area, everything felt alarmingly real. I could already imagine tonight's text from my dad (*"How to go, kiddo!"*). He'd want every detail—who I'd met, what I'd done. How I fit into it all. Dad was a high school coach, and our football was grass stains and bootlegs. This was a billion-dollar industry that drew a hundred million viewers. When I took a last look at the hulking stadium, a sunbeam bounced off the upper deck, a mocking wink.

The lobby had thick carpeting and plush seats, and while I waited I cycled through positions: shoulders back, hands folded at knee, feet together. Straight back listing left, elbow not-so-casually on arm of chair. I was experimenting with my purse on my lap and one hand through the strap when the revolving door spun and admitted a stocky guy about my age with the preppy confidence of someone who knew his way around a boat. *Another intern,* I thought, my heart lifting, *thank God.* Then I noticed the red Bobcats ID clipped to his belt loop, strained to read it, and looked up to see the puzzled smirk of someone wondering why a stranger was staring at his waistband. Before I could stammer anything guaranteed to make the situation worse, the guy saved me from myself, gave an awkward laugh, and walked on.

Any confidence I'd been faking was shot, and I gripped the arms of the chair like I was about to be launched into space. At the sound of a whistle traveling down the hallway, I pressed my shoes hard into the carpet, and a moment later the whistle entered the lobby, its source a blond man with skin so tanned he resembled a burnt roll.

"You're Poppy," he said as we shook hands. From the way his hairline inched up, I guessed he was in his late forties, and his teeth were unnaturally, distractingly white. "Poppy Benjamin. Man— that might be the most football coach's daughter's name I've ever heard."

"My mom is southern," I said by way of explanation.

"Got it, got it. It's cool, though. I mean—Brent. Also weird."

I didn't think my name was weird, but I forced a laugh.

"I'll tell you what," he went on, "I'd rather be the swimsuit judge at Miss Medicare than get here this early. But that's why we have you, right? Let's walk."

The offices were surprisingly corporate. I didn't know what I'd expected—Astroturf carpets and people walking around in helmets?—but other than the hulking stadium attached to the building, it could have been any other workplace. Media Relations had its own annex through two secured doorways, and Brent paused to scan a badge at each. "Your badge—we'll get that next—is all-access, since you're going to be doing papers and press clips. They have to be on Mel Aberford's desk by the time he gets in, and he's a thousand so that's early. Like, grapefruit juice early. I'd shoot for six thirty, just to keep it tight."

"Yes, for sure," I said quickly, recognizing the name of the team's owner. To get here by six thirty, I'd have to leave my apartment no later than five forty-five, a thought that made my teeth ache.

Over the next few hours, Brent shared a thousand details—the weekly schedule, how to use the giant copier, the credentialing process. I itched to take notes, but he spoke so confidently ("And you know, obviously, a season credential would be for legacy media, national guys, people like that, but we use day passes for the rest—unless they're in the division or we'll probably see them in the play-offs. And then for the photographers . . ."). I nodded and nodded and nodded, because I so badly wanted to be someone who just got it.

And the introductions—I'd had no idea how many people worked here, and it didn't help that Brent threw out nicknames like a Russian novelist. "B-rad," he said, high-fiving one man in the hall. "Meet Poppy B." I resorted to a trick my dad used with incoming freshmen and gave everyone an alliteration anchor. Just Julie was the sour-faced media relations admin who closed her office door without saying a word. Reedy Richard for the tall, thin director with his wire-rimmed glasses and graying auburn hair. Unlike Julie, he stopped to talk, but his eyes never left the bulky Nokia in his hand.

"Normally we'd start you slow in training camp," he said, "but you're going to have to pick things up fast and pitch in. Brent handles the day-to-day with the beat writers—locker room access, press conferences, interview requests. And Julie," he raised his chin toward the closed door, "keeps us all in line. She's the real boss around here. Do you have a boyfriend?"

"I . . . no."

Richard sighed, like he figured I'd say that. "It's easier if the girls do, but that's okay. You might want to buy tops one size up, though." He circled his palm in front of his chest. "Just to avoid any issues."

I forced myself to nod, to smile, but my burning cheeks betrayed me. This dress fit, but I wouldn't call it *fitted*—was it? And the neckline—maybe it was college-fine but not professional-fine. I snuck a glance at Julie's door, wishing for the kind of look that women give each other to say *that's gas you're smelling, but I've got you.* She didn't exactly seem the type.

"Oh, and the DeMario thing—" Richard began, but just then the landline in his office rang, a sputtering tone with an extra beep echoed at the end. Richard all but ran for his desk and snatched up the receiver. "Asbel, hi."

"The GM," Brent said from the corner of his mouth. "Never pick up when it's his extension—he doesn't want to talk to you—but *make sure* Julie or Richard gets it before the third ring. Very, very important."

"What happens if they don't?"

Brent clapped me on the shoulder. "You get fired." He laughed like he was joking, and then trailed off like he wasn't.

*

The pressroom was at field level, directly below the offices. It was only ten minutes until availability, and so I should have turned left out of the elevator, but instead I went right, toward the bowels of the stadium. It was dark here, cool and cave-like, with cement floors and exposed industrial piping. As I hurried past a row of empty equipment carts and the huge bay where the team buses pulled in before games, the click of my heels echoed, syncopated against the *drip drip* of something above me. I followed the sounds of grunts and whistles, the stomach-twisting crack of helmet against helmet, to where light spilled into the hallway from a pass-through, and when I reached it, 120 yards of green bloomed.

Coaches prowled the sidelines in athletic shorts and aviator shades, whistles dangling from their lips. On the field, black practice jerseys flashed against white as the groups moved through their drills. The quarterbacks, in their red no-contact jerseys, stood with their position coach, who jammed his index finger at something on his clipboard. I pressed myself against the cement wall of the tunnel because I wasn't supposed to be here, but I couldn't help it. I needed to watch.

I don't think I'm supposed to love this as much as I do. Seeing the needle thread of an eleven-inch ball spiral for fifty yards before precision landing on a fingertip gives me the same helium feeling in my chest that other people get from a power ballad. It's an earned miracle that fills me to my edges until I *have* to scream, I *have* to cheer, because watching that kind of thing silently could kill a person. So far, using the laminating machine upstairs did not have the same effect. It felt miles away from here, from the grass. I breathed in deeply, trying to catch the scent of it, but it was FieldTurf and only smelled like the little rubber pellets that flew into the air every time someone hit the ground.

Back in the pressroom I hurried to the podium to place my tape recorder near the microphone. It was already surrounded, and I was trying to decide if I should layer or nudge when someone grabbed the recorder in the center and dumped it at the podium's edge. "You're the new intern?"

I nodded. "Hi—Poppy."

"Bernie. You make the transcripts, that means your recorder goes right there. We want the best audio, because I am not typing this out for myself."

"Oh, okay. Thanks for moving yours."

Bernie pointed to one still in place near the middle. "That's mine."

"The most important thing about the transcript," said a bearded man in a Springsteen T-shirt, "is to get it up as fast as possible. The last intern typed like a toddler with broken fingers."

"Toddlers can spell a lot better than that intern," said a reporter in jeans and a checked blazer. He didn't introduce himself, but according to his credential, his name was Steven and he wore that blazer a lot.

I tried to cover my absolute horror at them talking about me this way next season by pivoting the conversation. "Oh, do you have kids?" I asked Steven.

"Probably."

Then the room fell silent as Brent walked in, followed closely by Red Guillory.

I'd expected Coach Guillory to look like my dad, but he was much younger, almost young enough to be one of the players. With bright, expressive eyes and cropped black hair, he could have been sort of hot—in a nineties-action-hero kind of way—except that his nose looked like it had bounced off two helmets going in different directions. He leaned forward to grip the sides of the podium with both hands and said into the microphone with a boyish grin, "You guys got any questions for me today?"

Bernie raised a finger and Brent nodded to him. "Red, talk a little bit about Chicago's secondary. Is that something you're concerned about, with such a young corps of receivers?" *Concerned about young receivers??* I wrote in my little notebook.

Coach Guillory nodded. "You know, we like our guys, we trust our guys. We've seen some good things out of them through camp, so I think they're going to be okay. This is a real test for them straight out of the gate, but with A.J. in there controlling the huddle they're in some of the best hands in the NFL." He flashed his teeth. "If they can't make something happen with a quarterback like that, it doesn't matter who's in the secondary."

As the questions flowed, I had to keep consciously bringing my focus back, to make sure I was actually *doing* the job instead of geeking out about finally being here. Five months earlier I would have still been in my dorm, hand slamming into my nightstand while I blindly reached for the Tylenol to combat the effects of Thirsty Thursdays. There should be a program for easing slowly and safely into adulthood, like the way astronauts return from space in stages so their legs don't crash out from under them.

After I'd filled three pages, Brent called out, "Last question for Coach," and then, pointing to Steven, "Steve-O—go."

"I guess I'm going to be the one to say it," he said with a little shrug and a glance at the wall of cameras. "Expectations are high here, given the success of the last two seasons, and then the team Asbel Perez has put together during the off-season. How do you handle that pressure, or respond to that—or I guess, how do those expectations filter into what you're trying to accomplish in the locker room?"

Coach took his time with this answer, waiting so long that I was able to mark down the entire question. At first I thought he was thrown and needed to gather his thoughts, but the way he stood there, brow smooth and open, was too calm, too confident for that. As the seconds ticked audibly past from the gym-class-style clock on the back wall, I realized he was doing it on purpose. Coach was milking the moment until the silence was complete and every person in the room had drawn forward, like we were being sucked in by his very breath.

"Steven," Coach said finally, "what you're talking about are outside expectations and outside pressure, and I realize that's what gets people buzzing, but it doesn't have anything to do with us back there." He hitched his thumb toward the locker room. "For us, we go into every season expecting to win every game we play, and that makes this year no different. We're going to focus on our work and our preparation. We're going to beat each other up a bunch in practice, and we're going to play sixteen one-game seasons." He stood up straight and grinned again. "But I will say this—we're undefeated right now, and I sure as hell don't plan to start losing."

*

"So," Brent said as we rode the elevator back upstairs, "the DeMario thing. DeMario Jackson? Top draft pick defensive end out of Illinois?" I nodded. "Richard wants a featured blog with him and I don't want to do it, so that means you've got your first assignment."

"Great." I stood up straight and clicked my pen—real work. "Should I ask him—"

"Oh, no. DeMario's not doing the blog. Just write it for him. Make it up."

The elevator dinged, and Brent headed down the hallway, me a half step behind. "But I've . . . never even spoken to him."

"Neither has anyone reading it. He's got a cockney accent and a hard-on for puns, for all they know."

Okay. Okay, blog with the team's marquee rookie who I had . . . probably *something* in common with, right? I could write about being new. I could write about . . . liking football. This would be fine.

At the annex, Brent straddled one of the vacant chairs by my desk, and I swung my seat around to face him. He snapped his fingers, then smacked his fist against the other palm, *click-thud, click-thud, click-thud.* "So like Richard said this morning—we're down a full-timer." Richard had not said that, but it explained why I was being brought on after training camp. "That means you're the coordinator now, congratulations. I mean, you're the intern, but . . ."

"I get it." Intern's stipend, no health insurance. I wondered what had happened with the actual coordinator, and who I might be able to ask.

"Incredible experience, though. There's not another intern in the league who'll get to do what you're doing." Brent grinned with Chiclet teeth. "And we can manage it. I mean, I'm great, Julie's great. Are you great?"

"I . . ."

"Poppy." Brent leaned closer, tilting his chair onto two legs. "Are you great?"

There were thirty-two teams in the NFL. Most media relations departments had a vice president, a director, and a coordinator, which meant ninety-six people in the entire world got to do this job—and you could guess how many of those were women.

I imagined forgetting to take off my Bobcats ID card and—oops—walking into a supermarket with it still hanging from my neck. I imagined going through the playoffs, living and dying with every snap, not just as a fan, but as someone on the inside, someone whose coworkers' *jobs* depended on whether the team won or lost. I imagined the pride in my dad's voice as he told everyone from his golfing buddies to his dentist what his youngest child was doing with herself these days.

I looked Brent straight in the eye and flashed my own, less brilliant smile. I felt my ponytail bounce against my shoulders as my head bobbed. "I'll be great."

CHAPTER THREE

NOW

I was a marionette, offering a tight-lipped smile here, a sympathetic grimace there, while inside my brain revved like tires in the mud. My entire adult life had been built around the routine of football season, where July meant training camp and March meant starting the new media guide, and every week in between was subdivided into a lockstep schedule grinding unforgivingly forward. Today was Friday, which should have meant the coach at the podium ahead of open locker room—but instead there was no coach, because he was dead.

The room was full to bursting, every chair taken plus an out-growth of bodies that pressed to the walls. There hadn't been this many people here since the run-up to our last Super Bowl, when a much younger version of myself had peered in from the anteroom and shivered at the assault of lights, the shortage of air. "The trick," Red had said then, coming up close behind me, "is to think of each set of eyeballs like a battery. They're not grabbing a piece of you, they're *giving* you what you need to get it done." Then he'd clapped me on the shoulder as he passed, arms swinging, stride confident and wide.

It was just me here now, and Red was gone. I stood behind the podium holding up a white piece of paper and leaning into the microphone, counting mechanically from one to ten. This should have been Chloe's job, but I wasn't about to put her up here in that shirt. It wasn't her fault. She hadn't known about Red until after she got to the stadium, and as I hit eight I realized I could have just grabbed her a hoodie from the pro shop. An entire store's worth of solutions, and it hadn't even crossed my mind. I needed to pull it together.

"Whadya think, Pop?" called Rodney, my second-in-command. I'd dispatched him to deal with the crush of newcomers, to handle the greetings and the questions and the minutiae while I did the important work, like counting to ten. He stood at the back of the room holding up his hand with fingers spread. "Five minutes?"

"If that." I leaned into the microphone. "Guys." The room instantly fell silent. "We should be ready to go here in about five minutes. Thanks."

I caught a glimpse of myself in one of the monitors, a somber, professional woman in all black. My long dark hair was knotted in a low bun, and my skin, always pale, looked ghostly today, white marble with blue veins. Over the years I'd trained my wide, expressive hazel eyes to go flat and doll-like, to give nothing away. Today there was nothing for them to hide. I was empty.

I shifted my gaze to look out over the sea of people and try to draw energy from them the way Red did. To feel them fill and lift and bolster me until I could do this. But it didn't work. Whatever magic he'd bottled, whatever alchemy he'd found, it worked only for him.

*

My inbox was on fire. I'd instructed Edward to run interference on any phone calls, but I could still hear it ring, over and over again. "Sorry, Poppy," he said as he squared a stack of message slips to the outer corner of my desk around seven. Edward compensated for his height and surprisingly deep baritone by speaking softly, and the effect, even on a day like today, was soothing. He sounded like a late-night radio host from the kind of show that faded and then caught again as endless miles of highway unfurled beneath the tires. "I handled everything I could, but some of them only want to talk to—"

"It's okay. Thank you. You should get out of here—I'm just going to be catching up on some stuff for a little longer."

"Anything I can help with?"

"Nope."

He hovered for a beat, then knocked his knuckle twice on the desk, pressed his lips together, and left.

The next time I looked up, blue-light glasses perched at the end of my nose, it was nine thirty. The rest of the annex was dark. A vacuum hummed from somewhere on the other side of the secured door, but otherwise the building was quiet. Everyone was gone, home to their families or out to a bar, or wherever else could help them process the unimaginable truth that Red Guillory was dead.

I had other plans.

From a garment bag on the back of my office door I removed a midnight-blue gown embellished with a dusting of sparkles. I have the shape of a retired opera singer—short and compact but spreading, my hourglass curves, so effortlessly tight in my younger years, softer now, like a Band-Aid that's been peeled off and reapplied. For a minute I imagined changing into cashmere-blend lounge pants, closing my eyes above the cool eucalyptus scent of my retinol patches while a weighted blanket anchored me to my bed. I sighed, shook off the vision, and yanked down the dress's stiff zipper.

Ten minutes later my hair was loose, my heels were swapped out for a swankier pair, and I'd layered new, darker eye shadow over the old. I had just flipped the light switch when something tickled the base of my neck. The office was silent, save for the metronomic tick of the gold clock on my bookshelf. My eyes swept over the empty chair, the cluttered but organized desktop, searching for the source of my unease. They landed on the recycling bin. Clicking my tongue, I crossed to it quickly and tried to squat, but my mermaid gown wouldn't allow it, so instead I lifted the entire bin and set it on my desk. I pushed past transcripts from earlier and a notice from HR offering bereavement services until I found the handwritten envelope. I pulled out the note and stared hard at it, running my thumb over the ink. Then, with a huff of frustration at myself, I slid it back into the envelope, opened my clutch, and stuffed it inside.

*

On the short drive to the Syracuse Aquarium, the words of the note rolled around my head.

I know what you did.

Tell the truth or pay the consequences.

You have five days.

It had to be a coincidence that this note came today. When you read something like that on the same morning a dead body is found, the *what you did* part jumps right out. But I hadn't done anything. The words meant nothing to me. And yet the note kept buzzing, a fly trapped inside the car, and I felt safer somehow knowing it was nearby, where no one else could see it.

"Here, thanks." I handed my keys to a valet and hurried past a tripoded sign announcing the Salt City Women's Annual Gala. The rain had stopped, but the ground was wet with cold, dark spots that threatened to turn into ice as the temperature dropped.

The main wall of the ballroom was a floor-to-ceiling shark tank, dimly lit in shades of blue and purple. Pale creatures glided out of the darkness before disappearing back into the gloom with a flick of their tails. The opposite wall of windows overlooked the inky black of Onondaga Lake, and the ballroom felt suspended between them. I spotted Faith Jackson with two other women at a high-top near a carving station. I'd known her for a long time now, ever since she'd started dating our star defensive end. Now DeMario was the team's co-captain, and he and Faith had three boys under seven who all called me "Miss Pop."

"Hey!" Faith said when I approached, dark eyes wide with surprise. "You didn't have to come tonight—I mean, I assumed you wouldn't."

"Oh, no, I'm fine." I pretended not to notice Faith's frown and extended a firm hand to the other women. "Hi—Poppy Benjamin, Bobcats media relations director."

"Ashley," said a woman with an inch of dark roots and a small compass tattoo on her wrist. "And this is Corynne. We're both with the Northside Animal Shelter."

"Oh, with the hang-in-there billboards? I love those."

The women exchanged sharp glances, and Ashley put a hand on Corynne's arm. "Those are for the Animal Shelter of North Syracuse. People conflate them, but they're a kill shelter and we—"

"—would *never* do that," said Corynne flatly.

Fuck.

"Of course you wouldn't. I'm so sorry. Today has been . . . extremely challenging, and I'm still a little out of it." I inhaled shakily for good measure and was horrified that my throat really did thicken, like it had been waiting all day for permission to do so. Well, permission denied. I raised my chin and pressed my tongue against the roof of my mouth, while both women's expressions instantly softened.

"We were just telling Faith, we are so, so sorry about Coach Guillory." Corynne had a dark bob that was shorter in the back than the front, and it shook when her hand went to her chest. "I couldn't believe it when my husband told me. He's been crying all day."

"It's been a hard one." I cleared my throat. "But it would mean so much to Coach Guillory to know what an impact he'd had on the Syracuse community."

"I mean, he *is* Syracuse, you know?" said Ashley. "Or—shit, was. I just can't wrap my brain around it. Fifty-one!"

"You know," Faith cut in, her palm at my elbow, "we're talking about this and I'm thinking, man, this girl has really earned a drink today. Let's go fix that empty hand, Poppy. We'll see you guys at the table?"

"Do you want my job?" I asked once we were a few steps away. "Because that was impressive." We were walking along the tank, and the movements within coupled with my too-high shoes threw me off-balance. I reached out a hand to steady myself against the glass, then yanked it back when a gaping mouth slid into view.

"Uh, pass. One of my husband is plenty, thank you. I don't know how you deal with eighty of him."

"Eighty DeMarios would be fine. How's he doing, by the way?"

". . . Okay? Stressing about what to say, because everybody in there's looking at him." I understood that "there" meant the locker room. "If it was anyone else, he'd—"

"—ask Red," we finished together.

"But you know D. He'll come through. How are *you* doing?"

"I'm fine, really. I'm sure it will hit me at some point, but today was busy and tonight's busy and tomorrow's busy, so I'm fine."

"Hey." Faith stopped, and my heart rate kicked up because I was holding it together, but that didn't mean I could keep holding it together. A waiter walked by with a glass of merlot on his tray, the thick, sticky color of blood on floorboards, and for one terrifying second my lower lip wobbled. Then Faith indicated her dress, a black tea-length gown with slashes of yellow. Her lipstick was an impressive scarlet, and her hair was slicked back into a tight bun at the nape of her neck. "Can I ask you—does this make me look like one of the fish?"

My first real smile of the day bloomed. "In the *best* way."

Once I had my vodka soda, we found our seats. The surface of the table was so covered by the elaborate place settings that there was no room for my phone, so I tucked it between my right thigh and the chair. Directly across the table from me, a man I vaguely recognized from the State Fair planning committee was trying to meet my eye, but I snapped a placid expression on my face and turned toward the stage, relieved that for the next hour I wouldn't have to talk to anyone.

Local news personality Donna Boyer was MCing, and she stood in a disco ball of a dress holding a collection of note cards.

I gripped my clutch, my own little note buried inside, as Donna flashed startlingly white teeth. "We're here tonight to celebrate the incredible women in our community who are reaching back and lifting up the ones behind them, especially our Sister Stella Zuccolillo honorees—Mirror Mirror Bridal and Rainbow Papers. And I'm so happy to see so many *men* in the room, because supporting and furthering the careers of women is not just a women's issue. So good job, guys."

I broke off part of a roll and popped it into my mouth as a polite ripple of laughter and applause moved through the audience. It was the first thing I'd eaten since lunch, and for one million dollars I couldn't have said what that meal was.

Donna's pretty face grew serious. "This is a cause we want to celebrate, but of course it's a tough day for that, because as a community we are hurting. Syracuse lost one of its icons today, and I know that many of us don't particularly feel like celebrating."

The roll turned to dust between my teeth. I could sense Faith trying to catch my eye and looked away. Beneath the table, I folded my hands in my lap and squeezed them together so hard that they vibrated.

"It's tough," Donna acknowledged, "it's really tough. But in the spirit of tonight, and in the spirit of this amazing organization, I want to acknowledge someone who is experiencing this loss as sharply and as fully as any of us."

Oh no.

"This person has been a lifelong champion of women in the ultimate male-dominated field. She was an early infiltrator and has kept that door open behind her. She seeks out female interns. She is a role model, and a mentor, inside and outside of her organization. If we need an auction item—and there are some great ones tonight, I'm telling you all right now—this woman is there with a donation that knocks our socks off. She's here tonight, and we want to support and lift her up as much as she has supported us—Ms. Poppy Benjamin! Poppy, where are you? Stand up!"

Deep vertigo split my center as I stood and arranged my lips in a demure smile. The entire room stood too, turned to me, applauding. Some wiped tears that I knew were for Red—it was all for Red, this outpouring of emotion, of gratitude. I was just the conduit for what a city in mourning wished it could say to its fallen hero. "Thank you," I mouthed to each side of the room. "Thank you."

When it was finally over and I sank back into my seat, Faith reached her hand out to squeeze mine. Her palm was warm, and I could feel her trying to press some comfort and strength into me, and I couldn't take it, I couldn't be here for one more second. I broke away and pushed back from the table. "Bathroom."

My pace stayed brisk but controlled until I made it to the ladies' room, where I slammed the button on the hand dryer. At a loss for what else to do, I slammed it again and again, until it got stuck, and a constant stream of hot air blasted from the nozzle.

Fuck this day. The boning in my dress had broken through and was skewering my ribs just below the bra line. The lights hurt my eyes. I needed to get out of here. I thought of where I really wanted to go, and a small sob escaped because that was closed to me, now more than ever. Now for good. I would go home, to my empty apartment, where the automatic thermostat had surely reset itself to sixty-five *again.* I would put on that certain pair of sweatpants I'd kept, so oversized that even with the drawstrings pulled tight they barely stayed above my hips, and crawl between cold sheets where I could finally cry while no one needed anything from me.

Two short, firm breaths later, I was ready to go back, but I'd barely made it past the water fountains when Ashley came out of the ballroom, eyes scanning.

"Oh, great, there you are. I hate to ask this, I'm sure it's been just the worst day, but a lot of our donors have been asking to meet you. Do you think you're up for it? Just a few? It's the Red thing, you know, they—"

"Of course." My eyes were flat again, my lips stretched wide. "Of course, whatever you need."

*

I couldn't get away before the gala's bitter end, when the lights came on and the band packed its instruments away. Even then, waiting in the scrum near the coat check, I shifted from one sore foot to the other while the owner of a local restaurant chain known for its chicken tenders held forth about Red.

"You know, it's been a tough few years," he was saying, "we got spoiled. Those Super Bowls, all the playoff runs. I love it as a Bobcats fan, and when you run a sports bar it's money in your pocket, too. Everybody wins, right? Right?" He elbowed me directly on the broken boning, his braying laugh covering my gasp. "But we're loyal, we bleed Bobcats red. Anything the team ever needs, we could collaborate. Actually, do you know who I would talk to about stadium concessions? We've been trying to get our foot in there since the nineties."

I was just about to rattle off our fan club phone number when my clutch shook as the cell phone within vibrated—never a good sign after midnight, and my stomach sank further once I recognized the number. "I'm so sorry, I have to take this." I ducked into the ballroom, where the lights were on and the staff was breaking down the tables. I pressed one ear closed with my middle finger to block out the noise. My back straightened, my voice deepened. Notwithstanding my gown and heels, I might well have been back at my desk. "Poppy Benjamin."

"Poppy, it's Sandra. Things got messy and the police are coming. He wasn't involved, but he's here and I figured—"

"I'm on my way."

Shit, shit, shit. I abandoned my wrap at the coat check and headed straight outside. "Just give me the keys—I'll find it," I told the startled valet. My car was near the back of the lot, and I jogged before breaking into as much of a run as I could manage. The exit was clogged with tipsy donors heading home, so I drove the wrong way out the entrance and merged onto the highway.

Downtown was still bustling, the turning point of a Friday night when one wave was going home and a smaller, rougher crowd was heading out. People lingered at street corners, making threats or plans, while I willed the lights to work in my favor and rolled through stop signs without pressing the brake.

I slowed down outside a club with giant pink-neon lips out front and bright yellow letters between them that read LOOKY LOU'S. Some people were smoking by the door, but there were no cops yet—good. I pulled into the alley, where Sandra was waiting for me at the employee entrance. "I'll get him!" she called.

I hopped out and opened the passenger door before two burly men emerged carrying a third whose feet dragged lightly across the ground. His white shirt was soiled with something that had also splashed onto his sneakers, and his dark eyes rolled backward as the bouncers deposited him into my car. The air reeked back here, the antiseptic tinge of old vodka warmed and blasted outward by an industrial exhaust vent.

"Heeeeeey, Papi!" Our starting running back laughed at his own joke as I reached across his chest to click the seat belt in place.

"Alec."

I pulled out of the alley as fast as I could safely manage and was two streets away when we passed the police cruiser en route to Looky Lou's. I exhaled deeply. At least something had gone right today.

"Big night?" I merged back onto the highway, heading for the city's wealthy eastern suburbs. I was going for stern, but when my eyes darted sideways and met Alec's lazy grin, I couldn't help smiling back. I didn't want to think about what it said about me that I felt more comfortable driving through the city's late-night crowd and bailing out a drunk football player than I did with a bunch of movers and shakers at a gala.

"Needed it." He stretched his arms overhead, thick as gym class ropes and rippling with muscle. He was drunk, for sure, but much less than he'd acted while leaving the club. He'd wanted Sandra to call me. "Thanks for picking me up."

"Again," I retorted, but there was no heat behind it. "What was the fight about?"

"I don't know, I don't get into that shit. I was just vibing." He turned, apparently just noticing my outfit. "Sorry if I interrupted something. Where the hell were *you?*"

"Oh, Syracuse's hot new club—the aquarium. Going nuts with a bunch of donors. You're lucky you weren't in that fight—the hospital sponsored three tables, so half the doctors in this city are drunk on champagne."

"Not you, though."

"No. I had a feeling I might need to drive tonight." I kept my eyes on the road but felt Alec shift beside me. This wasn't the first, or fifth, or fiftieth time I'd swooped in to remove a Bobcats player from a sticky situation. We have good relationships with most of the clubs and hotels in town, and I can usually count on a call before things get embarrassing for the team. Alec was a different case, because he wasn't doing anything wrong. He just didn't want a record of his having been at a place like Looky Lou's.

"You know," I said, breaking the silence, "if you ever want to start going in the front door instead of the employee entrance, you'd have support."

"From *you.*"

"From a lot of people."

"Like A.J.?" he muttered.

"What's that supposed to mean?" I risked another glance over. "Has A.J. been giving you shit? Because that's not okay, Alec, I don't care who—"

"Oh, really? What are they going to do?" Alec took on an announcer's deep affectation. "'Thanks for the Super Bowls, A.J., but we're gonna have to cut you loose.' No, man—he's not going anywhere." I sighed, but he was right and we both knew it. "It's fine, Pop. It's no big deal, and I need that man to give me the ball."

I eased the car into Alec's circular drive and put it in park. "Can you get inside okay? I'll wait here to make sure."

He held out his fist for a bump and opened his door. Then, with one foot on the ground, he said, "He said the same thing you did— Red. About how I'd have support. I appreciate you both."

My gut spasmed as I watched Alec shuffle up his front walkway and navigate his key into the lock. He turned and flicked two fingers off his forehead in a salute, and I flashed my headlights before pulling out.

I was so tired my hair hurt. If I closed my eyes, if I could just—blink this all away, maybe I could undo it. Maybe we could go back to the way things were, the way they were supposed to be.

A sharp horn blared and I jumped, yanking the car back into the lane I'd drifted from because that's what ten seconds of self-pity brought. Of lack of focus. No more of that now. There was nothing to do but go home, go to bed, and hope that things somehow made more sense in the morning.

CHAPTER FOUR

FIFTEEN YEARS AGO

Friday morning I drove to work with my flashers on and my nose an inch from the windshield, begging my wipers to keep up with the assault of rain. Every passing truck doused my little Jetta in waves of muddy water, and by the time I pulled into the stadium fifteen minutes late I was shaking.

I ran through the parking lot, my shoes instantly soaked, retrieved the mail cart, and then headed back out into the storm. Water streamed down my hair and into my face as I bent to gather a sopping pile of newspapers, their pulp and ink scent set loose by the rain.

Back inside my shoes squelched, bursting the office's early-morning silence step after step like a toddler kicking a pew. Mascara ran in streaks to my neck, and my skin prickled against the air conditioning. Beneath my soaked white sweater I could clearly see the outline of my bra—and then some—and I still had ten hours of work ahead of me.

I was going to have to hold each of those papers under the bathroom hand dryers and hope there were enough salvageable copies to get through my delivery list. As I blasted them one after the other my pulse became a ticking clock while I fell to twenty minutes late, then twenty-five.

"Good lord," I said, catching myself in the mirror. A wet paper towel took care of most of the mascara, though it left my face red and splotchy. I tried fitting myself under the dryer, but the angle was impossible so I ran back to my desk and found the men's size-large Bobcats hoodie that Brent had given me yesterday ("Use a hair tie or whatever"). It looked ridiculous and fell almost to my knees, but it covered me, and I zipped it to my chin.

Mel Aberford's secretary took the dripping stack from me like I'd handed her a pile of racoon guts. She also had a sharp glance for my sweatshirt, but said nothing, and I went slinking off to the coaches' wing.

"Please be getting coffee, please be getting coffee," I muttered as I came up to Coach Guillory's office, but no such luck. He was at his desk wearing a white Bobcats performance shirt with red sleeves, and just as I stepped in the doorway he popped two pills into his mouth and swallowed them dry. I hitched, but he saw me and waved me in.

"Did you forget your swimmies today?" His voice was deep but pleasant, and his face split into an unexpected smile.

My ears prickled. "I'm—" I gestured down at myself, "so sorry about this. I don't normally wear . . ."

"Hey, I'm not getting on you for it." He laughed and indicated his own shirt.

It was warm in the office, and it smelled like greens and spice. The desk held a little rubber football and a framed photo of Coach with what I assumed was his family. The carpet was nicer in here, thicker, and the window looked out at Onondaga Lake in the distance. I tucked a soaking-wet strand of hair behind my ear and bit my lip. "Thanks," I said, meaning it. "Have a good da—"

"Where the fuck are the papers? Is the intern water-soluble, is that the problem here?"

At the sound of our general manager's voice booming down the hallway, my throat tightened. I didn't know whether to hurry out there and get him his papers or hide behind Coach Guillory's desk, and before I could decide, the voice came again. "Has anyone considered hiring someone who knows what the fuck they're doing? Instead of their friends' kids?"

That snapped me out of it. I didn't know anyone here, and neither did Hank and Nadine Benjamin of Arkana, Ohio, thank you very much. I'd earned my spot through four years in my college athletic communications department, unpaid summers working whatever events would take me in Toledo, and a lifetime of football following me home. I shot Coach an apologetic look and hurried from the office, but to my surprise, he followed directly after.

"Mr. Perez," he said, clapping a hand on the GM's shoulder. "I apologize—that's my fault. Poppy delivered my papers fifteen minutes ago, and I held her up talking."

More like two minutes ago. I willed my cheeks not to flush.

Asbel's lips twitched, but some of the fire left his eyes. "She was . . . with you?"

"Just some welcome-to-the-Bobcats chat." Coach Guillory grinned boyishly. "Since we're both newbies."

Asbel looked profoundly disappointed at being denied an ass to chew out. He took in my wet hair and hoodie, muttered, "I guess it's casual fucking Friday around here," and stalked off down the hallway.

"You didn't have to do that," I said quickly.

"Neither did he."

I pressed my lips into a thin smile, then nodded before hustling off with the remaining papers. It wasn't until I was swiping my way out of the coaches' wing before I thought to wonder how Coach Guillory knew my name.

*

The morning was a whirl of transcribing, copying, and mailing. Staff could use the dining hall downstairs, but only from eleven to twelve to ensure we didn't overlap with the players. The clock on my desktop flashed eleven forty-five, so I double-checked that my lanyard was around my neck and booked it down the stairs.

As I approached the bottom, I heard voices near the elevator bank.

"No, it goes Abby, Intern, Casey, Jen, Julie," said the first.

I froze. That was basically every woman who worked in the office. Did that make me "Intern"? I had to be. I held up and pressed myself against the wall.

"No, dude," said a second voice, "Intern, Abby, the reporter with the tattoo, Casey, Jen, Julie."

They were ranking us. I didn't even recognize these voices. They didn't even know my *name*.

"It's employees only," the first voice insisted. "And interns, because you can't leave an ass like that off the list."

"Oh, for sure." There was the slapping sound of a high five, followed by laughter. "If we're doing fronts, Abby's first, backs, Intern's first. Three-sixty cam, I'm going Abby."

There was a soft *ding*, and then the voices cut off as the elevator closed, but I was still anchored to the stairwell. My cheeks were on fire. Was I supposed to be flattered? Insulted? I was mostly just shocked—and grateful that they hadn't changed their minds and taken the stairs.

It was late by the time I got to the cafeteria, and so I threw whatever looked ready—a congealed slice of pizza and an apple—onto my tray and walked quickly toward the door. I would eat in the stairwell, where I wouldn't bother anyone and no one could look at me.

"*Hey.*"

I jumped, sending the apple tumbling from my tray. It went rolling and spinning along the floor. When I turned, a Jeep Cherokee of a man—hulking, bearded, Celtic cross tattooed on his neck—was staring down at me.

He jabbed a meaty finger at the clock on the wall. "It's 12:02. What the fuck are you doing in here?"

Everything went white. I looked wildly for the apple, but when I half turned to see if it was behind me, I remembered the comment about my ranking and whipped forward again. "Sorry—so sorry," I managed. "I was just—I'll—"

He held the terrifying expression a beat longer, then broke into a wheezing laugh. He clamped a hand the size of a child's mitt on my shoulder, knocking me further off-balance and sending the pizza to the edge of the tray. "I'm just fucking with you—don't worry about it." He walked off toward the grill station, chuckling to himself while the rest of the players filed in.

I righted my tray and blinked furiously. Okay. Okay, okay, okay. This was fine. Be cool, it was a joke. Did I want to be some invisible little mouse who everyone just ignored? *No.* That was . . . cool of him to tease me. Nice. It was a nice thing. Gets the heart rate up.

"Hey." The same word, but this time said through a smirk. I turned to see the guy from the lobby sitting with two other young people, who'd obviously just watched everything. "Oh, here." The guy unclipped his ID badge from his belt loop and held it up jokingly for my inspection. "Or I can stand up if you want?"

"Very funny." At least he knew what I'd been looking at and didn't think I was a sexual predator.

"Come on, come sit." I shuffled to their table and took the empty chair, trying to suck in great gulps of air to cool my cheeks without looking like a fish.

"I'm James," he said. He had a square jaw and thick brown hair that swooped across his forehead in a way that made me wonder if his ears were magnetic. "Have you met everyone yet? This is Abby. She's in marketing." The name pinged—Abby ranked one ahead or behind me, depending on who you asked, and now that I'd seen her myself I could firmly conclude that yes, I should be flattered. I caught her looking me up and down, but with soft eyes that seemed more curious than judgmental.

"And this is Mohammad—Mo—with IT."

"When," said Mo, a big man with impressive sideburns, "not if—*when* you mess up your computer, please promise you'll call me first before trying to fix it yourself. I've got a graveyard full of desktops that didn't deserve what was done to them."

"I will."

"I'm Asbel's assistant," said James.

Working for our general manager would have scared the shit out of me, but James radiated a prep-school confidence. In fact, none of them were old enough to have been here very long, and they seemed so comfortable, so sure of their places. "Don't worry about Chaser. He's pranked everyone more than once—it's his thing. And he's the best nose tackle in the league, so we live with it."

"He's so dumb." Abby rolled her eyes. "He's gotten my ears so many times with the Freeze Spray I can only wear studs." Trainers used Freeze Spray on in-game injuries to instantly ice and numb an area. In high school I was once holding out a water bottle to one of my dad's players when my pinky got caught by the blast, and I could have snapped that finger off at the knuckle. The thought of someone sneaking up behind me and spraying it that close to my face made me shudder.

"He swapped my water bottle out for one full of smelling salts," admitted Mo. "But I managed to vomit in private, so—who's the winner there?"

I laughed—genuinely, for once—and settled into my chair. Sitting with the three of them, for the first time all day, I felt my shoulders release. "I thought his name was Chase."

"Chaser's his nickname," James said. "Everybody with the team has one—you know, Lemon is Lemmer, Miller is Mills, Herrod is Roddy, Mackey is Mack."

I remembered Brent's introductions that first day. *B-rad, meet Poppy B.* Ugh. There was even more to learn. "What are yours?" I asked.

James hitched his thumb toward Mo. "Mo Money."

Mo shrugged, looking supremely unbothered. "It's better than Mo Problems."

"My last name's Worthington"—*Of course it is,* I thought—"so I got JWorth."

"Right."

"And you . . . what's your full name?"

"Poppy Benjamin."

"Pop-Tart," James and Mo said in unison. Abby smiled and rolled her eyes, and I wondered why I hadn't heard her nickname.

James spread his hands. "Take it as a compliment. You're a real Bobcat now."

*

Sunday dawned clear and cool. After a week spent typing and sorting, rushing from place to place and generally trying not to make a fool of myself, it was time to remember why I wanted this job so badly in the first place.

"Soak it in," my dad had instructed me on the phone the night before. "Your first NFL game—I hope it's the first of hundreds, kiddo. I'm so proud of you."

I wished he could be with me as I pulled into the parking lot outside the stadium, because it wasn't fair that I was here instead of him. He absolutely could have coached at this level—and he'd had the opportunity. His first job was as a college grad assistant, and he was offered a full-time position assisting with special teams after that. He was on his way up the ladder—but then he married my mom, and they had my older brother, Jeff, and my parents made choices. This job was all-encompassing. It was weekends and holidays, and my dad was school plays and dance recitals. He wasn't willing to miss Jeff's lacrosse games to watch film. He didn't want someone else reading bedtime stories to my middle brother, Luke, while he hopped a team charter to Arizona. My dad had a choice, and he chose us. And now I was standing here, with this amazing opportunity, because of what he sacrificed to give it to me.

Later today these lots would be filled with tents, portable grills, cornhole, DJs, pop-up bars, face-painting stations, and bounce houses—not to mention eighty thousand rabid fans. It was the first Sunday of the NFL season, and I, Poppy Benjamin, got to be a part of it.

About an hour before kickoff, I saw James (I would *not* be trying to pull off JWorth) by the staff elevators. His arms were filled with snack bags of popcorn, and he nodded at them and said, "Asbel gets testy during the games—salt helps."

"Yeah, I can imagine."

"What do you mean?"

"Oh, just," I backtracked, "it's a big day, and since it's the first game, but I'm sure—"

"I'm kidding." James said. "He's a nightmare." The elevator dinged, but he ignored it and allowed the doors to close. "So—how did a nice girl like you end up in football?"

"Excuse me?" I balked. "Did you ask Brent that?"

"I know how Brent ended up here—lifetime supply of free gum."

This time when the elevator opened, he stepped in and swiped his badge to access the suite level. "You ready for today?"

"I think so."

"I hope so," he said. And then, as the doors closed, "This is the fun part. Well, the other fun part."

I smiled as I walked to my seat, because to me it was all the fun part, and it was really nice to feel like that wasn't something to be embarrassed about. Every morning I drove to work in the dark. At night I drove home in it. If I wasn't needed at practice, I could go the entire day without seeing the sun, and it was completely worth it for the view of the field at six thirty when the sky was navy and the lights were off but the stadium somehow still glowed.

The stadium pulsed with fans, cheerleaders, coaches, trainers, mascots, yellow-coated security guards, beer vendors, and of course, the players. When the team ran onto the field to the driving soundtrack of AC/DC's "Thunderstruck," the roar of the crowd lifted my hair from my neck. The cheerleaders signed the anthem in ASL, and then a flyover swooped above our heads, a cannon fired, and the return team was on the field, hopping in place to get themselves hyped for kickoff. The crowd gave a collective "Ahhhhhhhh-hhhhhhhhhhhAHH!" as foot connected with ball, and we were off.

Three hours later it was over, and the Bobcats had improved to 1–0 with a decisive victory.

That night I stood in my shower, eyes closed, with the water set as hot as it would go. My feet ached. My shoulders were sore. The hours were murderous, the pay was pathetic. And I fucking loved it.

I stayed in the shower so long that the water pooled around my feet. Grabbing the hair catcher and setting it on the side of the tub, I wrapped myself in a towel and lay on my bed, staring at the ceiling. Then I reached for my laptop and scrolled through Facebook. Most of my college friends had found entry-level jobs in New York, and they posted a constant stream of banal updates like "Amanda is . . . getting coffee for ten" and "Layla is . . . never taking the L train again." It all sounded so boring compared to the things I was doing. I'd much rather be following up on a credential request from the Playboy Mansion than taking lunch orders from eight levels of middle managers. How could I imagine myself as one of millions when I could be this special instead?

CHAPTER FIVE

NOW

The rain continued on Saturday, setting the private runways at MillionAir glistening under the floodlights. It was only four o'clock, but the gloomy skies combined with the end of Daylight Saving Time made this feel like a night flight.

I inched through security, pecking away at my phone. If it seemed crazy that, less than forty-eight hours after our head coach's body was discovered, we were flying to New York without so much as naming an interim replacement, that's football. The games don't stop when someone collapses right there on the field, so they certainly weren't going to stop for this.

A text interrupted my typing.

Eight o'clock in the usual place. Tell no one.

I quickly closed it and looked over my shoulder, where I was met with nothing more than a puzzled smile from Rodney. "I thought I felt a fly," I said.

"You think MillionAir lets flies in here? They shoot them at the gate." Rodney spent more time in the weight room than most of special teams, and aside from the mandated suits for travel, it had been years since I'd seen him in anything other than a Bobcats polo.

Today he'd snuck a dryfit shirt under his jacket, and I supposed he'd get away with it since we had no coach to enforce the dress code. "Birds, on the other hand . . ." he started, but I waved him off.

"Just—no. Not today."

"They have to 'let' them in. A private airfield? *This* is the surveillance they want."

"Rodney, you know that the only thing stronger than your love of conspiracy theories is my hatred of your love of them, right?" He'd never admit it, but I was sure he was the one who gave Raj those flat-earth shirts. That all birds were replaced with surveillance robots in the seventies was one of his favorite theories. I couldn't count the number of times he'd solemnly recited that birdwatching goes both ways. He didn't even *believe* this shit, he just liked riling people up, and given the events of the past two days, I was in no mood to be riled.

"You've never seen a baby pigeon. That's all I'm saying."

"We're doing beverage service, right?" I asked our flight attendant, Clarissa, once I was seated. It was only forty minutes from Syracuse to the Meadowlands, but I badly needed a drink, even if I was technically at work. This didn't count, I reasoned—sky rules.

The players shuffled toward the back of the plane to spend the flight napping or continuing the high-stakes poker game that had been going on since Week 1. Coaches sat in the middle, and staff was up front, although after takeoff I often headed back to catch someone I'd been chasing that week while they had nowhere to run. Not today. I would not turn around. I would not risk catching sight of the empty seat three rows behind me.

Alec held his fist out to bump as he passed. There would be no other acknowledgment of last night. We wouldn't mention it again, until the next time.

I tucked my phone inside my purse, where it brushed up against the little envelope, still along for the ride.

I know what you did.

Tell the truth or pay the consequences.

You have five days.

The weather followed us through the atmosphere, and even above the clouds we bounced along through bad turbulence. After drinking my cocktail in two long sips, I laid my head back and listened to the soft *tink* of ice cubes jumping around in the glass. I allowed my feet to slip out of my heels and flexed them. That damn note. If it had come any other week, I would have just tossed it away, maybe without even opening it. Red's death, and where I was while it happened, had unmoored me. My entire life felt as suspended in midair as the plane.

"Hey."

I jumped at a pat on my elbow and twisted to see our quarterback, A.J. Caufield, glaring at me from beneath one of those stupid Baker boy hats.

"Hey there. How are you holding up? Feeling okay about tomorrow?"

"I keep getting these messages."

I'd downed that vodka way too fast, and now it was smacking me around. Two consecutive late nights and the swooping of the plane weren't helping either. Still shoeless, I struggled to my feet and clamped my hand on the seat back to steady myself. "Messages from who?"

"How about every reporter I've ever met wanting to know about Red? I haven't talked to half of these guys since I was in college. I don't even have the same cell number now. Did you give it out?"

"A.J., come on. Have I ever done that?"

He flexed his wrist to show off a diamond-encrusted Apple watch. "Look," he said, scanning through. "Look at all this shit. What am I supposed to say?"

"Nothing. Ignore the ones you want to ignore. Tell the others you're still processing everything. Given the circumstances, no one's going to bother you beyond that."

"Good, because I shouldn't even be dealing with this—that's *your* job." His finger was way too close to my face. I wanted to bite it. "I'm in charge of the football, you're supposed to be taking care of the press. And you know my brand is media friendly, Poppy. I'm not damaging relationships because you're dropping the ball."

"Yes, I know that's your brand. I'll handle them—we have availability tomorrow morning, and I'll make sure everyone knows I'm here if they need anything before then. You just focus on the game. If someone reaches out who you don't want to talk to, tell them I said everything has to come through me. Okay?"

After an uncomfortably bumpy landing, I couldn't get off the plane fast enough. Rodney and I usually helped the ops people hand out per diems and then babysat the production meeting at the hotel, but tonight he was on his own.

"What if they ask about Red?" Rodney said.

"Of course they're going to ask about Red." The production meeting gave the broadcast team a chance to talk to the players ahead of the game, to get some tidbits and background to mention on air. "Give everybody a line on their way in the door—first time they met Red, what he meant to them, winning one for him tomorrow, whatever, it doesn't have to be Shakespeare. But," I put up a firm finger, "keep it focused on Red the person, not the death. We're in legacy-building mode."

Upstairs, I dumped my bag in my room and swapped out my suit skirt for tight jeans. Keeping my heels, silk shell top, and blazer, I applied a shade of lipstick I wouldn't wear to work and fluffed out my hair.

My phone buzzed with a text from Asbel.

Police agree with Lexi. We'll talk Monday.

I sank onto the cheap hotel duvet, sour saliva flooding my mouth. *Murder.* I felt the word between my ribs. *Police* hit higher up, a hard bubble near my sternum. It was suddenly all horribly, impossibly real.

I wanted to run down to the production meeting and shove Rodney out of the way. I wanted to hold on to the players' mouths during the interviews and flap them up and down so I could control every single word that came out of them. I wanted to call the Syracuse police and demand that this stay quiet, that no errant photos of the crime scene—*crime scene!*—get passed from phone to phone, no thoughtless sound bites be delivered to a whole different tribe of reporters who would now be on this story. More than anything, I wanted to go back two nights and undo everything I'd done. I knew, logically, it wasn't my fault that Red was dead, but what did logic have to do with it?

But in the end I couldn't do any of that, and so I called a car service and headed to Hoboken.

*

I walked briskly off Washington Street and up the steps of a gastro-pub still reeking from last night's misadventures. Inside was dark and scene-y, with brass fixtures and a polished wooden bar running the length of the room. Young professionals were stacked three deep around it watching the baseball playoffs. The booths were deep and high-backed, and I found who I was looking for near the back, in the third one from the restrooms.

"Hey, stranger," said Nisha from her seat by the window. "I'm glad you still came. What a week."

"Well, I heard they serve alcohol at this bar." I slid into the empty side of the booth across from her and nodded toward her glass. "What's that?"

"Whiskey." Her dark, glossy bob swept across her jaw as she lifted her chin. "My most dependable relationship." Nisha was an NFL advance scout, which meant her job consisted of constant travel and sitting alone at the end of press boxes taking notes—not exactly conducive to a productive personal life. She had large, dark eyes, a sharp jawline, and a sharper tongue. "Listen, I'm not great with awkward things, and this is the *most* awkward thing. I figure the period in your text meant maybe you're good and maybe you're not, but either way you don't want to talk about it."

"That's about right."

"Thank God. I mean, we can if you want to. But thank God." She balanced her coaster on the edge of the table, flipped it up with the backs of her fingers, and caught it. Our friend Dayanna taught us that—she could flip and catch a stack of ten—and we'd all picked it up as our go-to party trick and bar fidget. Nisha, I knew, could flip a three-stack in her sleep, so her intense concentration was a way of having something to look at other than me.

"Go ahead," I said finally.

"I'm not saying a word."

"*Say* it. I know you're just barely holding it in."

"Okay . . . Has Peter checked in?"

I wished there was a pillow I could hold to my chest to make it hurt less when I heard his name, the way you hugged one to your stomach to cough after surgery. "No. And I doubt his fiancée would be too excited if he did."

"Oh, shit, Pop. I'm sorry."

"It's okay." And if it wasn't, I couldn't change it anyway. "Listen," I said, trying to save the mood, "can we put in for some apps? I burned a lot of stress calories this week I'd like to start backfilling."

Annika arrived next, tall and ice blond. She hung her trench coat on the hook outside the booth, then leaned in to hug me. "Hi, sweetie. I am so, so sorry about Red." After I waved her off, she said, "I almost didn't make it tonight—Joanna broke up with her boyfriend yesterday. A better mother probably would have stayed with her, but all she really wants to do is make sad TikToks."

Nisha and I nodded like we could relate, which we couldn't. Annika, the oldest in our group, was the only one of us to marry or have kids, and her daughters were, predictably, highfliers—the heartbroken Joanna was studying feminist theory, and Carolyn was in her second year of law school. I'd always thought that if my mother was more like Annika, if she'd had her magic balance of warmth and drive, we might talk more than once a month.

"Are you okay, Anni?" Nisha asked. "You look . . . tired."

"That's not even a creative way of telling me I look like shit, that's just telling me," she said. "I'm fine, though. Drinks?" I nodded toward Nisha's whiskey, then turned around to watch the sea of twentysomethings part as Annika approached, placing her palms gently on a back here, a shoulder there. More than one of the young guys in half zips checked her out as she leaned over to talk to the bartender. Annika was in-house counsel for an NBA team, where the rosters were small but the egos were astronomical. As she liked to remind us, every free throw was a close-up, and her players were superstars in a way that most of mine, buried beneath their helmets, would never be. Annika was supposed to focus on contract issues and arbitrations, but more often found herself dispatching non-disclosure agreements like an Old West sheriff spraying bullets.

I checked to see if Rodney had sent an SOS, but my phone was disappointingly quiet.

"You get AM radio on that?" asked Nisha. The phone was an Android, pre-COVID vintage, and it had certainly seen better days.

"We're locked into this sponsorship. The players have the latest and greatest—not that they use them. Staff gets these."

"Just looking at that thing makes me feel old."

"We are old. A girl I used to babysit for is an obstetrician now."

Annika made it back at the same time the food arrived, and the three of us clinked our glasses. The wings were electric orange with a scent that tickled the back of my throat, and I made an executive decision to steer clear, going instead for a too-hot bite of melted cheese.

"Oh my God," moaned Nisha, wiping her mouth with a cloth napkin. "These are so good. Cocaine is illegal and wings are not. Explain that."

I sipped my whiskey, which slid harmlessly down my throat without a fight. It hadn't burned since my midtwenties, and I sorely missed the sensation of fire moving through my body, of how alive it used to make me feel. Tonight I wanted that burn to distract from the strain growing lower, deeper inside of me.

"Who's that?" Annika indicated the TV, where the broadcasters had been joined in the booth by a third man.

I gave her a funny look. "You don't know Clem Phillips?" He'd been one of the top quarterbacks in the NFL for a decade before his retirement last year and was now a fixture at anything with a ball and a camera. He rose from his stool and raised both arms over his head as an outfielder made a particularly acrobatic catch.

"Yeah, of course I know Clem. I mean the guy on the side."

Hovering at the edge of the frame, barely in view, was a man with short black hair and what could have been a shadow or the hint of a new beard. He had full lips, strong eyebrows, and skin the color of a worn penny.

"Omar Kadeer," I supplied. "He's—"

"Hot as shit," Nisha broke in.

"I was going to say A.J.'s agent. Probably Clem's too, since he's there. Those sneakers aren't going to sell themselves."

"Forget Clem, I'd buy sneakers from that guy." She glanced toward the door and raised her chin. "They're here."

It was no surprise that Dayanna and Sarah arrived together. The rest of us were scattered—Nisha in San Francisco, Annika in Wisconsin, and me in Syracuse—but Sarah lived here in Hoboken and Dayanna was just across the Hudson in Chelsea, and more often than not when we arranged the group Zoom, they appeared from the same screen, toasting with the actual clinking of cups while we raised our glasses into the air. Both murmured their condolences about Red, but again, I waved them off. Tonight wasn't about that.

"Hear ye, hear ye," Nisha said as the two of them filled in the booth. "We're all present and accounted for—let the airing of grievances begin."

"Go ahead, Poppy," Dayanna said. "I've been thinking about you all week. It's everything, isn't it? The work side, the personal side. And the whole city must just be . . . There's no escape, for a second."

Something broke off in my chest, because she got it, exactly, and that was a reason not to talk about it. If I did I would completely fall apart. Losing Red was foundation-shaking. *Murder, he was murdered. Someone murdered Red.* I took a slow sip of my drink. "You got it," I said, "and actually I would love to talk about your stuff instead. Take a little vacation from it."

Dayanna squeezed my shoulder, while Sarah said, "Yes, absolutely. If you want distractions, I have a good one." Sarah's hair somehow gets redder and curlier when she's worked up about something, and tonight it exploded out over her bomber jacket like a sunrise. "There's a new woman at the *Post*, Audrey. She's young— maybe two or three years out of school. On the first day I kept half an eye on her in the locker room, but she seemed fine. I go do my thing, get a few quotes for a story I'm working on—fine. Then I walk past her at Gary Huker's locker just in time to hear her say, 'Oh, wow, that's a . . . tough choice, Gary.'"

"No!" We'd all heard about a certain hockey player's famous "would you rather" hypothetical, a truly disgusting choice between inserting twenty anal beads or licking a used tampon. He dispatched it to new reporters as a little test to see how flustered he could make them, and it always worked, but it hit differently when the reporter in question was female. It was like the world's suckiest magic trick, making you feel embarrassed and ashamed when you hadn't done anything at all.

We'd all dealt with shit, but Sarah might have had it the worst, practically speaking. As a sportswriter, she competed with male colleagues who freely handed out their cell phone numbers, bonded with sources over late-night drinking sessions, and generally made themselves available at all hours of the day and night. What felt like relationship building from a middle-aged man read completely differently from Sarah, who could no longer open her texts on public transportation because she received so many unsolicited dick pics from sources and colleagues.

"Poor girl." Dayanna shook her head. She could relate, since she'd once had a coach tell her, in her own office no less, that she had a "body for sin." She headed community relations for an MLB team, and so she poured that body into gowns for lots of charity galas where alcohol was served. Everything bad gets worse with alcohol. We all remembered the time her team's Gold Glove– winning shortstop grabbed her by the face and dropped a Bugs Bunny–style smooch fully on her mouth, after which *Dayanna* was called into team president Buster Gibbs's office to defend her out-

fit, choice of lipstick, beverage selection, and overall professional-
ism.

"I took her out for coffee after," Sarah said. "She was more than
a little shell-shocked."

We raised our glasses. "To Audrey," we said in unison, and then
Sarah finished, "May she get assigned a beat far from Gary Huker."

We called ourselves the WAGS. Traditionally that's Wives and
Girlfriends, meaning the partners of professional athletes, but in
our case it was Women Against Groping Shitheads. We all worked
in sports. We'd all progressed into the upper levels of our fields, and
we all needed a safe space to vent the kind of crazy shit that came
with these jobs without being judged for it.

The few times early on I'd relayed a similar anecdote to my
brothers, their response was to ask why Audrey wouldn't have
reported it. To who? For what? There was work to be done and a
long line of people willing to do it for low pay without complaint.
We were lucky to be here, we were all so *grateful* to have jobs that
made people at parties say, "Oh, cool!" And if young Audrey made a
fuss, what kind of assignment do you think she could expect to get
next? The only athletes such a "humorless" and "sensitive" reporter
could hope to get near again would be the horses at Belmont Stakes.
I hope this isn't going to be a Dayanna situation was shorthand in the
WAGS for someone in sports being particularly sports-y, because
Day had once overheard old Buster say that to a woman broach-
ing the topic of maternity leave. Dayanna had never taken one,
but she did have an ovary removed after a cyst the size of a grapefruit caused gasping pain over a six-month period. It grew so large
because she waited for the off-season, and her white-knuckling was
rewarded with a comment about whether she really had to make
"that face" all the time.

This was our dumping ground, the place we could vomit up
every aggression, be they passive or micro, and know we could wake
up the next day without a mental hangover. Pumping and dumping
was what kept us sane.

As the food disappeared and the drinks were refilled, the conversation turned to a story Sarah's outlet had broken earlier in the week.

"Deanson was already a coach there when it happened?" Nisha asked.

Sarah shook her head. "Grad assistant. So it was Deanson's first job after graduating, and he and John Doe would have been on the roster together for two years."

The story involved a top-tier college basketball program, where Shep Deanson, a former player beloved in the manner of under-sized white shooting guards on rural campuses everywhere, had been head coach for the past twenty years. A John Doe had recently come forward with claims that one of the assistant coaches sexually abused him while he was a player in the nineties.

"But once Shep *was* named coach," Annika said, "he fired him, right?"

Sarah shook her head. "That part isn't really clear. He moved on, but not until a year later, and nothing was ever formally reported. Deanson's never going to survive this."

"But—"

When they all turned to me I faltered for a beat, then fur-rowed my brow and pushed on. "Is that fair to Deanson? I mean, he's head coach now but he wasn't when it happened, he was just a grad assistant trying to start his career. What could he have really done? And if this had come out back then, we wouldn't be hold-ing Deanson responsible at all. He's more culpable for the same response because of subsequent success?"

"You sound like that writer for the *Pacific*." Annika smiled. "What's his name? Josh Youngerman? His whole thing is about can-cel culture and male witch hunts. He's the kind of writer where the story starts out pretty reasonable and you're thinking, okay, he's made some good points here, that's fair, yup, okay, I'm with you, I'm with you—and then there's just a *hard* left turn and all of a sud-den you're knee-deep in an incel manifesto."

Dayanna, sitting next to me, was staring at the table with her thick, dark ponytail pulled over one shoulder, twisting it absently into a rope. Of the five of us, she was usually the quietest, but tonight she looked a million miles away. I nudged her. "You okay?"

"I'm fine."

I knew that line. "Day, what's up?"

"It's dumb, truly, especially with your week. Something happened a few days ago that I haven't been able to shake off, but it's probably one of my idiot players thinking he's funny."

"What?" Nisha prompted. She had a strange look on her face that matched the tickle at the base of my throat. We'd been sharing these stories with proud detachment, passing them around like war correspondents, but the atmosphere at the table had shifted, thickened. Suddenly we could hear the bombs.

Dayanna sighed. "I got this note."

It couldn't be.

"Tell the truth?" Sarah said after a pause. She flashed her usual wry smile, but it wobbled at the corner.

"Or pay the consequences." Annika folded her hands on the table.

The bar erupted as one of the teams hit a home run, and in the ensuing roar we stared at each other, Dayanna looking sick, Annika serious. Nisha's arms were folded across her chest, and Sarah's lips were pressed together. When the noise level dropped, we hung in suspended animation, no one wanting to speak first, each hoping the others would dismiss it, would laugh it off. But none of us could.

My note was still in my purse, and I wondered if the others had brought theirs, if all the time we'd been sitting at this table we'd been secretly surrounded. Ambushed.

Nisha broke the silence. "Well, obviously, someone's messing with us." She flipped a stack of coasters but missed the catch, and two tumbled to oblivion under the table.

"Who?" Sarah said. "To one of us, okay, but who would send this to each of us? Who even knows we're friends?"

"It's not a secret."

"Isn't it?" Sarah shot back, which made me think. It was true that I'd never consciously kept my friendship with these girls quiet—who would care?—but I also hadn't advertised it. We weren't the type to post group shots online, and this type of hangout, where we saw each other in person, was exceedingly rare.

"We don't know that it was only sent to us," said Annika, ever logical. "What if some crazy sent it to every woman in sports he could find? We're all in staff directories, our information's public."

"Mine came to my apartment," said Sarah quietly. Inside my glass, the ice cubes danced. My hand was shaking again. The stadium gave me some level of distance, for whatever that was worth, but knowing that someone had used a pen to write out Sarah's home address, had breathed on that envelope, licked it, and sent it to the place where she slept made me shiver. And Sarah lived *here*, in Hoboken. I was sure it was mailed like the rest of ours, but nonsensically it felt possible—likely, even—that whoever sent them was at this bar. Studying us.

Nisha made a face. "Okay, so someone's fucking with us. It has to be. *I know what you did?* I mean, come on. *We*," she gestured back and forth across the table, "haven't done anything."

"Not collectively."

Sarah's words sat like a pound of lead as my mind raced again across the years, examining every decision I'd made in my role with the Bobcats. There were lots of things that could get me fired if they became public, because that was my job. I was a professional sword faller-on-er, and the reason I was good at my job was because those things stayed buried.

"What about the five days?" Dayanna said.

"Four, now."

Nisha gave Sarah a look. "Listen to yourself! A fake note with a fake deadline that scares you into revealing some embarrassing little secret. You guys, we have all seen shit like this before."

That was true. Pro sports was rife with dares, hazing, and pranks. It started at training camp, when the rookies had to stand on the lunch tables and belt out their alma maters with mouths full of marshmallows. How humiliated would I feel if this came from one of the stadium ops guys and I'd spilled my guts like a teenage girl whose diary gets grabbed at a sleepover?

But of course, the other WAGS didn't know what I knew. Not about Red.

"You guys. My note came the same morning Red was found." I dropped my voice to barely more than a whisper, and four heads bent forward. "We're not sharing this—Sarah, seriously, you can't—but they're thinking it wasn't an accident. Or natural."

I couldn't say it, just let the implication sink in. Everyone looked stricken. "Oh, Poppy," Dayanna murmured.

Nisha hitched, her dark eyes hard. "That's horrible, yes, but for our purposes, it's not the worst thing in the world, right?"

"Nisha!" Annika snapped.

"I'm serious," she went on. "*Five days.* That's proof that these aren't connected, because Poppy got the note the morning after Red was killed. If she doesn't spill her guts, what are they going to do, kill him again?"

"*Shut up!*" I hissed. The bar was packed, that strange balance of there being so many people around that none of them could hear us, but it was still a public place, and it was still my job to bury this. Or, not bury it, shit, keep it quiet. How was I supposed to feel? *Oh, thank goodness, an* unrelated *murder.* Nisha was right that the time-line made no sense if the notes were connected to Red. But it also made no sense that they weren't connected. We each got one? On the day he was found? Each scenario was more ridiculous than the other.

I slammed the remainder of my drink and put the glass on the table harder than I meant to. It landed with a *thwack.* "I should get going. This is reminding me I have a shitstorm of a day tomorrow—we're announcing the interim coach, and A.J. is being A.J." Dayanna stood to let me out, and I slid quickly off the bench.

"Poppy, stay," Annika said. "We can talk through this together."

I shook my head. "Nisha's right, they're just pieces of paper."

"They're *not,*" Sarah insisted.

"It's all of us, Poppy," Dayanna said quietly as she hugged me goodbye. "We'd all be screwed."

"That's comforting."

"I just mean, you wouldn't be alone."

My breathing didn't slow until I was in a car on my way back to the hotel. Ever since Asbel called with the news about Red, it was like my bones weren't set properly, and whenever I thought about where I was that night, what I was doing while Red was dying, my chest seized. I couldn't have helped him. I didn't know, I couldn't have known. But I should have. Somehow, I should have. I forced myself to count the lampposts as they streaked past in steady, even increments, to box breathe, to blink.

I waved to our ops director, stationed in the hotel lobby to make sure the players made it back by curfew, but continued toward the elevators without stopping. "Big night out?" he called after me.

"Oh, you know," I replied, pushing the button repeatedly. "Just taking in some local culture."

As the elevator swooped its way to the thirtieth floor, I leaned against its mirrored wall and closed my eyes. I hadn't slept for the better part of two days, my stomach was a mess of alcohol and fried foods. I flashed to an image of Peter, his easy smile, the thermal blanket effect of being wrapped up inside one of his hugs. Pulling out my phone, I opened Facebook and hovered my finger over the search bar, eventually letting the hand drop when the elevator doors slid open. Looking scratched an itch, but it never helped, and in this case would make things significantly worse.

I kicked off my heels and flopped onto my bed, staring at the bad hotel art of a sailboat on the wall. On the day after Red Guillory was murdered, Nisha, Annika, Dayanna, Sarah, and I had each received a pernicious little note. It was with me now, warming the bed from inside my purse. I could have sworn it glowed. The notes might mean nothing, or they might be a clue to what happened to Red. To what was about to happen to the WAGS.

We were five of the most powerful women in sports.

And if Sarah was right, we were being hunted.

CHAPTER SIX

FIFTEEN YEARS AGO

I opened my door and sighed to find another yellow Post-it note stuck to the outside. My landlady, Flossie, had started leaving them a few days ago, passive-aggressive offers to let me borrow the vacuum or little tips on how to clean. I was so tired—dead tired—every second I wasn't at work, the last thing on my mind was scrubbing the oven, which I'd used maybe twice. The notes made me feel like a child who hadn't picked up her room, and I resisted the urge to ball this latest one up and drop it onto the floor of the foyer. That door was mine—I was paying for it—and sticking things on it felt like she was pushing her way into places she shouldn't be. I imagined Flossie hovering outside the door while I was sleeping, breathing against it and pressing the brightly colored notes against the only barrier between my space and theirs.

I called my parents on the drive to work. It was strategy, the early hour making it more likely that my dad would be the one to pick up, but this time I wasn't so lucky.

"Hey, Sunshine," said my mother. I let my head loll to the side because I *hated* that nickname. She thought it was hilarious since I'm naturally much more stormy, but every time she trotted it out, it felt like a peek into the daughter she wished she'd had instead. The smiley, uncomplicated one. "How has it been going? Are you being careful?"

"Like avoiding paper cuts?"

"You know what I mean. You're around all those men all the time and—"

"Jeff's around men all the time."

"Your brother works in *finance*. Will you stop being obstinate? You're a beautiful young woman, my dear. You need to take care of yourself."

I pictured the Post-it, still hanging from my door, tiny yellow hands on its nonexistent hips. "I *can* take care of myself. I don't need you hovering. Just—let Dad know I called."

*

After lunch I was updating the email distribution lists when Brent tossed me a media guide. "Cut it up," he said, "and make yourself some flash cards."

"I already know everyone's number. Even the practice squad."

"I'm going to need you to be able to recognize them without their numbers on." When I realized what he meant, my face flushed deeply, and Brent squinted. "That's not going to be a problem, is it?"

You couldn't be in media relations if you weren't where the interviews took place, and unlike in college, here that meant hanging out in the locker room. It was awkward under the best of circumstances, but when the average football player was six foot two and you stood a full foot lower, it was *not great*.

I thought about my mother, who had never once congratulated me for getting this impossible-to-land internship. Who thought I needed an electric fence around my desk to protect me from the big, mean boys, because of course she'd never bothered to ask what my job actually entailed. Of course she assumed they wouldn't respect me. Of course she thought they wouldn't see me as a real member of the team.

I smiled at Brent and raised one shoulder in a casual shrug. "No problem here."

When enough time had passed, I slipped out of the annex. James held up his hand for a high five as I walked through the executive section, and Mo gave me a nod when I passed IT but stayed focused on his screen. I was about to turn right toward the ladies' room when a body slammed into mine and pinned me against the wall.

"Whoa—hip check!" Neil from accounting was on me just long enough to say the words before he stepped back and crinkled his eyes like we were old friends when in reality that might be the first thing he'd ever said to me after "Hi, I'm Neil." "Look alive, Poppy." He walked off whistling down the hall while I sucked in breaths. Then I let myself into the ladies' lounge attached to the bathroom and sank into an armchair. The carpet in here was pink. A small sign designated it a breastfeeding space—although who could find time to get pregnant while working these hours, I couldn't imagine. A glass bowl of stale potpourri sat on an end table, along with a wicker basket of tampons.

A minute later Abby came through the door. "Hey," she said casually, and then, seeing my face, "*Hey*. What's going on?"

"Nothing. I'm fine."

"You look fine."

I sat up. Abby was petite, with blond hair and peachy cheeks, but had the kind of hard twinkle in her eye that suggested she could probably teach me new swear words. Her makeup was more cocktail hour than business casual, and if anyone had advised her to buy tops one size up she had clearly ignored them. Women like Abby terrified me, because they were fully formed in a way that I wasn't, but she was here, asking, and just then I needed someone to talk to.

"I came in here to process the fact that I'm going to be doing naked locker room stuff and got . . . *hip checked* on the way by—"

"Neil?" She lowered herself into the other armchair. "Such a creep. Last year he commented on how all the team-issued gear is in men's sizes and asked me for my measurements so he could look into getting something specially made. Not my size—my measurements."

"*Accounting* was going to have something specially made?"

"Exactly."

It was our first real conversation, and as flustered as I was by the one-two punch of the last ten minutes, it brought some hope. I badly needed a buddy here. Maybe it could be Abby.

She sat forward and put her hands on her knees. "So—talk to me about naked locker room. Are they going to be, like, naked-naked? They don't even grab a towel or anything?"

"I mean, I've heard that most of them do think it's weird and they wear towels, or they get dressed really quickly. But my college boss told me some straight-up hang out naked. It's like a power move, to try to make the reporters uncomfortable."

"And the media relations interns?"

"*So* uncomfortable—not that I want to admit that, because . . ." I trailed off, and Abby raised her shoulders in a way that showed she got it. If I said anything, it meant that a woman couldn't do this job as seamlessly as a man, that I needed some kind of special treatment. And with hundreds of people lined up behind me dying for my spot who'd need no extra thought at all . . . I could never take myself out of the running like that. The only thing for it was to make myself easy to hire. Unproblematic. The only thing to say was nothing. "Everyone's name is above their locker, so until I learn who's where, I'll just walk around with my eyes angled up and pray like hell I don't bump into anything."

She pointed a French-tipped nail at me. "And that's the difference between men and women—praying not to bump into anyone versus hip-checking them in the hallways."

*

On Saturday I stretched out on my little sofa in a tank top and man-sized pair of Bobcats sweats. With the team in Indianapolis, I had the day off and intended to take full advantage, sleeping until ten, pushing through five loads of laundry, and organizing my closet. Dave and Flossie had invited me to a barbecue, but I got out of it. Flossie probably would have tried to teach me how to clean the grill. There would be no college football for me today either. My plan was to catch up on *The Hills* and order enough Chinese food to carry me through both lunch and dinner.

But by the time Justin Bobby wore his combat boots to the beach, I could not get comfortable on the couch. I hugged a throw pillow, tucking my feet beneath me. What was the team doing now? They'd be landing soon, then breaking out at the hotel for position meetings. Brent would help with production. And I was missing it, bounced back to the outside like everyone else. It was fine to have a break, but not when it all continued without me, because that meant I didn't actually matter. I wasn't the one making any of it happen.

I was crabby and had meat sweats from so much takeout. Both things, I figured, would be helped by a long shower. In the mornings before work I barely had time to wet my hair, so it felt downright indulgent to stand under the showerhead and let the spray beat against my back. I moved so that my shoulders would be directly under the water and let my head hang forward, eyes closed.

After a minute I opened them and looked at my toes. Water was pooling around them. I stepped out of the spray and turned around to get a better look at the drain.

The hair catcher had been replaced.

CHAPTER SEVEN

NOW

On Sunday morning I dressed quickly, stopping in to the team breakfast only long enough to grab a granola bar before catching the first of three shuttles to the stadium. I had no appetite, and so the snack was decorative, something to take up space inside my purse besides the note.

Given the circumstances, New York was generous enough to let us use their pressroom to introduce our interim head coach, even permitting a Bobcats backdrop for the cameras.

"I can't imagine," Jayson, the New York media relations director, kept saying as he unlocked the press entrance hours ahead of the typical game-day timetable, and then when I thanked him, "You'd do the same for us." I wasn't so sure about that, but I thanked him again and adjusted the signage.

"Five days."

Jayson was behind me, and when I heard those words I whipped around so fast that my hair hit my face. "What did you say?"

He smiled, confused. "Fridays? I was just saying we're going to try half days on travel weekends. We'd been thinking about it for a while, but Red was so young, it really hit home. The stress of these seasons is something else."

"It certainly is." I grimaced and grabbed his hand in my most matronly gesture, then drew in a shaky breath like the air was causing me pain. It had the intended effect of terrifying him into leaving the pressroom.

I stared down at my purse. Over the course of my career, I have talked my way into the back of a police cruiser and then talked myself and one of our safeties back out of it, uncharged. I have stood before a naked Super Bowl loser in the postgame locker room and convinced him to put some shorts on and face a room full of reporters waiting to ask why he dropped the game-winning pass. Once, I reduced a three-hundred-pound lineman to tears after he called me the C-word under his breath. I am not easily intimidated. But I knew, beyond all doubt, that if I slid my hand inside that purse where the note was, it would come out with bite marks.

Thirty minutes later Nate Hoonan, our newly temporarily promoted former offensive coordinator, stood at the podium for his first press conference blinking like someone had yanked the curtain back halfway through his shower.

"You'll signal when it's time to start, right?" he'd asked as we took the short walk from the locker rooms to the pressroom. Mid-sixties with kind brown eyes and a full head of white hair, Nate was a good man and a good coach, but Asbel had told me he wasn't even on the list of interviews for our permanent replacement.

I tried not to think about the thousands of times I'd made the same walk with Red, whose confident stride and tendency to enter the pressroom with a thunderous clap of his hands contrasted so sharply with Coach Nate's timidity. If I'd ever suggested that Red watch for my signal to begin, he would have given me that knowing smirk and then left me somewhere halfway down the hallway.

"I can do that," I told Coach Nate. "We'll plan for around five questions, but if you get in trouble tap the podium twice and I'll cut things off."

The pressroom was jammed. The camera bank aimed at Nate looked like the set of a space epic, and I could see the sweat glistening off his forehead from my spot just beyond the backdrop. Nate's fingers were white at the tips from gripping the podium. His neck bobbed as he dry-swallowed. In my crisp navy suit, hair pulled back into a complicated ponytail, I forced all thoughts of the note from my mind. This was happening now, I was needed *now*. I coughed and, at Nate's reflexive glance, caught his eye. Slowly, I lowered my chin and raised it back up. I would look out for him. I would call on friendly media, trusted media who knew better than to beat him up with tough questions on a day like today. I had his back.

Nate drew in a breath that strained the front of his shirt, then huffed it out straight into the microphone. The assembled reporters cringed as hands flew to ears, and Nate reddened but pushed forward.

"I know you all never expected to see me here," he said, "and I'll be very honest with you—I didn't either. But as we so often tell our players, this is a game of next man up, and we're all at some point in our lives called upon to take that step.

"Red Guillory was my friend. We coached beside each other for more than ten years, and I consider it a privilege to have watched a man like that up close for so long. As a person and as a coach, he's set an incredible example that I know all of us will try to live up to every day. I'm sure you folks understand I can't answer any questions about the circumstances of Coach's death." His voice broke on the last word. "There's not much I understand about it myself, and we're going to leave all of that to the people who . . ." He stumbled here, and I nodded, encouraging. "Who do that. What I can talk about is football. We have a room full of young men back there who have worked very hard, and who will continue to work hard. And we'll be honoring Coach Guillory with that work."

I couldn't smile under the circumstances, but I squinted at Nate and nodded once in a way I hoped conveyed that he'd done well—very well. I stepped one foot onto the dais and pointed to a familiar face near the front. "Brian?"

As the press conference rolled on, I stepped back, relieved that Nate was pulling through. Soon enough they'd choose the real coach, and I'd have someone else to figure out, to cater to, to cover for. But for the next little while, Nate was not going to be a problem.

What would my career have looked like if a Nate had been in charge all along? Easier, for sure, because I would have told Nate what to do and he would have done it. No Super Bowls, probably, which would have meant shorter seasons and fewer one-hundred-hour weeks. It would have left more of me to give to the other parts of my life—it would have made it possible to *have* other parts of my life.

I shook that thought off before it could settle in and make itself comfortable. The truth was I knew in my bones that without Red I wouldn't be the professional I was today. He had challenged me. He'd pushed me, hard, and I'd learned to live and then thrive under that pressure. Easy was nice, but hard was good, and I, like so many others who'd come through this building under Red's tenure, had become the strongest, best version of myself because of him.

I owed him.

*

We lost, obviously.

New York was a strong team, and we were in a tailspin. The play-calling was a mess, with A.J. throwing pass after pass to empty patches of the field while frustrated receivers waved their arms. But that was nothing compared to watching our co-captain, DeMario, stumble and fall mid-stride with no one else around. He lay face-down, pounding the turf with his fist and clutching at his left leg, and a collective *oof* went through the press box, followed by the sound of twenty writers frantically typing.

"How many things," groaned Rodney, "are we going to heap onto the giant pile of shit this season is becoming?"

"Look, he's getting up." DeMario put each of his arms around a trainer and hopped back to the tunnel, keeping his left leg bent at the knee.

"That's not up—that's hoisted."

I sighed from my toes and twisted around to Chloe, seated in the row behind me. "Go down to the locker room please and see if you can get an update out of the trainers. At least enough to hold everyone over."

The final score was 46–3, our lone points coming on a field goal against New York's second-stringers late in the fourth quarter. We were now 1–5 on the season, coachless, and the back half of our schedule was a showcase of the league's top teams.

"Don't worry," I told Coach Nate when I met him on the sideline to escort him to the pressroom. "They're more interested in DeMario right now than you."

"Considerate guy. What's Doc say?"

"'Lower-body injury'—you know the drill. Anything more than that, tell them we're waiting to get it checked out when we're back in Syracuse. And don't get drawn into speculating."

Normally I would never boss a head coach around like that, but Nate was not quite meeting his blinking quota and seemed a little stunned. Stunned led to sloppy answers, which led to bad quotes, which led to more work for me. The team bus was already running in anticipation of a quick exit, and I needed Nate to mumble through a few stock answers and get on it.

But the very first question was a curveball. It came from Isaac Dorchester, a pocket-sized national writer known for flirting with the line between tabloid and sports, and I never would have called on him. Instead, when I pointed at a local reporter because he looked new and timid, Isaac took advantage of those same qualities to push in front of him and ask his own question.

"I'm hearing Red's death is now considered suspicious. What can you tell us about him being found with the back of his head bashed in?"

My mouth dropped open. Could one of the girls have . . . ? Nate looked at Isaac like he'd peeled his face off to reveal something putrid, and I recovered myself enough to say, "Okay, we are going to shut this dow—" before Nate cut me off.

"How *dare* you, sir." His voice was low and steady. The stunned look was gone, his gaze now locked in on Isaac like a heat-seeking missile. He was drenched in sweat from the effort of coaching his first NFL game. The whistle still hung around his neck, and as he leaned forward it tapped against the microphone, adding a heart-beat to a room otherwise so frozen it seemed to have none. I was appalled—completely appalled that even a bottom-dweller like Isaac would be crass enough to throw something like that out in a nationally televised press conference. Involuntarily, I pictured Red's thick black hair mottled with blood, Red soaked in red. I imagined pain. Pain and panic as he fell beside the heavy executive desk he liked to drink behind with his feet up. As he waited for help that never came.

It set my teeth chattering, which was my only excuse for not stopping what happened next. For not grabbing Nate and pulling him from the room before he calmly stepped from behind the podium, waded into the press, and punched Isaac Dorchester full in the face.

CHAPTER EIGHT

FIFTEEN YEARS AGO

The Bobcats won again on Sunday, and then the next three Sundays, putting them at 5–0. Game 5 was a blowout by halftime, and so Coach's decision to go for it on fourth and long in the fourth quarter was the first thing Bernie asked about in the presser. "Why pile on like that when you're already up twenty?"

Coach Guillory's massive shoulders lifted in a shrug. "I'd say kicking a field goal there is piling on because it's an automatic three points. If we go for the first down, you know, at least we're giving them the chance to stop us."

Brent's low whistle was lost in the chatter of the room. Coach Guillory smiled as if the whole thing was a joke, but there was a new hardness behind his eyes. A new heat coming off him.

The vibe inside the building changed with the color of the leaves. It was stiffer now, tighter. When a receiver dropped what should have been a long-range touchdown in practice, A.J. upended a cooler, sending a wave of ice and multicolored bottles of sports drink all over the sideline. In his red no-contact jersey he looked like a matador's cape but acted like the bull. "These fucking busted routes!" he screamed. A ball boy crouched to scoop up the ice, but the safeties coach grabbed him by the collar and yanked just as A.J. drove his foot into the cubes and drilled them into the stands.

The credential requests ticked up with the same frequency as the wins. The team had become a national topic of conversation, and with that came the first whiff of heightened expectations. The daily clips packet of media coverage grew longer. More often than not when I heaved up the stack of newspapers outside the stadium in the mornings, it was Bobcats red staring at me from the place of honor on the back cover. It felt good to win, and the excitement of game days carried us through the grind of the weeks that followed, but now, I noticed, when the final whistle blew the roar of the crowd held more relief than joy. We'd survived another week.

"Congratulations," I told Coach Guillory when I dropped off his papers. He was hunched over his computer, brows deeply furrowed as he muttered something to himself about stunts, but he flicked two fingers off his brow in a light salute. When he bent his arm, his sleeve rode up to reveal the bottom of what looked like a nicotine patch—a weird contrast with the water bottle full of neon-green liquid celery at the side of his keyboard. Smoking and juicing didn't exactly go hand in hand, but maybe it was a way to manage some of the stress without actually lighting up.

"Oh hey, Poppy." I was halfway out the door but spun on my heel. "You know employees are allowed to use the gym downstairs, as long as it's not during training, right?"

"Oh, no, I didn't realize that."

"I can tell you like to take care of your body, and these hours— they're way too crazy for a regular gym."

He looked the same as always. Red Bobcats dryfit shirt, elbows on his desk, open, pleasant smile on his rugged face.

I can tell you like to take care of your body.

The back of my neck itched as I played with the beaded bracelets at my wrist. I'd all but ignored Richard's one-size-larger rule and was wearing flared dress pants and a short-sleeved fitted sweater. Was this a compliment? A little reminder to stick to the dress code?

That easy smile didn't match what I was reading into it. Someone under the kind of pressure Coach was facing took time out of his day to try to be nice, and I read the worst, darkest meaning into it—like a complete baby. *You loser.* I made sure my smile back was twice as bright as normal.

"Thank you," I said. "I'll make sure I get down there soon."

When I finished the papers, I detoured to the kitchenette for some coffee before going back to my desk, because I needed to shake myself out, to get out from under my constant, suffocating awkwardness. I lingered over the little metal tree of K-cups, walking my fingers over their tops like I knew the difference between Colombian dark roast and breakfast blend. There were mugs for employees in the cupboard, but I stuck to Styrofoam even though its filmy taste transferred to the coffee. I watched the black spill against bright white, quick drips, and then a steady stream. When I drew in a deep breath, the scent of it filled my nose, bringing to mind as it always did memories of my father.

Twice now I'd repeated my experiment with the hair catcher, and twice it found its way back into the drain. Flossie was definitely going into my apartment while I was out.

I'd always known she was a little much, between the obnoxious notes and asking me last week how her "dollhouse" was doing. But knowing for sure she'd been in my private space ruined the appeal of the little apartment. Now I sat on the sofa instead of lying down. I kept my dirty laundry in a pile on the floor of my closet, because I didn't want the landlord who wasn't supposed to be in there to think I was messy. And at least when I was home, I knew there was no one *currently* in the apartment. All day long at work I squeezed my pen, picturing the lock sliding backward, the knob turning, fuzzy pink slippers padding down my hallway. That was my space! The last thing I needed was another mother hovering over me, picking at me. The whole situation was making me weird over things that were actually helpful, the *coach,* for God's sake, taking time out to tell me to feel free to use the gym. And I had the nerve to twist that. I carried my coffee to my desk, thinking that as long as I held a cup of steaming liquid, no one would press me against the walls.

After spending a few hours updating the all-time stats lists,

I headed into the locker room with the beat writers, eyes up, recorder in hand. Out of habit, I followed the group to A.J.'s locker, which overflowed with supplements and designer freebies stuffed in behind a copy of *On the Road.* Bernie caught me looking at its creaseless spine and nudged me. "Think that's a nod to us?"

"To impress you?"

"No—because Kerouac's a *beat* writer."

Brian quipped, "'I saw the best minds of my generation destroyed by Madden.'"

We quieted down as the interview began. I was straining to hold my recorder close and trying to keep mental notes when someone behind me said, "Hey—Ponytail."

DeMario Jackson—mercifully in workout shorts—waved me over to his locker. He was a wall of muscle. He looked like he tossed cars around for fun. I hesitated, and Bernie, seeing what was going on, indicated his own recorder and mouthed, *I've got you.* I crinkled my eyes at him and ducked out of the huddle.

"You're writing that blog?"

DeMario had bright, expressive eyes and a mouth that twisted easily from resting pout to playful smirk. His shoulder-length locs were tied in a low, loose ponytail, and the sleeves of the T-shirt he pulled on fit like blood pressure cuffs.

I stammered. "I—my boss told me—well, Brent—"

"I asked you—you're writing that blog?" I nodded and he pulled a face. "How're you going to write a blog that's my blog and not talk to me about it?" He pulled a printout from his locker and read from it in a high, thin voice, bobbing his head as he spoke. "*I'm so excited to play Chicago. The city has a special place in my heart since my college days—*" He stopped. "Does that shit sound like me?"

A rush of heat flooded my cheeks, my ears, my neck. I'd *told* Brent! Hadn't I said this exact thing? And what was I supposed to say now, that I *wouldn't* keep doing what my boss had assigned me to do? "I'm really sorry. I'll see if I can switch it to another player—"

"I don't want you to switch it. But include *me.* Talk to *me.* We should do it together."

Now I was completely thrown. "Seriously? Every week?"

"Hey—I've got a lot of feelings. You and me are going to blog them out." He moved his hand back and forth between us. "Blogging buddies."

"Okay." I grinned, relieved. "Blogging buddies."

*

"How the hell did you get DeMario to do that?" Brent asked after the first joint blog went live. He and I were in the stadium waiting for an ESPN commentator to finish filming her stand-up. Normally this was a solo babysitting job, but with Monday Night Football coming up Brent was in full hovering mode. It was mid-October, one of the first really cold days of the year, and we were both in red Bobcats coats. For once I was grateful for the man-sized team gear, because the enormous coat hung past my knees and helped block out the frigid wind swirling through the stadium.

"I guess . . ." I grimaced, a mouth shrug. "He's a fan?"

"Yeah, right." We laughed, rocking up onto our toes to keep warm. "Good for you, kid, that's a big get. I can't believe Coach G gave him the go-ahead."

"Maybe he doesn't know about it."

"Well for God's sake, don't tell him."

A flash of something on the other side of the stadium caught my eye. I squinted across the field—there it was again, one section to the left. Whatever it was moved fast, not in the stadium bowl but inside along the concourse, and each time it passed the rectangular opening to the seats a shock of red split the concrete.

"What the hell . . . ?"

The figure made its way around the end zone, which was when I realized it was *James,* full-out running.

"Poppy, here you are—come on. We gotta go."

"*Me?*" My stomach cramped as I flashed through emergencies. Was there a fire at my apartment? Had something happened to my dad? James held up one hand while he caught his breath, and I steeled myself, straightening my spine and setting my shoulders against whatever I was about to hear.

"It's Chase—he switched the labels for the Coke and the Diet Coke on the soda machine."

I started at him blankly. "What the fuck are you talking about?"

"He switched them—to be a dick, like he always is. You know that ticket-sales girl is always talking about Atkins and ketosis. He's down there now watching to see if she drinks the regular soda. You've got to go do that, and then we tell him you have a condition that makes you react chemically to high-fructose corn syrup. It crashes your nervous system, I don't know, you'll make it up but we prank the prankster. Finally, we get him."

"*James.*" I wanted to use the heel of my hand to push his face away from me. He could get away with frat-boy bullshit as the assistant to the GM, but I was the media relations intern. My job was to shut up and stay out of the way, and here James was suggesting, in front of my *boss,* no less, that I walk away from work to go pull a prank on one of the players. "That's really obnoxious, and we're working here." I turned to Brent, an apology halfway out of my mouth, but stopped when I saw his face.

"Poppy." His voice had gone hoarse, and he was gazing into the distance with a thousand-yard stare. "Last season I pitched a community event. The offensive line built a playground for inner-city kids. We took pictures of them putting the slide together, hoisting up the swings, burying giant tires in the sand. A month later, I got a notice of suit—thick paper, on legal letterhead—saying the slide had collapsed and killed two kids."

"Oh my God."

"It was fake. Chase made the whole thing up—had a lawyer friend draft the letter so that when I looked up the firm it had a website and everything. I was practically pissing blood for three days until he finally told me, and then he took a photo of my face and kept it on the notice board for the rest of the season."

Brent put a hand on my shoulder with a pained squint like he was about to tell me the real fate of my childhood pet. The hand gripped. He sighed. "Play ball with us, Poppy."

*

"Okay." James coached the three of us as we rushed back along the concourse. "Drink the soda and sit down with Abby to eat your lunch, but keep putting your hand against your stomach. Then start to sway in your seat like you're dizzy. Abby's going to call for a trainer, and Deon will bring the backboard. Then we'll carry you out."

"I'm going to actually be sick."

"That's perfect."

We stopped outside the cafeteria doors, my shoes pointing left and away. This was a bad idea. On so many levels, I did not feel good about playing the starring role. Then James cupped his hands around the edges of my shoulders. Standing squarely across from him, the full heat of his dark-brown eyes looking dead into mine, I felt fingertips dance up my spine. James gave me a squeeze. "We're all counting on you, Pop Tart."

The cafeteria was much more full of staffers than it should have been at this time of day. Great—spectators. They mixed in with the players, buying food or sitting in little groups, but I knew that it was set dressing, like a scene from a spy novel where an entire train station is filled with decoys to make a private space feel public. There were too many eyeballs, all aimed at me. I hated it.

I grabbed a tray and slid it slowly along the metal rails by the hot food, stopping once to scoop a bowl of room-temperature pasta salad. The soda machine was at the end, and as I got closer I focused on lifting my shoes instead of dragging them. I wanted to be included, to be *in* on the joke, but in a perfect world I wouldn't actually *be* the joke. Glancing toward the doors, I saw Brent, arms folded, nodding encouragingly. *We're all counting on you.*

I filled my cup from the fountain marked Diet Coke, jumping at the *errrrrr* of the machine when it kicked on. Abby was at our usual table, looking impressively casual as she ate her salad.

"Hi, friend," she said when I sat down. "Thirsty?"

It's a joke, they're hazing me, just like they make the rookies wear coconut bras and sing island-themed karaoke. And once they do that, once they get through it, they're part of the team.

72

I picked up my cup and downed it.

"Poppy," Abby said two minutes later at unnatural volume. "Are you okay?"

"Yes." I forced myself not to look at Chase, "But it feels like the skin on my hands might be melting. There's no corn in this salad, is there?"

"No, but the Coke might have corn syrup."

"It can't—this is *Diet* Coke. I'd *never* drink regular, it could kill me."

Not for nothing, but I will say it got a lot easier to avoid looking at Chase once my head was immobilized by the backboard.

"Don't worry, Poppy, we've got you!" James called from his place near my feet while I bumped and bobbed my way out of the room. "Just focus on shallow breaths, okay, nothing too big. We'll call your parents so they'll know what hospital. Also—do you have a DNR?"

They carried me like that all the way through the bowels of the stadium and out the ambulance bay. "Commit, commit, commit," James muttered as we rushed past two members of the bewildered grounds crew. He and Brent were holding the board near my feet. Deon, the head trainer, walked briskly beside me, his face hidden behind a baseball cap and giant aviator shades. I didn't even know the two guys carrying the end with my head, although I was pretty sure the one on the left worked in the video department. None of them would make it through an egg-and-spoon race without cracking it, I could say that much.

Once we were in the parking lot, Deon unstrapped my legs, abdomen, and finally my head. I rolled it roughly across my shoulders, trying to counteract the cramp, while Brent stared at his Nokia.

"Lewis says Chaser hasn't swallowed once since you hit the deck. DeMario told him we don't give the interns health insurance so you'll have to go after him in court to handle the medical bills. Ha—he said all kinds of things come out in those depositions and asked if he remembered Puerto Vallarta. Chaser might cry, this is amazing."

It was freezing out there with the wind whipping across the miles of open parking lot. I'd left my coat outside the cafeteria, and so I had only my thin cardigan to block the cold. A nearby flag snapped and stretched at the top of its pole, and I shivered and rubbed my arms. "I'm going to try to finish those game notes, unless you want me to organize the headshots first."

Brent shook his head without looking up from his phone. "You're not going back in there."

"What?"

"Chaser thinks you're on your way to the hospital. You have to get out of here. Take the rest of today and tomorrow off, lay low over the weekend, and then we'll see you Monday for game day. Really try not to leave your apartment, though, I don't want anyone to see you out and about."

"You can't—" I had to stop myself from stomping my foot. "You cannot be serious!" I gave up cooking food outside of a microwave for this job. I, at twenty-two years old, moved my bedtime to ten p.m. just so every day I could enter an unwinnable battle royale to be the first person inside the building. I hadn't seen my family or friends for months, because the job was too busy and too important for something as basic as weekends. And now I was being sent home for *four days* for the sake of a prank?

Mo came down the hallway with a bulky black computer bag slung over his shoulder. "I brought you a laptop so you can keep up with everything. You're home, but you're not, you know, off." I glared as he handed it over, and he gave me a little wave.

Brent shot me with his finger gun. "Hey, great work today—see you on Monday."

*

But it worked. After that I wasn't just some intern. I was the girl our breakout rookie chose to blog with. I was the one who'd finally pranked Chase. I was Poppy fucking Benjamin, and people I didn't know said hi to me in the halls. Chase himself gave me a grudging fist bump when he saw me in the locker room after Game 7. "Okay, Pop Tart," he said as the rest of the team whooped and waved their towels. As we clicked through Games 8, 9, and 10, the team stayed undefeated, the pressure rose, and we members of the Bobcats pulled closer and closer together.

It was a feeling I'd chased my entire life, that ride-or-die comradery that comes from long hours and high stakes. It's the pang of jealousy watching an Oscar-winning cast climb onstage to accept their award, all arms around each other's shoulders and inside grins. It's the way Peace Corps volunteers in conflict-heavy areas end up at each other's holiday tables for life, or how a band's cramped and smelly tour bus feels like a never-ending summer camp you're not allowed to attend. There's something about a group of strangers choosing one another day after day that makes anyone not chosen feel discarded. Passed over.

But now I was in. I'd given something of myself, and in response the team made me one of their own. I stopped automatically parking in the back row of the staff lot even though it was almost empty when I arrived in the mornings. I ditched the Styrofoam, bought a mug from the pro shop, and put it in a place of pride right near the front of my desk. I left my staff ID on during after-work errands, angling myself so that the cashier could catch a glimpse.

The Bobcats had chosen me, and I chose them.

CHAPTER NINE

NOW

The team's mood was so heavy I was amazed our plane stayed in the air. "We're not doing anything tonight," Asbel had said on the tomb-silent shuttle to the airfield. "But I'll see you in my office first thing."

"That info wasn't from us. Isaac must have a contact with the poli—"

"Don't. Tomorrow."

I ducked my head and nodded.

The good news is, you looked great, Dayanna sent to the group chat.

Kiss Coach Nate on the mouth for me for finally punching out Dorchester, Sarah added.

I was grateful for them, always, but while I read the texts I swallowed and swallowed and swallowed. If we'd all gotten that note, why was *my* coach dead? Why had *my* press conference devolved into a melee? This wasn't an escape room the five of us were working through together; it was *Mystery Science Theater,* with me stumbling around trying to escape a monster while they watched and made commentary. I was alone. Completely alone.

It was my job to keep certain things quiet. I'd failed, and that pissed me off. After struggling through the past few days, I'd hoped that the game would be a reset because no matter how much people loved Red, they'd always love football more. Instead, Isaac's question reopened the wound. It brought attention back to the nasty particulars of Red's death, and now it would almost certainly spend another week as a main story. Internet sleuths would get involved, like this was all a game, morbid memes would be generated and used in joking tweets. We'd moved into a new phase now, the one where People Knew, or thought they did, and what came next was Demanding the Details.

Coach Nate sat alone on the plane. No one went near him. Sometime after we leveled off, Rodney climbed over my knees and plopped himself next to me. He stared at the seat back, then whispered, "Did you know anything about that?"

I shook my head, eyes wide, because the story might be out, but this I could still do.

"Man," he said. "He's dead either way, but I didn't know it was like that. When I heard they found him on the floor—"

"Lexi," I broke in, naming Red's wife. "Lexi found him on the floor."

"I thought he was just lying there. Like he was about to start a set of sit-ups or something. You know, too many . . ." Rodney mimed popping pills. He half stood, took a long, slow look around the plane, sat again. Then, even softer than before, he whispered, "You think he did it?"

"Who?"

Rodney bulged his eyes meaningfully and inclined his head toward Coach Nate.

"Are you serious?" I hissed. "Of course Nate didn't do it. They were friends."

"Okay," said Rodney, hoisting himself out of the seat. "But there was only one way on God's green earth *Coach Nate* was going to head an NFL team, and a few million people just saw what happens when he loses his temper."

I knew two things: Rodney couldn't resist a good conspiracy

theory, and Nate wouldn't hurt a fly . . . except for today. But he certainly didn't kill Red.

Someone did, though, didn't they? And if it was true that most murder victims died at the hand of someone they knew, it was also true that none of us on this plane, who'd spent our days, our nights, our weekends, our holidays with Red, we who knew him best, who fought with him and revered him, and cursed him, and would have followed him off a cliff, could have done it. We just couldn't have.

A screech of memories flew past like a freight train. Hands up to block a spray of champagne in a Super Bowl locker room. Water dripping from my sweater onto a plush carpet. Red cheating at King Rummy, leaning in close with comically raised eyebrows to see my cards. The splat of raw fish against our bus window outside another team's stadium. Cheering. Laughing. Screaming.

I held out my hand, fingers splayed, and focused hard on holding it still, but I couldn't—it jerked and jumped.

It was barely five o'clock when I got home, a fact that didn't stop me from diving headfirst into my comfiest clothes. I crawled into bed in mauve sweatpants and an extra-large cream sweater to watch footage of Nate coldcocking Isaac as the day's sports coverage churned on. A *SportsCenter* anchor quipped, "If the Bobcats had showed that kind of fight on the field, they might have lost by less than forty."

*

Asbel was a hands-off general manager in the sense that he felt our win-loss record spoke for itself and stayed out of media relations, which made my job much easier. Now, with one dead coach and another attacking reporters on camera, the first thing he said when I got to his office Monday morning was "Close the door."

I perched on the edge of a heavy hard-backed leather chair. Asbel sat forward with his elbows resting on his desk, fingers tented together. His thick gray hair and strong eyebrows were just the same as the day I met him. I was terrified of him back then—the way those dark eyes would flash just before the screaming started. It took me a while to learn that was mostly window dressing, to focus on what he did instead of what he said.

Asbel inclined his chin toward the clips packet at the edge of his desk. The top page was an angry image of Nate's fist connecting with Isaac's jaw, Isaac's skin caught mid-ripple from the impact, his eyes wide behind his glasses. "That idiot got himself suspended."

I grimaced, but it wasn't exactly unexpected. "How many games?"

"Three. It was five, but I yelled at someone."

"Who are you going to have fill in?"

"The hell if I know—you want to do it?"

It figured. Rodney's pot stirring aside, Nate was the mild-mannered coach of my dreams, so of course he snapped on his first day and was already gone. I rubbed at the space between my eyebrows.

"Punching out Isaac Dorchester," mused Asbel. "If I could, I'd give him a raise. Granted, he laid it on a little thick with that 'honoring Red's memory' bullshit, considering."

"Considering?"

"Nate was in here last summer making the case for his turn. I had to sit through a whole PowerPoint deck of ideas for revamping the offense—and you can tell how good those were, considering yesterday he couldn't find the end zone with a map and a fucking headlamp."

"That's crazy."

"Keep your friends close."

So Nate had gone behind Red's back to take a shot at the top chair. I phrased my next question carefully. "Was that something you were considering? A change?"

As grimy as it felt now, after ordering 315 roses delivered to Red's funeral to match the Syracuse area code, it would have been justified. Coaches like Red had a long leash, but the memory of that initial wave of success was fading. The second Super Bowl was eight years ago, when half the guys on our roster were still in high school.

Last year we would have missed the playoffs entirely if the rest of our division wasn't so weak, and the 1–5 start this season all but guaranteed we'd be eliminated before Thanksgiving.

Asbel scoffed. "We're not in the business of firing coaches here. Especially someone like Red, who's earned a little loyalty."

At that word, I looked at Asbel long and hard, but his brow was smooth and there was no trace of irony in his voice. Most GMs served at the favor of their team's owners, but Asbel had been here so long under an owner who held some of the last first-person memories of the Battle of the Bulge that he *was* the Bobcats. Together, Asbel and Red, with A.J. as their quarterback, had enjoyed the kind of long-term stability almost unheard of in professional sports. They were an unimpeachable unit.

But I had been here just as long as Red. I also had standing with this team. And Asbel of all people should acknowledge that I already knew plenty about loyalty.

"It's not like it would have been out of the question," I said finally. "He was losing the locker room, especially A.J., and on Twitter the fans have been screaming—"

"I'll be sure to check in with DonkeyBallz69 before making any personnel decisions going forward, how about that?" Asbel snapped. "Does that work for you, Poppy?" I pressed my lips together, because I knew better than to push any further. Not today. "Oh, and since you brought up A.J.—you two are going to be spending some quality time together."

"No. I—"

"He's a malcontent, and I don't want him running his mouth while things are so in flux, so from now on, you're with him at every event—community relations, branding. I don't want him so much as calling his mother without you doing the dialing. You got it?"

I nodded, grinding my teeth to dust. This was purely punitive for questioning his decision-making about Red, and we both knew it.

He went on, "More fucking good news—DeMario's out."

"How long for him?"

"For good."

My hand went to my mouth. "How can that be? He walked off. He's—*DeMario.*"

"He was DeMario. Now he's a relic with his third ACL tear and a contract that expires at the end of the season. He's not going to stay on for rookie money, and I can't pay him more than that to hold up a pair of crutches on the sideline. He's done."

My heart sank to the industrial carpet. In the time I'd been here hundreds of players had come and gone. Some were nightmares, most were perfectly nice and treated me with courtesy and respect, but there weren't many I'd call an actual friend. DeMario was different. Our blog was the first big thing I did right—that was a gift he gave me, one that showed my bosses I could add real value around here. It also signaled to the other players how I should be treated, because if DeMario Jackson thought I was okay, I damned well must have been.

Beyond that, we'd had fun together—goofing off at endless media days, standing backstage at late-night talk shows after the Super Bowl wins. We'd been to the White House together more than most low-ranking members of Congress. We were both thirty-seven, and people had the same regard for defensive ends at that stage of life as they did for unmarried women. I loved Faith, I loved their kids. DeMario was, without a doubt, my favorite player. And now, one bad angle of his foot against the grass and it was over.

"I just talked to Deon this morning—DeMario doesn't even know yet," said Asbel. "He's smart enough to figure out it's season-ending, but the rest . . ." I nodded numbly.

He squinted at me, chewing thoughtfully on the inside of his lip. Then he nodded once, like he'd made a decision. "There's something else. The results from Red's preliminary toxicology report came back."

"I thought that took weeks."

"I don't ask what they do, Poppy, I just call up and offer good tickets, and they tell me what I want to know."

"Anything interesting?"

"Yes."

"What was it?"

"Nothing."

"I don't understand."

Asbel spoke slowly and meaningfully. "There was nothing in his system—no drugs, no alcohol, no medications."

That was stranger than it sounded. Red was a former athlete, which meant he took a great-aunt's handbag worth of meds to manage the aftereffects of all that crashing and jolting. His affinity for alcohol was well documented by anyone who'd seen him after three p.m., but Asbel and I were close enough to know it was more than that—Red needed those drinks. In recent years it had started to show, a collection of permanently strained blood vessels across his nose and face like a sunburn. He'd grown a beard to hide the ruddiness of his skin, but it couldn't reach the tops of his cheeks, and it did nothing to camouflage the puffiness around his eyes. Red drank every single day—he had to. He drank straight past the warning labels on all those prescription bottles, he drank before he got in cars. He even drank before games. It was something people in the building had started whispering about, often in the same breath as our win-loss record, but Asbel wouldn't hear it. He hired Red a driver and kept an overflowing basket of breath mints outside his office.

Now Asbel was telling me that on the night Red Guillory was killed, not a single substance oozed through his veins.

"What does it mean?"

"It means I don't know what the fuck is going on, and I don't like not knowing what's going on, Poppy."

You and me both.

"So what do you want me to do, solve the murder?"

"No, just avoiding assault charges at our press conferences should do it—do you think you can handle that?"

I intertwined my fingers and squeezed—I never fidgeted in front of Asbel. "Should we still go ahead with the plans for the memorial?" We'd announced a Day in Celebration of Red Guillory. In addition to the tribute video, there would be Bobcats-branded tissues at every seat to let fans know they'd be crying and a bank of collection boxes for team-affiliated charities.

"Of course," said Asbel. His voice was firm. "The rest of us aren't dead yet."

My legs shook on the walk back to my office. "Give me an hour—please," I told Chloe when she tried to hand me a pile of messages, then closed the door behind me. When I turned around to face my desk, I stopped short. A frisson skittered from ankles to neck.

A small white envelope sat alone in the center of my desk.

Pulse pounding in my ears, I approached it like a bomb—slowly, and without taking my eyes off of it. It seemed to quiver, vibrating with the force of whatever would be inside. I knew before I was close enough to read it that the return address would say Truth or Consequences. I'd stared at the first envelope long enough to memorize their shape.

I allowed myself to the count of three, and then to ten. Finally, snatching it up, I ripped open the paper.

You know what you did.

Soon they all will too.

Tell the truth . . .

"It came in today's mail," Rodney called through the closed door. "Maybe you have a fan?"

"Only one?" I joked weakly. This time I could read the postmark—Queens. The Hoboken bar. That feeling of being watched. What if . . . ? Heart pounding, I put my head down on my desk and pressed my clammy forehead against the blotter, inhaling the scent of industrial cleaner.

My phone buzzed—a text from Bernie.

I heard from a good source that Isaac was right. Red was murdered?!

Don't know anything about it, I lied, then bit at my cuticle watching the ellipses dance as Bernie wrote his response, because Bernie was a good reporter and Asbel's admonishment to keep things under control was still ringing in my ear.

Another text popped up, this time from Sarah to the group chat:

I just got my mail.

Same here, came Dayanna's immediate reply.

Anyone want to clue in your West Coast friend? asked Nisha.

I was about to suggest we save it for a video call when Sarah wrote, *We got another note. If this isn't going away, we need to start thinking about a plan of action.*

Was it the same? texted Annika. *Was anyone else threatened? I'm not that comfortable sitting back and waiting for another Red.*

Bernie's response came through. *You're sure? Because with something this delicate I'd rather work with you to get it right than go off rumors.*

No one else is going to get hurt because it's NOT CONNECTED, I typed furiously to the group chat. *There's going to be a full-blown police investigation here and I don't want this shit in the chat history on my work phone so can we please save it for a video call?*

I knew this was hitting me harder than the others, but honestly, what were they thinking? These messages weren't private—not when subpoenas were involved—and we had to stop acting like this group chat was a safe space. It wasn't.

Was that meant for me?

My blood froze. I hadn't sent that to the group text, I'd sent it to *Bernie.* I'd be reporting *myself* for Red's murder if I'd read that out of context. The phone buzzed again, and I cringed so hard my teeth hurt. Maybe if I never read his response this would go away. Things would slow down and stop spiraling out of control, and it would all just . . . go . . . away.

Poppy, I'm a sportswriter. This is above my pay grade. But I don't know what to do with a message like that when a friend of ours has just been murdered.

I could hear my own ragged breathing growing louder and louder as the reality of what I'd just done sunk in. I couldn't let Bernie—*a reporter*—think I'd had anything to do with Red's death, but I certainly couldn't tell him about the notes. I looked wildly around my desk, eyes flitting across the lipstick mark on the rim of my mostly empty coffee cup, past a printed draft of Chloe's game notes, and landing on the clips packet. And then my breathing slowed.

It was time to snap out of it. I wasn't proud of what I was about to do—it wasn't nice and it wasn't fair—but right now I didn't have the luxury of either of those things. Picking up my cell phone, I tossed my hair back and set my jaw. I widened my eyes to the size of a doe's and tucked my chin, because it's scientifically proven that facial expressions can be heard over the phone. Then I dialed Bernie.

He picked up on the first ring, and from the hollow echo around his voice, it sounded like he was in his car. "What the hell is going on?" he said. "Jeez, kid."

I faked a sob and was surprised at how easily it came. "I can't imagine what you must have thought reading that, Bern, oh my God. I'm just . . . falling apart. It's too much, losing Red and being in the middle of the season. I just still can't believe he's gone."

"I know." Bernie's voice was softer now. He was a good guy, a fact I was going to take full advantage of. "Me too. But what . . . ?"

"Clearly I misfired that text—I'm such a mess! I'm so embarrassed, this isn't like me at all. But it's not what you're thinking, *obviously*. Can you even imagine?" I paused, sniffling directly into the phone. "It wasn't about Red. Ugh, you know already, so I may as well give you the story. I guess if anyone's going to write it, I'm glad it's you." I took a deep breath, pretended to gather my courage. "It was about DeMario."

*

When I hung up the phone, I stared at my desktop, holding the shock of what I'd done in my chest. It hurt. My chest hurt with it, and I was filled with the urge to vomit, to get it out, but there was nothing to be done because it was part of me. It was who I was. I'd protected myself. I'd kept my own secrets.

And I'd sacrificed DeMario to do it.

CHAPTER TEN

FIFTEEN YEARS AGO

Week 11 was the first time it happened. Somewhere, someone in the office whispered the phrase "'72 Dolphins," and from then on everything changed. The '72 Dolphins were the first—and only—NFL team to go undefeated. It took seventeen games to run the table back then instead of nineteen like today, but they were still the gold standard. And we were more than halfway there.

The air inside the building felt thinner, and like there wasn't enough of it to go around. The constant digs and pranks got a little harsher, a little sharper. We'd left the fun behind sometime around Week 8. Now it was a grind, week in and week out. Every team gave us their best shot. Every game was a war, and while losing felt like the end of the world, winning had become something else entirely. It didn't ease the pressure—it added to it. Game by game, brick by brick. We were suffocating.

Coach and A.J. had a heated exchange coming out of the tunnel for the second half against Carolina. While the rest of the players and coaches jogged around them, they faced off, Coach's finger in A.J.'s face.

"Teeeeeeen feet to the left," Brent sighed, waving his hands like he could push them backward. "We can't fight it out in the hallway without half of America watching?"

"What are they fighting about?" I asked. A.J. threw his arm out, indicating the far end zone, or maybe the scoreboard.

Bernie leaned back from his seat in the front row of the press box. "Brian can read lips. He says it's either *tuck this slit* or *duck Bisquick*."

"Definitely the second one," said Brent, and then, "Ohhhhh, come on," as A.J. knocked Red's finger away from his face and stalked off toward the sideline. "Nobody write that," he called to the already typing press. "We're all getting out of here on time tonight, I TiVoed *Survivor.*"

The first play from scrimmage was an easy handoff to the running back, who tunneled up the middle for one yard. Second down was also a run, this time for no gain.

"Let's see that cannon," Brent said as the team broke huddle. With nine yards to go to pick up a first down, we'd expect A.J. to throw the ball. Instead, they lined up in an I-formation, like we were getting ready for a short-yardage run.

"Uh, A.J.," said Brent. On the sidelines Coach Guillory was crouching with his hands on his knees, staring at A.J. like he was about to charge him. "I don't think that was the play call . . ."

"Looks like someone doesn't want to strain himself while they're up big," muttered Bernie, and I looked to Brent, confused. That made no sense—A.J. was a beast. If throat ripping was allowed in football there'd be blood all over his teeth. But Brent was focused on the field.

A.J. received the snap and handed the ball off to the running back, who was immediately stuffed for a loss of two. The punting unit jogged onto the field while the offense came off, shaking their heads. A.J. went directly to the bench to sit between two giant fans, and Coach stalked him over there and started screaming, gesturing angrily to the coach's box, where the offensive coordinator called the plays from. A.J. sat with his legs splayed and his shoulder blades against the back of the bench, but his face was stone.

"He wants to call the plays," said Steven. "I bet you anything A.J. was like, 'This one's in the bag, let me call them from the line.'"

"He thinks he's Jim Kelly," said Bernie, referencing a Hall of Fame quarterback from Buffalo who did just that.

"Steve's probably right," Brent said to me quietly. "I'll tell you what, though—he might just be Jim Kelly. A.J.'s going to be here longer than either of us. Maybe even longer than Red."

The defense did its job, and soon our own punt-return team was coming off the field. But during the TV time-out, Coach pulled our left tackle, Owen, aside and said something close to his helmet. Owen turned quickly toward Coach with his palms raised, like he didn't understand, but Coach just gestured toward the field, where the man with orange sleeves was walking off to indicate that we were back from commercial.

"That was weird," said Brent. The team huddled briefly, broke, and set themselves up for another run play. Nothing unusual there. But when the ball was snapped, Owen stunted to the right, picking up the defensive tackle in double coverage with our left guard and leaving a freeway-sized hole for Carolina's defensive end to come flying at A.J. and absolutely pancake him.

He got up looking furious and spit on the field, then dutifully executed a pass to the slot receiver on second down, picking up an eleven-yard gain.

Bernie twisted around in his chair. "Sorry, Brent. Looks like we already know who won *Survivor.*"

*

Monday morning I got to the stadium so early I worried my badge wouldn't work. Over the last few weeks I'd played around with the order when delivering the morning papers. Asbel was always first, but after that I sometimes started with the owner. Sometimes I did Richard's next, sometimes the assistant coaches'. The list was meant to cut the most direct path around the building—this desk, then this desk, then this desk—but I crisscrossed. I doubled back. I took detours.

Every day when I got to Coach Guillory's office, he was sitting at his desk, and I tried to ignore the flicker, that not-quite-identifiable feeling that tickled the space between my shoulder blades. He smiled. He was pleasant. It was more than any intern could expect from a head coach, let alone one in the middle of a historic season. But every day, I tried to figure out the timing of paper deliveries so that when I came into that office it would be empty. No such luck today.

"Cold enough for you?" he asked. I wasn't sure what to expect after all the drama yesterday, but he just seemed like Coach. It was three days before Thanksgiving, and since I'd come inside a light snow that probably wouldn't stick had started. I was wearing a fitted charcoal sweater over a pink-and-gray skirt, plus stockings that did very little to keep out the chill. "It sure is," I said. He indicated the corner of his desk, and I nudged a pile of folders inward to make room for my stack.

That should have been the end of it, so I gave a little wave, but Coach Guillory wriggled his shoulders against the back of his chair. "The air—this time of year. It's always so dry. Hey, can you help me out?" He turned sideways in the chair and angled his back toward me. "It itches right in the very center."

My pulse tickled my ears. He'd said it so casually, and I felt so young, like a third-grader who giggles at the word *bra*. It wasn't—he was just—

Our head coach was sitting there, back turned, asking me to help with something. And I was hesitating because . . . why, exactly? What was my problem? I had no answer, at least not one I could put words to.

Eyes on the carpet, I reached tentative fingers toward him until they met the artificial silkiness of his dryfit shirt. His back was taut, with broad shoulders built up by thousands of chest flies and rows and bench presses. The power in his body—the strength of it—cracked and sparked beneath my fingers while I clawed and unclawed my hand twice, sure he could feel my breaths on the back of his neck. Somehow, impossibly, sure I could feel his on the back of mine. He let out a deep sigh and let his head drop forward as my cheeks burned. I heard the soft shuffle of footsteps coming down the carpeted hallway and yanked my hand away. Jaw tight, my eyes skittering around the room, I turned and quickly left, almost bumping into Asbel on my way out the door.

"Sorry," I managed.

I could feel Asbel's eyes following me down the hall the same way I imagined I could feel Coach's skin caught beneath my fingernails. The fluorescent lighting glared down like a never-ending row of spotlights, and I realized I was practically running. I forced myself to slow as I moved through the main workspace, giving James a weak smile as I passed his desk. I made it back to Media Relations and sank into my chair to find two emails waiting for me. One, empty except for its subject line, was from James.

Everything ok?

The other was from Coach Guillory. I stared hard at it while a roaring filled my ears. Clicked.

That really hit the spot, thanks. You have magic fingers!

I deleted them both.

*

In a flurry of productivity, I finished the game notes, transcribed two long-form interviews for a piece Brent was working on, and helped several confused fans navigate the new light-rail schedule from Armory Square over the phone.

"Wow," said Brent, hovering over my desk with his BlackBerry in hand. "You have lightning fingers."

"What?" It came out a croak.

Brent turned the phone so that its screen faced me. "Those transcripts. You're faster than Julie around a tray of doughnuts. Nice work."

I struggled to calm my breathing, to slow my pulse. I fought the urge to push back from my desk and shake out my hands. "Thanks."

"You know, I used to be a Speedy Gonzales in my transcription days. I think it's because my mom made me take piano lessons—

don't tell anyone that, humiliating—but I can work my hands like no one's business."

"You're a Renaissance man," I managed weakly.

"Nah, I like Marriott. Better pillows." With a wink and a click of his tongue, he was gone. I looked into the admin's office to see if she'd registered the pinball effect—*ding! ding!*—of Brent's cringe-inducing comments. Her glasses were pushed on top of her head, and she was mouthing along to something on her computer. She either hadn't noticed or wasn't bothered. *See?* I chided myself. *You're being a baby.*

I grabbed my lanyard and headed toward reception. If anyone asked where I was going, I'd say I forgot something in my car. Maybe ten minutes in the cold would finally force out the flush my cheeks had been carrying since the morning. Maybe the bitter Syracuse winds would be the slap that snapped me out it.

"Hey, Poppy!"

It was Neil, from accounting. I was sure there were people I'd be less happy to see—Slobodan Milošević, maybe—but when he came bearing down on me with his sausage-like fingers and dusting of white flakes on his shoulders, I wanted to punch the wall. I wanted to bolt for the ladies' lounge, fling open the door, and scream, "SANCTUARY!" and then enjoy five minutes in a place where men couldn't paw at me.

"Hi, Neil."

"Nice skirt—love that schoolgirl look."

"I'm just heading out to my car for a second." I started to move around him, but he stepped to the side, blocking my path.

"Without your coat? *Iiieee.* It's freezing out there. You don't want to get goose bumps—or any other signs of the cold, right? Ha!"

"I'll be fine, thanks."

I all but pushed my way past him, crossing my arms tightly in front of my chest. His shoes squeaked as he followed me down the hall. "So what's your plan for Thanksgiving? Are you going home?"

"No." The team was playing on the road, so I could technically travel back to Ohio, but hard pass. I didn't want to fight the vicious traffic all the way down I-90, and for complicated reasons, Thanksgiving wasn't my favorite holiday.

I turned into reception, and Neil dropped back to let me through the doorway, then scuttled along until we were even again. "You know, my wife and I host every year, so if you need a place to go for dinner—"

"Actually, we already made plans."

Abby appeared out of nowhere and stood beside me so that the two of us made a wall across from Neil—me feeling like a rabbit trapped in the center of the road and exhausted from darting between the cars. Abby in her polka-dot blouse and heels no thicker than kabob skewers. Either one of us on our own would be physically unimpressive. Either one of us alone could be pushed up against a wall. But together we swelled to greater than the sum of our parts. Together we drove Neil from accounting all the way out of reception and back down the hallway with nothing more than two hard-eyed stares.

"Say thanks to your wife for us, though," muttered Abby when he was gone.

"Thank *you,*" I said.

"Don't mention it. Oh, and you totally can, you know. Come for Thanksgiving. My roommate is traveling, so it's just going to be me at my place."

"Oh, no, that's okay."

Abby arched an eyebrow. "You have plans?"

"I don't," I admitted.

"So let's just say that now we both do."

*

Abby's apartment was in a U-shaped complex of three buildings around a courtyard. Hers, the base of the U, had a common room with a large-screen TV and a pool table, a bar area, and a gym. It felt like a grown-up dorm, the type of place where *I* wanted to live, not the seventies-style attic I tiptoed around in because the insulation was so thin. Abby didn't have to time her laundry so that the dryer never buzzed after ten p.m., and there was no one here to sneak into her apartment and put their fingers on her private things. But the budget was the budget, and so Dave and Flossie's it was for me.

Abby opened her door in a black silk maxi dress and bare feet, a half-full wineglass dangling from her fingers. I immediately wanted to back away in my skinny jeans and one-shoulder blouse, but she reached out and squeezed my arm. "Cheers—yours is on the counter. Come on in. I have no idea how to tell when the chicken is done."

It wasn't until I hung my coat in the closet that I realized I should have brought something. Great—underdressed *and* empty-handed. Abby was probably already regretting inviting me.

I took in the apartment, chic and sunny with its light floors and sky-blue walls. The foyer blended into a kitchenette, which in turn became the living room on the far side of the breakfast bar. The coffee table held a stack of copies of *The New Yorker,* and I recognized a framed Ansel Adams photo above the sofa. The Mission-style furniture was basic but in good condition.

"It's gorgeous in here," I said, spinning to take it in. "And it smells like . . . did you say chicken?"

"I couldn't find a small enough turkey. My oven only fits chickens."

"Really?" I peered through the glass window at a tinfoil-covered bird. It did look pretty tight in there. I stood. "Okay, put me to work."

We chatted while I peeled potatoes and Abby dumped sliced apples into a premade pie crust. She mixed in scoops of sugar without stopping to measure or consult a recipe, just assuming that whatever she threw in would make a pie. And for someone like Abby, it probably would.

If I was home right now I'd be shivering under a blue-and-cream stadium blanket as Dad's team faced off against their crosstown rivals. My brothers and I would be passing a thermos of spiked coffee, warming our insides against air crisp enough to pink our ears and cheeks. I could almost hear the muffled *thwump thwump* of my hands as I clapped in thick wool mittens. I looked forward to that game all year.

But afterward, my brothers got to join Dad and his team for a pizza lunch while I had to go help my mom. We'd work in the kitchen side by side, which wasn't so different from this except that I hated being pulled away for no reason other than the fact that I was the girl. I resented my mother for making me peel and stir and sift and slice. She had always been jealous of how close I was with my dad, and she was always doing petty things like that to get between us. Every year while I stirred the cranberries I'd watch them pop and hiss in the pot and think, *I know what you mean.* But this year, someone else would have to make the sauce. I was busy doing something important, something the whole country was watching and following and talking about.

"I think we're ready." Abby broke into my thoughts. "Let's eat."

We filled our plates and carried them to the small square table marooned between the kitchenette and living room. The Dallas-Philadelphia game was on in the background, and we watched as we ate since Dallas, the defending two-time Super Bowl champions, had knocked the Bobcats out of the playoffs both times. They looked unstoppable again. The difference was that this season, the Bobcats did too.

The Dallas quarterback handed the ball off to his running back, who plowed forward three steps, pulled up, and lobbed the ball downfield. The receiver was all alone when he caught it, and he streaked to the end zone untouched. On the sideline, Coach Craig Washington, a six-foot-five giant with a shock of orange hair, pumped his fist. Dallas ran a dazzlingly fast, mobile offense that had earned the nickname Hell on Wheels, and people had already dubbed a potential showdown between him and Coach Guillory "Red vs. Red."

"Can you imagine us running a halfback option?" I asked. "A.J. would give up his endorsement portfolio before he'd let someone else throw the ball."

"What's a halfback option?"

94

I looked to see if Abby was kidding. She wasn't, so I gestured toward the TV. "What they just did—the quarterback gave the ball to the halfback, and then the halfback threw it instead of him. It's super rare." When she shrugged and took a bite of salad, I said, "Are you not that into football?"

"Not really." She put three fingers to her mouth while she chewed, then swallowed. "I want to be in marketing, but for something a little more important, you know? Maybe like an art museum, or for films."

I scooped up another forkful of potato. *Films* was one of those red-flag words that usually signaled someone I was not going to be very close with. And shouldn't a person who wanted to work at an art museum have deeper cuts on her walls than Ansel Adams?

"How did you end up working here then?"

"Oh, like everyone else—I had a connection. My dad's firm worked for the Aberfords and Mel liked him. And then Mel's youngest grandson is interning with my dad's firm now. That's just how it works, you know?"

Not really, no. That wasn't how it worked for me, but did that make me weird? Football was my life, it was all I'd ever wanted to do, and these jobs were so underpaid and hard to get that I'd just assumed everyone else at work felt the same. But was being at the Bobcats just another job to them? Was everyone laughing at me, skulking around the practice field and trying to sniff the grass?

Abby must have misread my stricken expression, because she gave me a sympathetic smile. "It's your first time away for the holidays, huh?"

Maybe that's what this was—she'd taken me in for the day like a lost kitten. I was wearing the wrong thing and fangirling over offensive schemes and yes, okay, maybe missing being with my family for the holiday, but I was also an adult.

"It is, but that's fine with me. Actually, I prefer it."

Abby cocked her head, looking at me with new attention. I'd surprised her and it felt good. "My Thanksgivings were not great either. My mom would spend all day cooking a huge meal and then every time I put something on my plate she'd do this little half cough. It was like a test." Looking down at tonight's dinner, Abby pushed the plate away and sipped her wine instead.

"My mom never stopped wishing I was someone else. And I guess that's her right, but don't *tell* me about it, you know?" I wrinkled my nose. "She calls me 'Sunshine.' Like, not in a nice way."

"*My* mom enrolled us in the Mommies and Minis doubles tournament at our club and then got mad at me when I played 'mannish tennis.' Like it's my fault Sloane Gimbsly has a shit backhand."

"Sounds like you were pretty good."

"Miss Junior Vermont Tennis Association Champion, 1996 through '98."

Abby refilled her glass and then tipped the bottle toward me. Most of my drinking had been from plastic cups in crowded bars, shots with degrading names like Redheaded Slut or Dirty Girl Scout. I could count on one hand the number of times I'd had wine without the word *zinfandel* involved, and I'd never tried the blood-red kind in front of me now, so thick in my mouth I almost chewed it. I'd had enough, but we'd bonded there for a minute and I didn't want to ruin it, and so I nodded, and we clinked.

My phone buzzed in my pocket. I pulled it out expecting to hit ignore on a call from my parents, but it was a text from an unknown number. "Sorry," I said as I opened it.

Happy Thanksgiving, Pop Tart. Hope you got your fill today.

James. A warming bubble rose through my chest as my free hand played with my hair. He was thinking of me? On Thanksgiving? I took a long drink and typed back, *You too. Go for the extra dessert.* After some thought, I added a winking emoji. Why not? It was more flirtatious than I would normally be, but I was out and chewing wine on my first Thanksgiving away from home. A little adult banter seemed appropriate.

Abby half stood from her chair and craned to see. "Okay— what's *that* about?"

"Just James." I snapped the phone shut and jammed it back into my pocket. "I don't even know how he got my number."

"Staff directory," said Abby. She pursed her lips in a teasing smile. "Are you into him?"

"Nope." I said it too quickly, but she was nice enough to pretend she didn't notice. "We're just friends. Not even that, really—we're like, work . . . people."

Abby raised her glass and winked at me before downing it. "Well, here's to work people."

*

"Poppy B," said Brent when he walked in Monday morning. From the looks of things, he'd gotten a fresh dye job and hit the tanning bed hard over the holiday weekend, but he sounded lackluster, a little less Brent-like than usual.

It was good to be back after so many days away. I didn't have any friends here outside of work, and Abby and I had already hung out on Thursday. I wanted to text James, but I *really* wanted him to text me, so I held off, and Mo and I didn't know each other like that. I'd considered making up an IT problem so I'd have an excuse to get in touch—maybe accidentally on purpose changing a few settings on my work laptop?—before realizing what a jerk move that would be during the break.

"Did you have a nice holiday?" I asked.

"Yeah . . ." He sighed. "Listen, kid, let's talk."

Nothing good has ever come from that opener, and my body was instantly on full alert.

Brent peered at me. "Did you spend Thanksgiving with that girl Abby? From marketing?"

"Yeah," I said, completely thrown. How would Brent know about that already?

"Don't hang out with her."

The words slapped me. That was outside of work, my private life, and it's not like I was hitting up P.F. Chang's with one of the players. Abby was just another female employee about my age. If I couldn't hang out with her, who *was* it okay to be around?

"Look." He leaned his elbows on the desk. "You're doing a good job here. We like you."

"Thank you," I managed.

"I want you to be here next season, and I think *you* want to be here next season, and so we both need you not to get fired." I was still reeling at the word *fired* when Brent continued, "Abby has . . . a reputation. That shit catches like viruses, and if people knew you were hanging out with her, her bad reputation becomes your bad reputation." He held up his palms. "I have nothing against the girl, I don't even know her. It just is what it is."

"What kind of reputation?"

Brent's eyes flicked to the closed annex door. "You know, her outfits are kind of . . . She likes to show it off, she likes the attention. And maybe she's not trying to snag a player, okay, maybe she just likes people looking at her, but it's not cool at work, you know?"

"Uh-huh." Pencil skirts. Fitted blouses and sweaters. Yes, they were tight, and yes, she looked great in them, but I tried to remember if I'd ever even glimpsed Abby's shoulders. And then it clicked—Neil from accounting. Abby was the one who helped drive him back, she'd sent him packing down the hall by fibbing that we'd be having Thanksgiving together. And then he ran to Brent, all concerned whispers. *I'm worried about Poppy. She's too good of a girl to get mixed up with someone like that.*

"I don't think she's missing too many happy hours at Thirsty Charlie's, if you know what I mean, and—look, I shouldn't be telling you this," his voice dropped even lower, "but last year she was fucking a scout. Major league sloppy, everybody knew about it. She would have gotten fired if her dad wasn't some big friend of the Aberfords. That's that nepotism shield for you, and it sucks, but it's the way the world works."

That was the way the world worked? Because it sure sounded to me like two consenting adults hooked up, and only one of them was in trouble. Was that because scouting was more important than marketing, or because the scout was a dude and Abby wasn't? My heart raced at the thought of the texts I'd exchanged with James.

If Brent knew about them, would he still think I was doing a good job?

Brent's shoulders relaxed, now that this Very Uncomfortable Conversation was over. He cracked his gum and patted my shoulder.

"Don't worry about it, Pop, you couldn't have known. I've got your back."

CHAPTER ELEVEN

NOW

Coach number three was also homegrown. Four years ago Dominick Russo retired from heading the tight ends and had worked in the front office ever since. I saw him most mornings in the kitchenette trying to decode the cappuccino machine, and now he would be at the helm of a multibillion-dollar franchise.

"I know it's only three games," said Rodney as we watched Chloe carrying a potted plant toward the coaches' wing. I'd dispatched her to help bring Coach Russo's things into Red's vacated space. "But don't sleep on that ficus for coach. We could get it a hat and some tiny sunglasses."

"Asbel knows what he's doing. Just do a find and replace on the release about Nate," I instructed, checking my phone for the millionth time. I'd just finished reading Bernie's story on DeMario, which had brought a flurry of demands for immediate availability. I had a blistering headache, and thanks to Asbel's new edict that I follow A.J. around, in twenty minutes I'd be on a bus headed toward the Adirondacks. *Don't forget,* hissed a little voice, *it's day four.* As if I could. "Or, actually," I amended, "forget it, I'll do that."

"Poppy." Rodney gave me the look he reserved for when I was

being, as he called it, Super Pop. It wasn't that I couldn't delegate, I just knew what I wanted and could do it better than anyone else, and so it saved time if I did it myself. I grudgingly sighed.

"Fine, you do it. Thank you."

Chloe returned, wiping dirt from her hands onto a paper towel so as not to stain her high-waisted trousers. She was young and bright, in sharp contrast to my own drawn, exhausted face. When had that happened? When had passing expressions of anxiety and concern become permanent, so that my baseline was a deficit I had to work against just to look normal? I took in Chloe's glowing skin and upturned mouth and felt like a fairy-tale witch lusting after her youth. "Chlo, can you go take this to Asbel to get his sign-off?"

"I can't—his door is closed."

"Really?" That was strange. "Since when?"

"Since the red-haired guy went in there. I saw him at reception when I was delivering papers."

I didn't know about any meeting with a red-haired guy—certainly not one that would have started at six thirty. None of our assistants had red hair, and neither did anyone in the front office.

Unless . . .

Asbel, *no.*

"I'll take the form."

"Go, Super Pop, go!" Rodney called down the hallway after me. I ignored him and broke into a near run.

"He's busy," Asbel's longtime assistant, Dot, said as soon as she saw me coming.

"Yeah, I just need this signed." Increasing my stride, I headed straight for his office door. Dot leapt from behind her desk to block me. "Excuse me. I *need* this signed. I'm leaving soon and it has to get posted." The blinds were drawn on the narrow windows to either side of Asbel's door, and I ducked and squinted, trying to make anything out through the slats. The move brought a look from Dot that I hadn't seen since my intern days.

"Leave it with me," she insisted. "I'll have him do it when he comes out." One of her eyebrows quirked above her glasses as she showed me the bottom of her chin. We stared each other down for a few more beats, but I knew a brick wall when I saw one.

"As *soon* as he comes out," I said, and Dot smirked.

Outside the stadium it was so cold that the sidewalk sparkled. I followed the stream of players in team-issued sweatpants and ski hats toward the two waiting buses. My winter-white dress coat looked great but tapped out at about fifteen degrees, meaning icy winds pierced it from all sides. I buried my hands deep within its pockets and hurried as fast as my ankle boots would allow on the frosted sidewalk. But then I stopped, forcing the crowd to split to either side, and looked toward the windows of Asbel's office. Of course, the blinds were drawn.

What if I just—didn't go? What if I stayed here and set up camp beside Dot's desk until Asbel opened the door and had to look me in the face when Craig Washington walked sheepishly out? He was the only person in football I could think of with flaming red hair, and there was only one reason he'd be in a closed-door meeting before dawn with our general manager. I should be *in* that meeting, explaining that Asbel absolutely *could not* bring on our biggest and most hated rival, the one whose name was inscribed on Dallas's stadium, in the wake of our beloved coach's death. Craig Washington had retired three years ago and still couldn't so much as fly over this state without being booed. Asbel wanted to give him Red's office? No, he could not do this. I wouldn't allow it.

"Yo, Poppy," yelled Raj from the steps of the first bus. "You coming?"

My shoulders slumped in defeat. Asbel was always going to do what he thought would win the most football games. The rest did not matter to him, least of all my opinion.

I climbed into the second bus, where the blasting heat had cleared only a credit-card-sized bit of windshield, and dropped heavily into a seat beside our CR director, Drea. Her hair was in its usual giant bun, and I had never in my life met a human being more committed to polka dots. We had very little in common besides professional perfectionism, but that was enough for me. I liked Drea. She was good at her job.

A few rows back, Alec was leaning against the window, his head-phones already in place. Across from him our backup quarterback, Will, was bobbing his head, bladed hands bouncing in front of him with the beat of whatever he was listening to. I didn't know him well—no one but A.J. had started for us since the launch of Face-book, and Will kept mostly to himself. Alec caught me looking. "He's old-school," he called. "It's A Tribe Called Quest." His tongue snuck out the corner of his grin. "What's on yours—Adele?"

I pulled a face, because having eighty brothers was more fun on some days than others. "Okay, she's actually very talented," I mut-tered. And then, to Drea, "Where's A.J.?"

"He's meeting us up there—on time, he swears. He had some-thing else this morning."

The drive to Fort Clinton took a little more than an hour, which the guys mostly spent on their phones. Drea was managing her emails, humming softly to herself. I should have been checking mine too, but I was restless, opting instead to stare out the win-dow. We were going the wrong way. I was itching to get back to the stadium, to demand details around everything I'd been so stupidly excluded from, and instead we were heading toward the Canadian border.

Drea looked up from her work and followed my glance outside. At this elevation the snow stayed from November through May, and the blur of gray-white covered the ground, the trees, the sky. A gust of wind shook the bus, and for a moment the road disappeared as old snow blew across it. She snorted. "What idiot scheduled this in the middle of winter? Oh right—me. Lovely day for a trip to the mountains." She turned to me anxiously. "You don't think any of them will get sick, do you?"

"You're fine," I said, but my mind had gone white at *day four.* The words were like an ice pick to the back of the neck.

What do you think, I texted Dayanna. I didn't have to specify about what.

Prank, she wrote back.

But who?

Instead of answering, she wrote, *Have I ever told you what my boss did when I first came on? He claimed Buster was self-conscious about his glass eye and not to look directly at him, and that our owner was deaf in his left ear. Both bullshit, but I spent my first-ever team dinner refusing to look at our president and yelling at our owner.*

I sent a laughing emoji and set the phone on my lap. I didn't believe the notes were harmless and neither did Dayanna, but for right now we would both pretend for the other that we thought things would be okay.

A stocky man with black hair and a red nose met us at the installation's gate. "We're glad to have you folks," he yelled. A vicious gust of wind caught my hair and whipped it around my face. I pulled my coat up over my mouth and nose.

Alec bumped my hip as he climbed off after me. "You cold, Poppy? We play in worse than this."

"I'm great. Just point me to the press box." My foot planted awkwardly on a set of frozen tire tracks, and I cursed my choice of ankle boots. There were patches of black ice scattered across the parking lot, and our next stop would be crossing the mud- and ice-covered grounds. And A.J. wasn't even here. I felt banished by Asbel to the ends of the earth.

And then, from the almost empty defensive bus, a heavily padded leg swung into view. My stomach clenched. *DeMario.*

"I didn't think you'd be here," I said, but what I really meant was *I didn't think I would have to face you so soon.* Shame bubbled sour and hot through my chest.

DeMario took his crutches from Drea and nodded toward the building. "I'm good. A torn ACL's not the worst thing in there."

The team trudged through outdoor training areas, gamely trying the obstacles despite the punishing cold. "I can't take a team photo until that jackass gets here," Drea said, removing her gloves to snap a picture of the offensive line by a decorative cannon. "Okay, guys," she announced, "we're calling it. Let's get inside and hit the bagels."

*

When we got to the cafeteria, I almost hugged the giant coffee carafe. The team filled their plates and then found seats with the servicemen and -women. I was trying to scrape the last bit of cream cheese out of its tub when A.J. finally walked in, followed by Omar Kadeer.

"What's up, gentlemen?" A.J. flashed his trademark half grin to an explosion of whoops and cheers. It was a magic trick of charm and dimples that made me want to pluck the hairs from his head one by one. "You guys are the *real* heroes."

"Obviously they're the real heroes!" I said to Drea, but she just gestured toward a beaming servicewoman having Raj sign the back of her jersey.

"He's here and they're smiling. That's good enough for me." She raised her camera and went to get photos.

As I watched, A.J. passed by Alec, leaned in close to his ear, and whispered something that made Alec's shoulders go stiff. A.J. looked at a particularly well-built serviceman, raised his eyebrows at Alec, then clapped him on the shoulder and moved on. "*Asshole.*"

"Excuse me." Omar Kadeer had come up behind me looking like a European fever dream in slim-cut jeans, an indigo blazer, and brown dress shoes with no socks (in this weather!). He was shorter than he appeared in pictures and more soft-spoken than I expected. "You're Poppy Benjamin. I've been wanting to meet you."

"Really?"

"Well, we move in the same circles."

We did not move in the same circles. Omar accompanied his A-list clientele to product launches in Dubai, while I spent lunch eating salad at my desk with my fingers. "I don't mean this to sound rude, Omar, but what are you doing here?"

He gestured toward A.J. "Keeping him company."

"Nice of you."

"He's our biggest client. There's a lot going on right now, with Red, the way the season is going. It's good to be nearby."

"So you want to make sure he doesn't say anything stupid to hurt his brand and your wallet. You know, if it's such a tricky situation here for A.J. you could always shop him around to other teams."

"So could you."

"Sure—except that he has an ironclad no-trade clause, which you wrote."

"Oh, that's right." Omar smiled, pulled out his phone, and started pecking at it.

"You could get him to waive it," I said, "make a trade to Miami or L.A., or somewhere else your face doesn't hurt when you go outside."

"Nah. His brand is here. His legacy is here. A.J. in any other jersey just dilutes that."

I watched the service members gathered four and five deep around A.J., who glowed under their attention. Most of them weren't even from this area, but they loved him because A.J. as quarterback of the Syracuse Bobcats was an institution. They'd grown up watching him, and now here he was in front of their eyes, a real live superhero. Branding was all about establishing a strong identity, and Omar was right. Changing the costume would damage that because people needed to hear his name and conjure one, concrete image—not Aaron Rodgers in a Jets jersey, or Peyton Manning in Broncos orange.

"You don't like him very much, do you?" Omar had put the phone away now and was looking at me with his head cocked, a smile playing at the corner of his full lips.

"It doesn't matter whether I like him or not."

"It's funny." Omar gave a little shrug and spoke over his shoulder as he walked off toward the group. "He says the nicest things about you."

*

"What kind of a mindfuck is that?" I ranted to Sarah later. I was outside the stadium huddled in the alcove by the main doors, where it was still freezing but at least the wind couldn't reach me.

From here, I could see into Asbel's office, which was dark. As soon as that light went on, he was getting a visit, and Dot had better just watch her toes.

"Is it possible he wasn't messing with you?"

I made a noise somewhere between a snort and a harrumph. "I've worked with A.J. for fifteen years, and if you showed up tomorrow in a brunette wig and sat at my desk, he'd call you by my name. And frankly, the wig is probably optional. There is no way he said actual kind things about me to *Omar Kadeer,* of all people."

"I like that we both realize that he is a first name–last name person—Omar Kadeer. What did he smell like?"

"Citrus sea mist with fruity undertones." The light went on. "I've got to go."

I marched into Asbel's office to find him looking up at me with a bemused expression, which pissed me off even more. "What the hell is going on, Asbel? I know you had Craig Washington in here this morning. *Do not* lie to me."

"I wasn't going to."

"Well—what the fuck? Are you bringing him in? You're lucky Red is dead because if he knew you were talking to Craig, he'd kill you."

"You don't think I'd hire him if Red was alive?"

"*Never,* you would *never* have—" Asbel raised his eyebrows as the penny dropped. "You want everyone to know that this wasn't in the works before. That you weren't planning to fire Red."

He picked up a pen and started scribbling, done with me. "Well, that, and there aren't any other future Hall of Fame coaches sitting home on their sofas just now."

Craig Washington was a brilliant coach, that part was undeniable. But he'd built his teams around players who could run the kind of flashy, quick-as-lightning offenses he favored. It took a very agile quarterback, someone who could read the defense and make a split-second decision on whether to run or pass. Someone who could handle the big hits that came from all that extra space between the offensive linemen, and the hazard of the trade that was a fat, juicy quarterback running with the football. Someone smart. Someone young.

Without looking up, Asbel said, "Everyone make it to the event okay?"

Goddamn it, Asbel. Of course I wasn't just babysitting A.J. as a punishment—Asbel would never waste my time like that, not when I could be doing something for him instead. He'd needed me to meet Omar Kadeer and get a read on whether A.J. wanted out. And through sheer luck and stupidity, I'd done it.

Now that I wasn't too annoyed to think clearly, I understood. Omar's cocky insistence that A.J. *was* the Bobcats was about branding, but also legacy. There had long been a debate about whether the team's success was down to Red or A.J. In our recent, leaner years, the conversation had shifted to whose fault it was. But with Red gone, A.J. had an opportunity to claim the glory once and for all. If we won now, it proved that *he* was the secret ingredient, that it was *his* brilliance that led to those Super Bowls.

Meanwhile, Asbel might like to seem tough, but he'd just hired the one coach who proved that he'd been planning to stand by Red, no matter how much pressure had been on him to make a change. And while Omar and A.J. were swanning into our CR event an hour late, Asbel was signing a coach who would prove that Red was the engine that had powered our success.

Because there was no way in hell that A.J., already geriatric in football terms, could run that offense.

Asbel was going to tank him.

CHAPTER TWELVE

FIFTEEN YEARS AGO

Game 16 closed out a perfect regular season. We freaking did it. On Monday morning for the first time in weeks people smiled at each other in the hallways. It wasn't the end. Even with a first-round bye, the playoffs would be a whole other level, and those battles were coming. But for now we had a week to breathe, rest, and celebrate the pretty major accomplishment of four months of undefeated football.

Somewhere around October Brent's boss, Richard, saw the trash can next to A.J.'s locker overflowing with unopened fan mail, and ever since I'd been responsible for answering it with Bobcats stickers, mimeographed photos, and cheerleader calendars. The upshot was that I had dibs on anything the fans sent in, and I thought fondly of Courtney from Utica, who'd mailed A.J. a Starbucks card "for their first date," every time she bought me a coffee.

The rest of the department was scattered on assignments, and I was three mocha truffles into a similar gift when James swiped himself into the annex. I stuffed the truffle box under my desk and grabbed an envelope from the fan mail bin, wiping my fingers on my dress pants.

We hadn't texted since Thanksgiving, although we still ate lunch together with Mo and Abby, and we both always refilled our coffee at one thirty. Or maybe I'd noticed that's when James usually refilled his and timed things accordingly, but we'd lean against the break room counters chatting and laughing until someone else came to use the machine. I imagined that James was impressed by how cool I was playing it, not the usual needy girl who had to ask "Are you into me?" or "Why did you text me on a national holiday and then never again?"

"What are you up to?" I said.

"Taking a break from the new college scouting assistant. His desk is right across from mine, and I need a little fresh air."

I finished copying an address on the envelope and dropped a fan pack inside. "No good?"

"He's kind of a douche."

"And you're saying he *doesn't* fit in."

"Poppy. He put his DKE letters on his cubicle."

"Oof." A wave of secondhand embarrassment washed over me. "That's awful, but I also feel kind of bad for him. It's not easy being new here, especially this season. Everything has been so tense."

"Yeah, and teams are tough to break into, but he's not doing a lot to embrace the culture, if you know what I mean." He nudged my desk. "Plus, you're not new anymore. You're a full Bobcat now."

What I would have given to have popped on my recorder thirty seconds earlier. To be able to fall asleep at night with my headphones on while that person saying that thing whispered into my ears in an infinite loop. I smiled at James, a big, goofy, embarrassing smile. His smile back was a slow, cocky lift of the lips.

"Listen, we're going out this weekend—Abby, Mo, and me. To celebrate the regular season. Do you want to join in?"

I forced myself to be cool. "Yeah—sounds fun." I thought a minute, then added, "And let's invite the new guy. So he's not left out."

"Fine." James pulled out his phone. "Let me get your number."

I laughed, and James cocked his head. "Oh—because, you know, you have it," I said in a rush as his brows folded inward. The look of confusion on his face sent my stomach tumbling to the floor. He didn't know what I was talking about.

That meant that James had never texted me, which meant that someone else had. And I'd flirted back. I'd sent a wink. Oh my God. *Oh my God.*

"Sorry, yeah, of course," I stuttered, fumbling with my phone. "Sorry, I was just thinking about a different . . ." *Stop talking, you full moron.* James let it go, but by the time he left he wasn't hanging over my workspace wall anymore but standing several steps behind it, his hands stuffed deep into his pockets.

As soon as the door closed behind him, I brought up the text from Thanksgiving. I'd saved it, reading and rereading the brief messages to myself while I wondered why James never made a move, why our text exchange had stopped there.

Happy Thanksgiving, Pop Tart. Hope you got your fill today.
You too. Go for the extra dessert. ;)
Shit, shit, shit, shit.

On brittle-boned legs, I walked into Richard's empty office and found a copy of the staff directory on his overstuffed bookcase. I sliced my finger on the first page and stuck it into my mouth, tasting blood, as I used my left hand to trace down the column of phone numbers. It didn't take long to find a match, and when I slid my finger backward toward the column of names, a boulder of dread anchored my stomach. I was going to be sick, gastric acids churning and roiling as they bubbled up through my gut and rested at the base of my throat.

I was in deep, deep trouble.

The matching phone number belonged to Coach Guillory.

*

I'd sent suggestive text messages to the coach. No one would care that he reached out to me first, because that was the deal. It was right there in the expression "locker-room talk," like the one we had downstairs. Like it was assumed this building was one giant man cave, enter if you dare.

Some teams, I'd learned, just didn't hire women—no fuss, no muss. Others made sure their female staff never interacted with the players, keeping them in the corporate offices like tigers prowling in a zoo enclosure. The Bobcats were special in allowing me to do my entire job, in letting me into the locker room with Brent and Richard. And this was how I repaid them.

I hurried back to my desk and dumped the rest of the truffles into the garbage, then dug them out and moved them to Julie's trash can. Their smell was overpowering, sickeningly sweet. I wished I could brush my teeth.

On Tuesday I forgot to set the copier to print the clips double-sided and came back from the bathroom to find an entire ream of wasted paper. It had to be done again, which meant I was late, but that in turn meant that Coach Guillory wasn't in his office when I got there. Setting the papers down as quickly as possible, my eyes snagged on the family photo on his desk. Did Coach's wife slip his phone off the nightstand while he was in the shower and go through his texts? He'd stopped playing only a few years ago, and I'd known enough college athletes to know their girlfriends checked their phones either constantly or never. Had Mrs. Guillory seen it? Was she going to come crashing in here one day to announce in front of everyone what I'd done?

By Friday my nails were gone, and I had a permanent ache in my jaw. This was my dream job, and I was fucking it up. Every success, every bit of ground I'd gained over the past few months, was slipping away as my head hung lower and lower.

During Coach's press conference, I sat ramrod straight in my chair, covered head to toe in a black turtleneck and hunter-green dress pants. I hadn't so much as shown my wrists since Monday. As Coach gave his opening remarks, I forced myself to look at him but not to stare. He was in a good mood—it was Friday, and they'd earned a weekend off to rest and watch other teams go to war. Coach's smile was easy, his back arched casually forward, and he cupped the podium's edges instead of gripping them.

"Come on, guys," he teased the packed media room, "give me a hard one." He looked straight at me and winked.

It was in front of everyone—from the *podium,* with cameras pointed at him. The air froze in my chest, a hard bubble, as I waited for accusing fingers to turn on me like swords.

But there were none. Beside me, Bernie nudged my shoulder and shot me a grin. Steven asked a question about whether it was important to Coach that the postseason path go through Dallas, and the press conference rolled forward. No one cared. They thought that Coach was being friendly and charming, and he was. And maybe everything was okay after all.

*

By the end of the day I was itching for our big night out. It had been a stressful week, I hadn't done anything social in months, and if I couldn't release some pressure there was no getting around it—my eyeballs were going to explode. I wanted a night to feel young and pretty. I wanted dollar drink specials and graffitied walls and pop music. I wanted to get drunk.

"We ride at nine," said Mo when I passed him near the coach's hallway toward the end of the day. He held out his fist to bump. "Bring quarters—they do a flip cup thing."

I put on a playlist from senior year of college and took a hot shower. Then, wrapped in a towel, I browsed through my closet and perused the section of shirts my dad didn't know that I owned. These were work friends, but it was after work hours. I could get away with being a little flashy, right? I thought about James's perfect hair, his cocky grins. The way he sat at lunch with his long legs out straight, crossed at the ankle under my chair.

Maybe a lot flashy.

I was halfway through my shirts when I pushed aside a wrap blouse and saw something that made my hand freeze on the hanger.

The next shirt—a tissue-sized number of silver satin with a tie back—was facing the wrong way. It was a small thing, something no one but me would even notice, but I was extremely particular about the way clothes hung in my closet, and this one was backward.

I squeezed the fabric between my fingers. It released a scent that set off spiders at the base of my spine—stale cigarettes.

All this time I'd assumed it was Flossie coming into my apartment, poking around her dollhouse, making sure everything was just so, but I'd been wrong. It was Dave. Dave hovering outside the door while I slept, pressing his hands against it to affix the Post-it notes. Dave's form filling my little bathroom, gliding back the shower curtain to reveal the space where I stood naked. Dave's footsteps padding across the shag carpeting, down the little hallway, and into my bedroom. Dave's fingers walking their way along the clothes in my closet and stopping at a shirt—*this* shirt, maybe the most revealing one I owned, and pressing it close enough to himself to transfer his scent.

It was so *violating,* and I had no idea what to do about it. Was I supposed to talk to Dave or Flossie? What if I was wrong? What if no one believed me?

I could not stay in this apartment for another second. I grabbed a shirt at random—black satin, with flutter sleeves—and pulled it on over skinny jeans. A pair of Uggs and I was good to go.

I would not worry about Coach Guillory flirting in public or my landlord touching my things in private or wherever James's head was at. I was twenty-two. It was my only Friday night of the season.

I was going out.

*

It was so cold that the snow crunched beneath my boots as I picked my way over the snowbank and down the icy sidewalk toward the entrance to Sloppy Hal's, a dive bar near the university section of town that really leaned into its name. The windows seemed to pulse out with each thump of bass, and a trail of abandoned cigarette butts led to the door. I handed my ID to a bored-looking bouncer, who shined a little flashlight at it but passed it back without looking down and waved me inside.

Abby, Mo, and James stood in a cluster on the far side of the giant bar that filled the center of the room. I had to push my way across the sticky floor and through the half-standing, half-dancing crowd to reach them.

"You made it!" said Abby, pulling me in for a sloppy hug. She wore dark flared pants that showed off her legs and a diamond-bottomed sleeveless top. Her cheeks were flushed a bright pink.

"Aren't you freezing?" I yelled, struggling to make myself heard.

"No." She indicated her cup. "Drunk blanket."

A hand clamped on my shoulder, and I jerked away at the touch. When I turned, James's palms were raised. "I just wanted to see what you're drinking."

Pull it together. "Sorry. I'm still cold, I guess. A rum and Diet Coke?"

"Good idea."

"Excuse me?"

"Because of the prank—the corn syrup. It was a joke."

"Oh. Right."

He made his way to the bar while the three of us bobbed our heads to the music. "Do you guys come here a lot?" I asked.

Mo shook his head. "Like twice a season. We're all too tired when we're not working."

"So when we do get out, we have to make it count!" Abby winked at me and downed the rest of her drink, which looked like it was made entirely of red dye 40. She leaned in uncomfortably close. I could smell the sugar on her breath. "Marketing is going to be insane now that we're in the playoffs. I have people calling *me* asking to work with us—like, *what*? And my boss said I could spearhead Coach Guillory's radio spot. Do you think he's kind of hot?"

I made a face just as James walked back with four drinks, then tried to course-correct with an overly bright smile. "The line was long," he said, pushing two of them into my hands, "so I loaded up."

I took a big gulp, which lodged in my throat like an air bubble. The thought of Coach Guillory and my texts and his itches brought up the same feeling as Dave and my shirt. It was like the entire world was made of fingers.

Meanwhile Mo, still caught in conversation with Abby, held up his hand and said, "*Please,* no work talk. Tonight—we dance." He held his forearm upright and made tight little circles in time to the music. Abby shimmied her hips, and the two of them bounced happily around to Usher.

I took another gulp from my first cup—was there any soda in there?—and locked eyes with James. He was staring at me intently, and my heart jumped. His sweaty hair was pushed back at an odd angle I was itching to fix. His jaw twitched as he swallowed. I watched the movement travel down his throat and to the base of his neck, right where his skin met his sweater. He leaned in, lips twisting into his usual smirk before it melted off his face as his gaze slid to the right to focus on something behind me.

I turned to see what could only be the new college scouting guy clap the disinterested bouncer on the shoulder as he walked in.

He was a human Ed Hardy T-shirt. His hair was black and spiked, his skin rivaled Brent's for fakest tan, and he greeted everyone, including me, who he'd never met, with hugs and ear kisses.

"This is Carter," said James, now suddenly several feet away and giving me a *you own this mess* look. "Carter, this is everyone."

"You guys fucked up already or what?" As opening lines go, it wasn't a strong showing. But when everyone else's bodies automatically angled away, I felt kind of bad for Carter. I hated seeing people left on the edge of a group, mostly because I was always so afraid it was going to happen to me.

"So you just graduated?" I yelled over the National blaring through the speakers. It was "Mr. November"—one of my favorites—but the drunken sing-along of the crowd made it impossible to hear. Carter threw an arm over my shoulder and pulled my ear to his mouth, and I forced myself to take a breath. To not treat every human interaction like an assault. It was *enough* of that tonight.

"Yeah—URI." I waited for him to ask me where I'd gone to school, but he just nodded to the music and scanned the rest of the bar.

"You like this song?" I tried again.

He shook his head. "Not really."

The DJ put on the Killers, and the packed bar cheered, including Mo, who pogoed in time to the music, slopping his soda onto the floor. Things were starting to spin for me, and instead of backing off, I kept sipping and sipping at one drink and then the other, until both cups were as empty as I wanted to feel.

"Mo!" yelled James just as Brandon Flowers sang that while he did have soul, he was not a soldier. I turned, surprised by the sharpness in his tone, and met his eyes. They were like onyx, hard and dark, and his jaw was tight. "Mohammad! Come outside with me."

"I'm not a machine," Mo protested, trailing after James through the throng of bodies in the middle of the bar. "I cannot just *leave* during this part of the song!"

Abby looked at Carter, then winked at me. "I'm going to the bathroom," she announced in a singsong voice. And then it was just the two of us standing there.

I bobbed my head a few times. Had I ever been less qualified to make small talk in my life? Finally I tried, "So you were in DKE?"

Carter yammered on and on about Greek life while I swirled the ice around my empty cup and tried not to feel the bass pounding behind my eyebrows. Every few minutes someone bumped into me as they made their way to or from the bar, and I was starting to sway on my feet. It was too loud in here, and way too hot. I needed some air. I needed to leave, but there was nowhere for me to go, no safe place where men didn't linger where they shouldn't and I could just be still.

"I have to go," I slurred finally, not caring that I'd cut Carter off in midsentence. James was the only reason I came out tonight anyway, and he was mad for some reason I couldn't understand—why was he mad at me? He bought me two drinks, and then he just got *mad.* I hated that look on his face, and I hated even more knowing it was for me.

What did I do?

Was I not friendly enough? He made that joke about the diet soda and I didn't laugh—I should have laughed more there. Things turned after Carter came, so maybe he didn't want me talking to Carter. But that didn't make sense, James was the one who invited Carter, wasn't he? I guess I invited Carter. But he had no problem with me talking to Mo . . .

I didn't understand it, I couldn't find the line. If I raised a fuss over things, then I was the no-fun police, but if I was too easygoing, then Coach Guillory thought it was okay to ask me to scratch his back. Did James think I was flirting with Carter, just by talking to him? Because I wasn't flirting, and if I didn't talk to him, Carter would think I was stuck-up. And where the hell was I supposed to look in the locker room, anyway? Who thinks naked media is a good idea?

I was done. I would say goodbye to Abby and then get out of here. Take a cab home, sleep with a bear trap at the end of my bed. I didn't want to be there, but I couldn't be here. I turned, scanning the dark bar for her telltale blond hair, but it was overcrowded thanks to the stupid nonperforming bouncer. Every inch of space was filled with people drinking, dancing, talking, laughing, just— being in my way. I went up on my toes to try to see over their heads. I scanned the length of the rectangular bar—not there. I looked by the door—nothing there. I turned and located the little hallway that led to the restrooms.

And *that* was when I saw Abby, pushed up against the wall outside the ladies' room making out with James like the plane was going down.

CHAPTER THIRTEEN

NOW

As a general rule, I leave the family stuff to my brothers. Jeff and Luke both still live in Ohio, and both married nice Ohio girls (Jeff's wife, Lisa, is from Indiana, but she had cheerfully relocated) and were raising nice Ohio children. I saw them at Christmas when the football schedule didn't interfere and for a week every summer, and whenever we played at Cleveland I got everyone tickets and tried not to feel irritated that none of them rooted for my team.

Now I was sitting in my car outside of the stadium FaceTiming with Lisa and Morgan, Luke's wife, who were at breakfast together in Morgan's sunny yellow kitchen. "It's so nice to have you 'with' us," she said, laughing, and I raised my Byrne Dairy to-go cup in a salute.

Lisa was all business. "So for Mom's seventieth." Both of them called my parents Mom and Dad, which was—fine. It made everyone happy on both sides of those relationships, so far be it from me to say how completely cracked I thought it was. "We were thinking of a full-family trip, because she's always wanted to and we've never done it."

"The kids really haven't been old enough," Morgan said. "But since Benny's *finally* potty trained," she put one flat palm toward the ceiling and briefly closed her eyes, "I think we're ready."

"The obvious choice is a cruise," Lisa said in her first-grade teacher's voice that made me want to break in with *Is that obvious, though, Lisa?* "But I also thought—if we can get all the kids' spring breaks to line up—maybe the Bahamas?"

Morgan grinned. "Is that where they have that giant slide that goes under the sharks?"

"From the pyramid, right. It's too much for Benny and Lola, but the big kids should be able to do it."

As the two of them chattered on about JetBlue points and chartered fishing boats, I watched my fingernails disappear into the Styrofoam of my cup. "This is a nice idea, guys, but I doubt I could get the time off, especially with everything going on right now."

Morgan and Lisa exchanged a quick look that, on Morgan's end, clearly said, *Let me handle it.* "Is there a time that would be better?" she asked. "Summer can be hard because everyone has camp, and then we can't do fall because Dad has football—"

"So do *I*."

Lisa's tone was flat. "It's Mom's seventieth birthday, Poppy. It's a big deal." There was no winning with her or Jeff. When I came home, I was the prodigal daughter who soaked up all of Dad's attention even though they were the ones who'd committed to living nearby, who helped my parents with weekend projects and sat through Sunday dinner every week. If I didn't come home or join them on a birthday trip, it was because I was too selfish and self-involved to care about anyone but myself. Given those two options, I'd take the one that let me sleep in my own bed and stay caught up on my emails.

"It's not all kids' stuff," Morgan put in. "There's a casino, and drinks are all included, and there's the beach and a spa. You could go golfing. You don't even have to see the kids!"

As if I didn't adore my nieces and nephews. As if not liking kids and not finding someone I wanted to have them with were interchangeable.

"Let me know the date," I said, mostly to get out of this conversation. "I'll see what I can do."

Inside I sent a flurry of texts to the group chat.

Can't you just get her tickets to Hamilton? Dayanna wrote.

Nisha's advice: *If you really loved her, you'd have a kid.* And then, *By the way, it's day five.*

As if we didn't know.

Nothing yet, Annika wrote. *I guess you were right, Nish.*

It's business days, Sarah cracked.

I slipped my phone into my pocket. If we couldn't be together today, then I'd keep them close to me this way. *It's nothing, it's a prank,* I repeated to myself, but my skin itched, and I wondered when I'd stopped believing it.

After a morning of meetings and checking my phone, I finally snuck off to the cafeteria around two. Nothing yet, and the chat had gone silent, but there was a lot demanding my attention at work. We were going to have to roll this new coaching hire out very carefully. Coach Russo didn't even know about it yet and was upstairs right now preparing for this week's game. Meanwhile Coach Washington's agent was finalizing his bonus structure and getting ready to file the contract with the league. Should I bother releasing the announcement on Coach Russo? It would look strange not to. Skipping it would only bring more questions and therefore more work for me.

Now that I was smelling the food, that moist plastic scent from the underside of the steam tray lids, the thought of it turned my stomach, so I stuck to coffee and sat at one of the small tables. It was quiet other than the drone of ESPN from a nearby flatscreen. If I had it my way I'd take a four-hour bath, read a trashy magazine, and come back to the stadium sometime around March. My recycling bin was overflowing with empty bottles. I couldn't remember the last time I ate something that came from the earth.

A red breaking-news banner flashed across the bottom of the TV screen beneath a headshot of Damian Jokiak. I sat up straight. Damian was the power forward for Annika's team, a four-time all-star currently starring in a nationwide ad campaign for breakfast cereal where he was dunked on by a squirrel.

Breaking news this afternoon as superstar Madison Blizzards forward Damian Jokiak is accused of raping and assaulting multiple women. A source familiar with the situation claims Jokiak choked and strangled the women before and while forcing them to have sexual intercourse.

"Oh my God," I breathed. Annika had worked with Damian forever. She *liked* Damian. I took a shaky sip of coffee as the broadcast continued.

In an unusual twist, also named in the allegation are the Blizzards organization and Blizzards in-house counsel Annika Smith. Smith is accused of having actual knowledge of these events, of offering the women hush money, and of coercing them to sign non-disclosure agreements threatening treble damages if the allegations were made public.

The cup slipped from my fingers and sent a wave of coffee across my white blouse. "Shit!" I shoved my chair back and stumbled toward the napkin dispenser, eyes still locked on the screen.

"Whoa, Poppy," said Mo, who had just entered the cafeteria with his laptop. "Are you okay?"

"I have to go," I managed. Leaving the coffee dripping onto the floor, I pushed my way into the stairwell, backed myself against the wall, and sank to the steps. It felt like a bird was trapped inside my chest, throwing itself against my ribs in its desperation to get out. The air was Everest-thin.

It was day five.

The story broke on day five.

This was real. And we were all on the table.

*

I managed to get myself upstairs to the Media Relations annex. "I'll be out for the rest of the day," I told Edward just as Chloe buzzed herself in through the doors. She took one look at my blouse and stopped short.

Edward blinked rapidly. "Today? But we're—you just—"

"I have to go. Rodney, you're the point person. Get rid of the little stuff and push everyone else off until tomorrow." I swooped into my office long enough to grab my purse and shove one arm through the sleeve of my ivory coat, letting the other side dangle. The liner was going to stain from the coffee, but I didn't care. I wasn't at all sure I could drive myself, but I had to get out of here and back to my townhouse.

Maybe you were right, Nish.

While Annika was typing that, ESPN would have been going over its story one more time, making sure it had at least two sources to corroborate the allegations, checking the spelling of Damian's last name. I had to get out of here. I had to be alone. I had to think.

By the time I got home I'd ignored calls from Dayanna, Sarah, and Nisha, all sent straight to voicemail. I barely even remembered the drive home. I peeled off my soiled clothes and wrapped myself in a bathrobe, a poor imitation of the comforting hug I wished there was anyone in my life to offer. *Do* not *think about him, do* not. *Do* not. My phone buzzed again, and for a wild second I thought that I was wrong, that Peter had somehow sensed that I was in trouble, until I saw it was a text from Nisha.

We're in the chat. Get on NOW.

Numbly, I set my laptop up on my bed and followed the link to our video chat room. The others appeared, pale and anxious.

"*Here* she is," Nisha said as she threw up her hands. "Now can we please figure out what the fuck is going on? Sarah?"

She shook her head, and her curls bounced wildly back and forth, escaping the edges of the frame. When we'd talked earlier, I could have pictured her with her feet up on the rust-colored sofa in her Hoboken apartment, oversized Penn State sweatshirt, thick socks. Relaxed and happy. Now she looked bled dry. "I haven't heard anything. I reached out to my contacts at ESPN, but everyone's being really tight-lipped. My one friend says they're under threat of death from legal not to spread any unsubstantiated rumors."

"Which means," said Nisha, "what they're reporting now must be pretty damn substantiated."

We sat in stunned silence. After several tense moments, I said, "Has anyone reached out to Annika?"

"I tried," said Dayanna. "Her phone is going straight to voicemail, and of course I texted, but I haven't heard anything back. God, she must be sick. And her daughters . . ."

It hit me straight in the gut. I didn't spend a lot of time thinking about what it would be like to have daughters. That wasn't going to happen for me, so thinking about it would be wasteful and unproductive. It wasn't worth thinking about the ways I would show my daughter that I valued her by meeting her where she was, at *her* interests, instead of trying to color her with my own pen. There was no reason to think through the ways I would support her, tell her I was proud of her and her career.

But Annika was a mother, and her girls adored her—so much so that the older one, Carolyn, was following in her footsteps at law school. I remember when Annika told us Carolyn had applied, she'd tried to toss the information off casually, modestly, but her shining eyes gave her away. They'd danced that entire conversation.

And when Joanna, the younger daughter, chose to major in feminist theory at NYU, Annika's husband, Grant, made a cardboard sign that read, I KNOW, I'M WRONG and wore it around his neck for a week while they all fell over laughing. The sweatshirt under the sign was NYU purple.

They were the success story, the family that had it all. This couldn't be happening.

And who was the source?

"Okay." Nisha licked her cracked lips. Her normally creamy complexion looked flat and bleached, and a strand of her dark bob was caught in her eyelashes. She didn't move it away. "Brass tacks time. This doesn't just affect Annika."

"We know," said Sarah quietly.

Nisha's voice was tight and higher than normal. "Whoever sent those notes actually blew up Annika over this—"

"Didn't she deserve to be blown up?" Dayanna cried. "We've all seen so much shit I can't believe I'm this surprised, but I'm just— shocked. I'm shocked that Anni would do such a thing."

"You don't know what she did or didn't do," Sarah put in. "You know how these stories take off—"

Nisha sneered. "Oh, because of the *media,* Sarah?"

"All I know," Dayanna said hotly, "is that I'm not going to live like this. Here's my deep dark secret—I dated one of my players. For two years. And if that came out I'd get fired and lose my career, and absolutely *nothing* would happen to him, but I didn't cover up a rape. I'm not going to let myself be put in the same basket as someone who would."

Her hand reached out and grabbed the top of her laptop and then she was gone, lost to the slamming of the lid. Nisha, Sarah, and I sat in heavy silence until Nisha broke it. "I get what she's saying, but it's still Anni and we're not giving up on her, right? *Right?*"

I tried to speak—"Right!" I wanted to scream. "Of course not!"—but nothing came out except a small sob.

Sarah rubbed her eyes and then looked to the camera with a thousand-yard stare. "First Red . . . then the letters . . . now ESPN. Someone planned this whole thing. They're going to pick us off one by one."

"We don't know that Red . . ." But I trailed off, because even I couldn't believe they were unrelated now. A rape cover-up and a murder. They were both too high stakes to be coincidence.

"Do we have a responsibility to tell anyone? What if this psycho is planning to hurt someone else?" Sarah bit her lip and looked at the ceiling. "I didn't want to say anything, because I thought I was being stupid, but now . . ."

"What?" I felt like I was sitting atop broken glass. One flinch, one move in any direction would slice me to pieces.

"I've been getting these weird messages on Twitter. I mean, whatever, that happens all the time, but these are really personal."

"Personal how?"

"So, one referenced where my car was parked, or at least, that's what I read into it. Another said something about the hat I wear on my runs."

"*Sarah!*"

"Okay," Nisha broke in, "but you said yourself you were reading into it. And I've seen your Instagram, you've definitely posted photos in that hat. It's the Alo one, right?"

"I don't think—" I started, but Nisha cut me off.

"I'm not saying don't be careful or whatever, but this isn't a Wes Craven production. Someone sold out Annika. That's fact. Anything else is just us guessing, and that's not helping anything."

"But Red—"

"Is dead, yes, but that was on day zero. It doesn't fit. It *doesn't,* Pop."

"Is that supposed to make me feel better? That there might be something *else* coming for me?"

"It's supposed to snap you out of it!" yelled Nisha. "And you, Sarah. We have to keep it together and *not panic.* We are women who know how to handle things, we do *not* lose our shit. We're going to keep trying to get in touch with Annika, and make sure Dayanna doesn't go rogue on us. Sarah, can you go by her place? Bring some fucking cupcakes or something?" Sarah nodded. "We're going to replace every password we've ever created, up to and including changing our own birthdates, if we have to."

"The second note was postmarked from Queens, and I had a weird feeling that night in the bar, like someone was watching us," I said. "Sarah, please be careful. I'm sure you already do, but walk with your keys between your fingers, check the back seat before you get in, lock the door before you buckle." The litany of car safety commandments my mother had drilled into my teenage self came out as though she'd possessed me.

"Go buy a hat or a sweatshirt or something and don't wear it out," Nisha suggested. "Just post a photo of it from inside your apartment. Then if this weirdo brings it up, you know he's just trying to scare you."

"I don't know if this is the time to be clever," I said. "We should probably avoid posting altogether for now. And don't go out alone at night."

"Do you do that a lot anyway?" Sarah asked.

"No." Although I had been out alone at night recently. On the night Red died.

"Keep it together," Nisha reiterated. "Whoever is doing this is not going to take us down."

"I'll let you know how it goes with Day," Sarah said. "I'm off today, so I can go over there in a bit."

I didn't have an assignment, so I just nodded firmly. "We'll talk soon." And then we signed off, and the ensuing silence made me feel more alone than I ever had in my life.

I sent Annika a text that read, *Here if you want to talk*. I hesitated, then added, *Love you*. It quickly changed from delivered to read, but no reply came.

Annika was a good wife and a good mother. She was an accomplished and respected attorney, had won awards for mentoring young female lawyers, and spent her very limited time off volunteering with an organization that helped women looking to enter the workforce apply and prepare for job interviews. Knowing what I knew now, maybe that work was less altruistic and more of a penance. Her name was going to be connected forever to the most despicable of crimes and an ugly propensity to shield the perpetrator from any responsibility. In the court of public opinion, Annika was as bad as Damian. Unless there really was more to the story. I, of all people, owed it to her to find out.

Poppy Benjamin, you will get through this, I told myself firmly, angrily. *Focus up. Do your job. And until we know what's what, keep a low profile.*

I was still holding my phone when a text came through from Rodney.

Asbel's looking for you. RG's autopsy is done and the police want to talk to all senior front office staff.

PART II

CHAPTER FOURTEEN

NOW

"I knew it," said Rodney.

Following another painful loss, we were side by side in the hall-way outside our main conference room, where two detectives had taken up residence. "Fact gathering," they called it, but that really meant "making sure not a single blessed thing gets done" because we were all wondering when it would be our turn to be interrogated. Asbel and I had planned to announce Coach Washington today, which meant we'd be introducing our new coach in the morning and then answering questions about the murder of the old one in the afternoon.

"It would take a lot of power to do something like that," Rod-ney went on. "You don't just half-heartedly smash somebody's skull—you have to be *strong*." I raised my eyebrows, indicating the powerful biceps of my gym-rat media relations manager, and he unfolded his arms, deflating the muscles. "The man spent his entire life in football. How many big-armed dudes did he come across— thousands? And he'd have to be tall, for the angle, because Red was tall. So if I was leading the investigation, I'd start with the wide receivers."

"*Are* you leading the investigation? Because otherwise we have quite a bit of work to get through today." My head was pounding, and the light hurt my eyes. For the fifth night in a row I'd fallen asleep with my glasses on and my phone in my lap, my battery run down from searching every corner of the Internet for updates about Annika. None of us had heard from her, despite repeated attempts to reach out, and the rest of us were in a constant cringe, waiting for our own detonations courtesy of the author of those notes. They might go off today or tomorrow or next week or never. My stomach ground away at itself, and I was subsisting mainly on alcohol and coffee.

I might not have a secret on the scale of Annika's, which I still couldn't wrap my brain around, but there were things in my past that would be problems. Big problems. There were things that, if made public, to save the team, I would have to eat. That would mean losing this job and everything I'd given up to have it. It would mean hitchhiking back to Ohio, where my smug-faced brother and sister-in-law would offer to put in a good word for me at the Millburn Turkey Farm, a Thanksgiving-themed all-you-can-eat buffet where the waitstaff dressed up like pilgrims. I wouldn't do it. I couldn't.

"I think Lexi did it," said Rodney.

"Red's wife? What happened to weight-lifting wide receivers?"

"Have you ever used a Pilates reformer? She's strong as hell."

"And the height?"

"Okay . . . back to Coach Nate. He's tall enough, he's got the rage. The motive. He just needed the opportunity."

"I'm taking *this* opportunity to go back to my office. Could you please bring the nice detectives some coffee?"

"It could have been Asbel."

I was a full five steps away when Rodney tossed that out, stopping me in my tracks. My pulse kicked up, and I turned. "Excuse me?"

Rodney shrugged. "What? He's tall and strong, and he had a coach problem . . . problem solved, you know?"

I was back beside Rodney now and dropped my voice. "I know you're just fucking around, but that isn't funny. Red was a real person, our *colleague,* and someone killed him. His kids don't have a dad."

Rodney nodded, chagrined. The office was warm, but as I walked back to Media Relations I rubbed at the goose bumps on my arms. It was true, of course, that none of this was at all funny, but Rodney being Rodney hadn't bothered me before because it was gallows humor, and what else were we supposed to do to keep putting one foot in front of the other? But that joke, *that* scenario, hit differently.

Because it had entered my mind too.

*

The detectives looked less like detectives than I'd expected.

I'd seen them coming and going as players and coaches shuffled in and out, so I knew what the two men physically looked like. But when my turn came on Friday and I was sitting across from them in the conference room, they were oddly less than what I thought they would be. Smaller.

"Thanks for meeting with us, Ms. Benjamin," said Detective Andrews. He was old enough to be my grown son or inappropriately young boyfriend, with dark hair and a face he couldn't quite make look serious.

"Poppy, please."

The other man, Detective Prager, was closer to my own age, not heavyset but husky, like he enjoyed both eating and working out. His brown hair was thinning, with a yarmulke-sized bald patch I could see only when he sat down. "We were hoping to be done by now," he said, then added with a wry smile, "we didn't know there were a million of you."

My smile back was tight. I wasn't afraid of them—I didn't kill Red—but I didn't want to be in here for long.

Detective Prager produced a list of questions and proceeded to walk me through them in a voice that implied he was getting sick of asking them.

"Are you aware of anyone who may have wanted to hurt Red Guillory?"

"Only about thirty-one other head coaches." Seeing the look Detective Prager shot me, I hastily added, "No, I'm not."

"Are you aware of anyone who made threats against Red Guillory?"

"No."

"Can you think of any reason why someone would have wanted to hurt Red Guillory?"

"No."

Here Prager paused. He slowed way down, letting the silence stretch until it marched around with jazz hands before saying softly, "Is there anything . . . you'd like to tell us about the night Red was killed?"

I shifted in my seat. "Well, he called me, as I'm sure you know." I gestured toward a pile of papers on the table. "And I didn't pick up. I assume you can tell that, too."

Prager nodded and pulled out a sheet of paper that I'd bet anything was filled with gibberish. "Yeah, we've checked out the call logs. Mrs. Benjamin—"

"It's Ms."

"Right, *Ms.* Benjamin. Did Coach Guillory call you often like that? Late at night?"

He arched an obnoxious little eyebrow at the subtext, and I chose my next words with intention, looking him straight in the eye. "He *did.* A lot of the players do too."

Detective Andrews choked on his coffee, and I relished the look of shock on Prager's face. *Mrs. Benjamin.* Ask me whatever you want, but don't play stupid games.

"I'm a contact for them when there's some kind of trouble— not this kind, obviously, but something that might embarrass them or embarrass the Bobcats. In the pre-Uber days I'd pick up drunk players so they weren't driving home, that kind of thing."

In reality it was much more likely that they'd call after they'd already done something stupid, like the time I swooped in to get a heavily inebriated linebacker who'd rolled his truck, created a cover story that he had epilepsy, and worked with Drea to create a year-long program of nonprofit events raising money for the cause. He got nominated for the Walter Payton Man of the Year award. But I didn't tell the detectives that.

"Okay," said Andrews, somewhat recovered, "but you didn't answer this time."

"No."

"Why not?"

"I was busy."

"At midnight?" Prager wanted to embarrass me, to save face, and his voice dripped with sarcasm. "I'm guessing there's someone who can corroborate that, then."

"No, there isn't."

"Where were you?"

I sat back. "That's personal, and since this is just an informal interview I'm sure you understand I'd like to leave it at that. I will tell you that I did not talk to or see Red Guillory after I left the stadium that night, I'd guess around eight fifteen. You can check my ID card swipe for the exact time. Can I ask you guys a question back?"

Prager and Andrews looked at each other, and then Prager shrugged in a way that clearly meant I could ask whatever I wanted but there wasn't much chance of an answer.

"The Guillorys had security cameras. Shouldn't your answer be right on that tape?"

"They were turned off," said Andrews. He opened his mouth to say something else, but a barking cough from Prager stopped him.

No drugs or alcohol in Red's system. No security cameras. What did that mean? What had Red been planning?

I stood without being dismissed. "Who can I send in for you next?"

Andrews consulted a list. "We'll take Rodney Dupree."

"Hey, Ms. Benjamin?" I was almost out the door when Prager spoke. His arms were folded across his barrel-shaped chest. "You know, Coach Guillory made a second phone call that night, and the person he called is the only other one who hasn't been able to give us an alibi."

"How frustrating for you. But you both seem pretty smart, I'm sure you'll figure things out."

I walked away with confidence, like the points of my heels were nailing the carpet to the floorboards, but in reality my suit was the only thing holding my body together. Everything I'd said was true—I didn't kill Red, didn't see or even speak to him after work that day. But I knew who else in this building Red called when he'd fucked something up, and as I passed Asbel's office I was careful not to meet his eye.

*

Halloween-adjacent games were always messy. It might seem like one had nothing to do with the other, but no one loves a costume like a bunch of people already wearing face paint and jerseys. The fans were always a little rowdier, a little drunker, and—depending on the team's record—either happier or meaner than normal. Our cheerleaders were dressed in Daisy Duke versions of Disney princess costumes. A group of fans with paper bags over their heads dressed as "Bobcats fans in December," and I saw at least three people dressed as Zombie Red Guillory.

That was the environment into which we introduced Craig Washington.

He jogged out with the team to a chorus of boos, his still-vibrant hair a perpetual spotlight. An arc of cups and wadded-up garbage from the stands fell behind him like a comet's tail. From the front row of the press box, the writers pecked frantically at their computers, a familiar blue bird flashing out from every screen.

"At least it's the right holiday for it," Rodney said, and then, when I raised my eyes dryly at him, "You know—boo?"

We won the coin toss and opted to receive, and as Atlanta kicked off I realized I was tapping my pencil against the press box table at triple speed. Raj, our kick returner, caught the ball near the ten-yard line and took off, managing to pick up twenty yards before being dragged down.

"All *right!*" I gripped Rodney's shoulder. Maybe Coach Washington was the change we needed after all. Our receiver-heavy offense trotted onto the field, huddled briefly around A.J., and then took their places.

"Jesus," said Rodney, seeing the way they lined up, with receivers stretched to both sidelines. "They look like a bag of spilled marbles."

A spread offense was so called because the players are spread out across the field, which means the defense has to do the same to cover them. It gives options to throw the ball and space to run the ball, but most of all it puts pressure on the quarterback to make split-second decisions because all that blue sky in the middle is like a magnetic field pulling defenders toward him. A great quarterback could shine in that offense; a shakier quarterback—or an older, less mobile one—could lose a tooth. It was time to find out if A.J. still had it.

The ball was snapped, and A.J. handed it quickly off to Alec, who ran forward for two yards.

"Okay, okay," I breathed. Two yards was fine. Two yards was a solid start.

When they lined up for second down, A.J., instead of tucking himself under the center, was several feet back in a shotgun formation. Rodney and I exchanged bracing looks. *Here we go.* A.J. clapped his hands, the ball shot backward, and he caught it, bouncing on his toes and checking down his receivers to see who was open. No more than three seconds had passed when—*splat.*

"*Oooooh,*" came the collective groan from the press box as A.J. peeled himself off the field. He shook out his head, huddled quickly, then sent everyone back to the line with another clap of his hands.

It was hard to watch. I hated A.J., but even I didn't want to see him leave little bits and pieces of himself all over the ground. His jersey was filthy, with half of the letters of his name smeared away.

"Terrific," I said, showing Rodney my phone. "'Ufie'"—all that was left of the CAUFIELD between his shoulder blades—"is trending."

By the end of the game, I couldn't blame the fans—those of them still in the stadium. It was always going to be bumpy transitioning midseason to a new offensive scheme, but A.J. was sacked seven times, two of which resulted in fumbles, and threw a pick-six. The defense, with A.J.'s crew going three-and-out more often than not, had spent the majority of the day on the field, and they limped toward the locker room looking like neglected ferns.

I rubbed my temples, staring numbly at the field. Beside me, Rodney snorted. "Well, that went well."

*

"Did you try to fix this yourself?"

I stood in my office with my arms folded while Mohammad tinkered with my computer. After that massacre of a game I'd watched two episodes of *The Americans* (late to it, loved it) before lying awake most of the night. I'd gotten up as soon as the clock struck an hour that could reasonably be called morning and made it to the office while Chloe was still delivering the papers, then spent a frustrating few hours fighting with my glitching computer. My nerves were shredded—any small movement sent a jolt straight down my synapses.

"No."

Mo stopped clicking around and gave me a look.

"Fine, yes."

"A graveyard full of desktops," he muttered. He stood. "Okay, well, you've killed this one, so I'll have Nikko bring a new one this afternoon. It's going to take some work to get everything configured, so you might want to pick up a project or something."

Exasperated, I abandoned my office, and I tried texting Annika again.

Thinking of you. Here if you want to talk.

There was no response.

What now? We got the first note the day after Red was killed. Three days after that came the second, and two days beyond that the news broke about Annika. Now it had been almost another week. Sarah was still getting those creepy messages, and my skin crawled any time I stood near a window for too long, but there were no notes and no bombs. What did it mean? And why involve Dayanna and Nisha at all if nothing was going to happen to them?

I took a lap around the building and passed the detectives, now interviewing Dot. The younger detective met my eye through the window, and I increased my pace, taking the coach's wing stairs down toward the dining room.

Coach Washington was there, with black coffee and a bowl of hard-boiled eggs. After a loss like yesterday's I wouldn't have gone near Red until at least Tuesday, but Craig seemed calm enough, if tired. "Coach," I acknowledged politely. I had about ten seconds before I needed to get away from the scent of those eggs.

"Poppy Benjamin. We picked a hell of a time for the bye week, huh?"

Each team gets one week off per season, and this was ours. It meant no players in the building, no media—just a quiet little murder investigation and a series of threatening notes. "It probably would have been nicer for you to start after the bye so you could have had a longer runway. Are you settling in okay? Anything I can do to help you?"

He grinned, and a web of creases spread from his eyes and mouth. "You can try apologizing to my wife, since she doesn't want to hear it from me," he cracked. "She just convinced me to retire, and now I'm back here with a whistle around my neck."

I pulled a sympathetic face. "It's a big change going from Texas to Syracuse."

"Oh, she's not leaving Texas. We've been married long enough to give each other some space."

Well, that must be nice. I knew that you started out thinking space was okay, that two people with busy careers could hold up their own skies and come together when it worked for them. That was how it had started with Peter and me. We were a perfect match, because who else could understand that I slept with my phone not on the nightstand but on my bed, right where my neck met the pillow? Who else but me would be okay with an emergency call that sent him stumbling out of a theater in the middle of a movie, stepping over purses and legs, then moving at a near run as he headed to the hospital? There was no guilt. There were no apologies.

And then, without warning, it changed. Peter wanted more of me than I could give. He planned trip after trip for us, crushed each time when I explained I had a game, I had training camp, I had to prepare for the draft. After a while it felt like he was planning those things *because* he knew I couldn't do them, so that he could get angry with me.

And then, last winter, he broke it off. And found someone more available. And by the end of the summer had proposed to her.

"Oh man." Craig's voice pulled me back. His cell phone, on the table beside the eggs, was lit up with a text.

"What's wrong?"

"They're saying Buster Gibbs had a heart attack. Nice, nice guy. He was manager of the Rangers for a while when we were both starting out, and our wives are real close, too. Actually, I'm sorry, Poppy, I should give Suzanne a call."

I nodded and spit out some platitude. A horrible, creeping dread spread up my back like a sopping-wet blanket covering my shoulders.

Buster Gibbs was Dayanna's general manager.

*

We need to tell someone, Sarah wrote to Nisha and me. *That's two deaths now.*

We don't know he's dead, and it's a heart attack, Nisha responded. *They're not that uncommon in portly old white guys. You seriously think someone took out Dayanna's GM because she slept with a player?*

Sarah had the decency to pause before responding, *Why not? They killed Red because of whatever Poppy did.*

I turned my phone off.

Dazed, I headed upstairs and toward my desk before remembering Mo was working on my computer. There was no media over the bye week, no players to deal with. I didn't realize I was hovering over Chloe's space until she looked up at me expectantly.

"Did you need me for something?"

"I—yes." Her desk was covered with envelopes and Bobcats stickers. "How's the fan mail going?"

"It's okay. A.J. gets a lot of letters from weirdos."

I know the feeling. I picked one up and skimmed it.

. . . wasting the best years of your career at a dying organization. You need a real team to show what you can still do . . .

Letters from weirdos . . .

"Chloe, why don't you and I go to lunch?"

*

Chloe, I learned, was a pollotarian.

"And what is the thought process behind that?"

We were at a Moroccan restaurant on Marshall Street in the center of the university district. It was casual—counter service open to the bustling kitchen, and hard-backed green booths filled with a mixture of Syracuse students and employees from Crouse and University Hospitals down the street.

Chloe lifted her chicken shawarma pita, an entire meal encased in a bread pillow that set my mouth watering. "It's an environmental thing. Like, red-meat animals belch methane and fish can be toxic, so chickens are the most sustainable meat source."

"And pigs?" I strained to sound interested. I didn't *dislike* the Earth, but cutting the plastic loops on a six-pack was more my speed on environmentalism. My fingers twitched toward my phone, still switched off in my pocket. I hadn't gone this long without looking at it in at least a decade.

"So, pigs are bad because the wild ones dig into the soil and that lets off all these gases. Domestic pigs are better, but they still spread a lot of waste."

I wondered how bread was for the environment because I was about five seconds away from knocking that pita out of her hands and shoving it in my face. What was I thinking, ordering a salad on a day like today?

I put my fork down and folded my hands. "Why don't you tell me how you're liking the internship."

"I like it. Or I did, before. I still like it, and you and Rodney are great, it's just—"

"It's okay. I know what you mean."

I wasn't sure what I was looking for here, except that the notes came through the mail, which Chloe delivered, and she also read every piece of crackpot fan mail that came to A.J. Maybe she'd, I don't know, noticed something or read something or just knew anything about anything that might be helpful. I watched her carefully for some sign I might be on to something and was startled to find her looking at me just as intently.

Neither of us blinked.

"It's a strange time to be here," I tried again. "I'm sure emotions are running high, and probably the mail . . . ?" Nothing. She waited with raised eyebrows for me to finish, looking polite and slightly confused. Chloe couldn't help me, this was a dead end. I sighed.

What *would* it be like to be the intern when the coach was killed? I hadn't thought about Chloe for a second in all this, hadn't checked in on her. Since Red died, I hadn't even done the usual mentoring like asking about her plans for next year and creating a contact tree to help get her there. I had no idea who killed Red. I couldn't explain what was happening to the WAGS or figure out what we should be doing about it, or even whether we were all still friends. But a young girl was sitting in front of me with hopes and ambitions and plans for her future, looking for some kind of leadership. And that, I could do.

I shot her a sympathetic smile. "It's not the same, obviously, but my first year was really hard too. It was the undefeated season and it should have been fun, but everything was just so tense. It was like a life-sized Jenga tower that got higher and higher but weaker and weaker, and nobody wanted to be the one who knocked it over."

"That was Red's first season, right?" Chloe's voice hitched slightly on his name, and I did some quick math to determine she would have been about seven years old at the time. I looked at her curiously.

"It was. Did you grow up a Bobcats fan? Do you remember that season?"

"I did, I—" She smiled, closemouthed and tight. "But also . . . Coach said something to me about it."

"He did?"

"Yeah—while I was delivering papers. He always talked to me for a bit when I'd bring his."

I swallowed, smiled. "Oh."

"He said—" Now Chloe was shredding a napkin, destroying it into a miniature snowstorm on the tabletop. "He said this year was like that one. Hard. Tense. He used the same word you did."

Several beats passed in silence. Too many.

He said this year was like that one.

"Chloe . . ." *Slow. Confident. Calm.* "Is there anything you want to tell me? Because I hope you know that you can do that—talk to me. If there's something I should know."

Once again, neither of us blinked.

FIFTEEN YEARS AGO

Thank God for hangovers. With my head pounding and my tongue fat and fuzzy in my mouth, Saturday was a blur of bed and couch, a horizontal day. I couldn't focus on how skeeved out I was by my apartment, or do anything beyond forcing in careful bites of crackers and slow sips of water. I barely registered the flickering images of the wild card games. The light hurt. The sound was muted. And every time two bodies crashed together on the field, all I pictured was James and Abby mashed up against each other.

By Monday I was physically better, but the mental hangover was still there. I stared blankly at my desk. How could so much have changed since Friday? I'd had Abby, the friend, and James, the crush. Now they were AbbyandJames. James didn't owe me anything. He didn't have to like me back. But Abby was supposed to be my friend.

Why did she do it? Abby *knew* I liked James. It was probably that poll, the fact that at least some of the guys here thought she wasn't the hottest one in the building anymore. Abby was jealous. Threatened.

"Poppy B," said Brent, his usual greeting. He smacked the light switch inside his office and hung his coat before heading to the kitchen.

"Good morning," I said to the closing annex door. I tapped my pencil against my notebook, considering. Brent had told me not to get too close to Abby, not to let her reputation bleed into mine. Because she *did* have a reputation. She dated that scout last year, and now she'd made out with James. And at the bar she said she thought Coach was hot too. How had I missed so many signs? She was no better than the random skanks sending A.J. fan mail spritzed with cheap perfume.

It really didn't make sense to base my work alliances on whoever happened to be female, I decided as I watched the copier belch out stacks of the clips packet. Abby and I didn't have much in common beyond that. Every day I tried not to be the girl who didn't know what she was doing, and Abby couldn't be bothered to learn the basic terminology because she was just here on her way to work in *films*. She didn't like football. She probably didn't even actually like James. Maybe he was just a step on the way to something else too, and she didn't care that I was interested.

I seethed as I delivered my clips, slapping them onto empty desks with an audible *thwack*. Who did Abby think she was? As if there weren't a million girls like her floating around every office in the country? She made the rest of us look bad, really. It was embarrassing. It was embarrassing for me that I'd hung out with her, and Brent was right to tell me to be careful. I was learning—friends at work weren't the people who said nice things to you all the time. Real work friends were the ones who looked out for you, who saw you reaching out to pick up the ice cubes off the ground and grabbed the back of your collar so you didn't get kicked. Brent was right when he said he had my back. That's what having someone's back looked like.

I ate lunch alone at my desk. I took the long way around to use the ladies' room at the opposite end of the building so I wouldn't have to pass Mo or James, and when James came through the annex, I grabbed my recorder and hurried off, muttering something about blogging buddies.

Monday grumpies? he emailed me midafternoon. I brought my finger down on the Delete button with the force of a lumberjack's ax.

My path wouldn't cross with Abby's on a normal workday, and so I didn't know how to show her I was freezing her out. It was so unsatisfying. I wished I was an ice-veined customer who could pretend she never existed, that I could put both Abby and James out of my mind and concentrate on heading into the playoffs undefeated during my first NFL season. But I didn't have that kind of composure, and I badly wanted Abby to know, unambiguously, that she was out.

I wanted to rumble.

I finally got my chance on Friday when she fell into step behind me on my walk to the far bathroom. I pretended not to notice and went on my way, but she caught the door I'd intentionally let fall shut and followed me in.

"Okay." She closed the door to the lounge, trapping us between the hallway and the actual bathroom. Her dress was a bright, look-at-me yellow. "It's the playoffs, so I could understand skipping out on lunch now and then, but not the entire week. And now you have to hide the fact that you're taking a bathroom break? You need to stand up to Richard. Or go to Brent, or something. You're only an intern, he can't treat you like this."

How could she be so dumb? "You think I'm hiding from *Richard*?"

"Aren't you?"

All my mirror-rehearsed rages failed me. Every speech I'd put together while brushing my teeth or practiced aloud in my car during morning traffic was gone, leaving me with nothing more than a gaping mouth and a hot neck. I barked out a frustrated laugh. "I'm not hiding from anyone, but I am avoiding you."

"Me?"

"Are you *kidding* me?" It came out as a roar, much too loud for the office, and I glared at her as if she'd been the one to yell. "Yes," I hissed, "you. You did what you did—at least own it. At least don't pretend like you don't know why I'm upset."

"Is this about Friday? James?"

"Oh, look at that, you do know why I'm upset."

"Poppy. What the hell? We were all out, it was a fun night. I thought you and Carter were going to get together. James and I both did."

"Just because I talked to him?"

"Because you *invited* him. You were weird with James all night, jumping away from him when he touched you, and then Carter showed up and you were practically purring."

"That's not—"

"And," Abby continued hotly, "maybe you forgot, but you told me at Thanksgiving you're not into James."

"That was—a month ago, and you were the one being all, 'Oh, here's to *work friends*,' so don't tell me you didn't know."

She threw up her hands. "Listen, Poppy. I know you're still in college mode, but I'm not a mind-reader. You told me you didn't like him, so when he asked if you'd said anything about him, I told him that—get this—you didn't like him! This is grown-up time now. You want to be the coyest little fish in the pond, this shit's going to happen."

"I'm sure it just broke your heart to pass that on, huh? You *knew* that wasn't true, and you said it anyway because you wanted James for yourself."

"Please. It's not that serious. I'd had a rough week—a rough *season*—and he was there and cute and into it. I don't have to sit back and wait in case you maybe, sometime in the future, decide you're interested in someone. I can sleep my way through this whole office if I want to, and it's not any business of yours."

"Is that your five-year plan?" I sneered. "I hear you're making good progress."

"Fuck you."

The door slammed, and Abby was gone, leaving me alone in the ladies' lounge. I closed my eyes and tasted the salt of a tear bump against my lips. When I opened them again, a streak of mascara ran in a vertical line down my face, splitting me into a Jekyll and Hyde. On one side I was the girl who walked into the stadium that first day looking for a friendly face, a trusted outlet, a confidant. On the other, I was a viper, scratching and clawing to claim space, to protect my spot. Did I have to be one or the other? Which version did I want to be, and which version would I have to be to stay here?

*

The snow crunched beneath my feet as I made my way to the car on the morning of our first playoff game. It was frigid even by Syracuse standards, with temperatures hovering around fifteen degrees and a real-feel below zero. Normally a game this important would be in prime time, but the powers that be at the League seemed to realize it would only get colder as darkness fell, so afternoon it was.

"This is some real Ice Bowl shit," said Brent once I'd made it to the press box. It was warmer here than outside but still too cold for human habitation. The wind found its way through the tiny cracks between the press box's all-glass front, causing a low whistle that brought my shoulders to my ears.

The field was barely visible from up here—everything was drenched in white. I could just make out the grounds crew, black specks studiously working to clear the yard markers and edges of the field. Swarms of stadium workers attacked the stairs with shovels while others cleared the paths in front of each row of seats. A cluster of players gathered by the tunnel, and I pressed my nose against the glass to get a better look.

"Are the linemen . . . Are those their bare arms?" Since football jerseys are short-sleeved, players usually wore at least one compression shirt as a base layer to cover their skin.

"They won't wear the sleeves. Think it makes them look tough."

Maybe there was something to that, since we were playing San Diego, but there was intimidation and then there was amputation.

"Go down to the supply room and gear up," Brent said. "We'll need you defrosted and functional for postgame."

With no seal to the outside, it was even colder in the stadium bowels, and I hugged myself as I hurried down the hallway. "Look alive, Poppy," called our equipment guy, Sam, as he drove past on a cart. "I left it open for you."

The supply room was a giant walk-in closet filled with Bobcats merchandise from throughout the team's history. It was lit by bare bulbs with chains I could reach only on my tiptoes. Most of the time it smelled thick and musty, but today the cold had wiped it clean—even the scent of the air was frozen. The walls were lined with industrial steel shelving stacked two high with faded cardboard boxes, and if you dug deep enough, you could find sweatshirts and hats with every logo the team had ever had. A pile of boxes had been pulled to the front, filled with sleeping-bag-sized Bobcats puffer coats, bobble hats, and hand and toe warmers. I grabbed a crimson coat at the top of the pile and shrugged it on. It was enormous. My hands were marooned halfway through the sleeves, and the bottom swished against the floor.

"You look like you're wearing a hot-dog costume."

I spun around—none too gracefully, in the giant coat—and saw James, arms folded, leaning up against the doorframe. He was wearing a sturdy, arctic-explorer-style goose down jacket that must have been reserved for people higher up the food chain than me.

"That's funny." I tossed my head with all the dignity I could muster and made a move for the hallway. "Excuse me."

"Poppy—wait." Now that he'd said it, I really could only picture my look as a hot dog, which made it incredibly hard to strike the kind of sophisticated indifference I was hoping for. I tried to fold my puffy arms, failed, and shot him an expectant look instead. "I'm sorry about Friday. No—" He grabbed my mammoth sleeve as I turned to leave. "I mean it. I've been trying to talk to you all week. I thought we were . . . you know, whatever, but then at the bar you seemed really cold. Not like—" He indicated my team gear. "You know. Unfriendly. And then Abby said—"

"I heard what she said."

He shook his head. "That was so bitchy, I can't believe her. I should have listened to Mo."

A small light flickered deep in my chest, a damp match against the wind.

"It was stupid," James went on. "*I* was stupid. And drunk, and frustrated, and she was, like, really in my face about it . . . I'm sorry."

So Abby had been the one to initiate things. The light held firm, small but steady. "You didn't owe me anything," I said, trying to sound nonchalant. "You and I weren't—I mean, we hadn't . . ."

James stepped closer. Even inside the supply room it was so cold that I could see his breath, an extension of him that bloomed out and beckoned. "I know. But I want to be. Do you?" My pulse kicked into high gear as nonchalant went the way of the buffalo. I nodded. James reached out, his arms circling toward my back and his angled jaw coming closer to mine—

And then we were cracking up, because his arms didn't fit around me in my giant coat. It was like trying to hug a sumo wrestler. The tension between us for the past week and the anticipation of our first kiss and the pressure of the game about to kick off and the sky literally falling outside—I clutched his arm to steady myself, I was laughing so hard. He reached for my face instead, cupping it with both hands, and pulled my lips to his, and we were still laughing, a fun and messy first kiss that felt like a fiftieth.

We pressed ourselves together, foreheads and cold noses touching, and stood there grinning like idiots, savoring the closeness and the warmth and the quiet before going back out into the fray. He grabbed the collar of my coat and whispered with mock sincerity, "the *hottest* dog."

*

The wind blew the snow sideways. My dad called weather like this the Great Equalizer, and it was true, because speed and skill were wiped out by the elements. In cold like this, bone crunched against bone. Running backs who hadn't fumbled all season could let a stiff football drop from frozen fingers and change the course of the game. Wide receivers who relied on their ability to streak down the field had their powers nullified as they slipped and slid across yard markers too covered in snow to see.

All those things were happening as the first half came to a close. Thankfully San Diego was even more affected by the elements than we were, and when the teams ran into their tunnels, the Bobcats were ahead a sloppy 14–3.

"Not a great day to be a statistician," said Brent. He stretched his arms over his head, flashing the top of his woven belt. "Hey, could you get me a soda? I know that's not kosher to ask anymore, but could you just do it?"

It was warmer in the dining area, where the steam trays below the press box meal fought mightily to keep the marinara sauce from congealing. A radio guy pressed a hot roll between his hands like a first-class passenger with a warmed towel.

The soda machine was blocked by a mass of red curls. A young woman in leggings and a long blazer was kicking its base and hissing curses as the Sprite dispenser let out nothing but air.

"Sarah?" I hadn't seen her since she was a senior when I was a freshman, but I'd never forget that hair.

Sarah turned and broke into a grin. "Poppy Benjamin! I heard you were doing something in the NFL. You're with the Bobcats?"

"Media relations. How about you?" I craned my head to see her credential.

"This tiny paper out in San Diego. I'm on general assignment, so I don't usually travel, but for this—"

"Sure."

"So how is all this? It must have been such an insane year. And you have A.J.—what's he like?"

"He's . . ." I so badly wanted to tell her, to vent like girlfriends. A.J. was spoiled and moody and unnecessarily difficult, but he was my team's quarterback and this wasn't school anymore. I was talking to a member of the media. ". . . super talented, you know? The whole team is amazing, with DeMario, and Coach Guillory . . ."

James passed through the dining area balancing four bags of to-go popcorn in his arms while trying not to let the buttered edges touch his suit. He tossed me a wink as he headed for the executive elevators to bring Asbel his favorite midgame snack, and a whoosh flew up my spine. I *kissed* that guy—he kissed me. In a supply closet! Bananas!

"I don't want to be weird or anything," Sarah was saying in a low voice, "but just . . . be careful around him. I've heard a few things."

I took a step back. "What kind of things?"

"It's nothing official—just rumors and stuff—but I guess he can be kind of . . . handsy."

I *wanted* him to be handsy! James was hot, charming, confident, and clearly on his way to success in the League. I'd just bet there were lots of girls who would welcome a little attention if he was willing to give it, but he was interested in me. He chose *me,* he'd kissed *me.*

"I'll keep an eye out," I said just as the announcement came that the second half was about to start. "Thanks for the heads-up."

CHAPTER SIXTEEN

NOW

Two gowns in just over a month had to be some kind of record. This event, though, on the white marble patio of a Charleston plantation, under a dripping canopy of angel oak so lush and thick it blocked out the stars, made the Syracuse gala look like the line outside a falafel cart around two a.m.

I was wearing a gold strapless bodice of handlaid sequins that bloomed into a tulle skirt. My hair was done in Old Hollywood–style waves, and my lips were a deep merlot. The event, thrown by a luxury brand whose name was synonymous with extremely expensive watches, was called A Time to Celebrate, and the guest of honor was the brand's main ambassador, one bruised, worked over, and extremely churlish all-star quarterback.

That meant by Asbel's new rules that I had to be here too, although I wasn't really. I physically might be clutching the stem of a white wineglass where condensation from the crisp liquid quivered against the sultry night air. I might be listening to the unfamiliar sound of southern insects harmonizing with the string quintet. But mentally, I was still in the booth across from Chloe.

"No," she'd said as casually as if I'd asked after her weekend plans, "there's nothing." But she was calm where she should have been confused, and I recognized too much of myself in her. Something was not right between Chloe and Red, but if he was dead and she didn't want to talk about it, where did that leave me?

When Chloe came on, we'd had "the talk"—*If anyone in this office ever says or does something that makes you uncomfortable, I want you to tell me about it. It's on them, not you, and you won't be in trouble, but I can't help unless you tell me.*

I will believe you.

I needed her to know that part, that she could come to me without fear of what would happen to her next. That I would stand up for her, that I'd use my position as a senior member of staff to be a voice for her. It was so very important that women do that for each other.

I doubted that today a Neil from accounting could pin young interns against the wall and be laughed off as over-friendly. It had been years since I'd heard a female trainer complain about "happy feet," where players wiggled their toes while their foot was propped against the trainer's chest for taping. But if everything had changed, it was also true that nothing had, and a girl like Chloe was just as vulnerable as I'd been, just now with shiny new packaging. Look at Nisha checking into hotels under a pseudonym. Look at Sarah's Digital Dick Museum, as we'd once dubbed her collection of unrequested photos, or the way Dayanna's GM, who seemed to be recovering nicely from his heart attack, spoke about her curves like she was Jessica Rabbit.

And we were the adults. We were the ones with a fair amount of aggregated power.

Chloe was a thousand times more self-assured than I'd been at her age. She gave unsolicited feedback to her boss on the day after the franchise's icon was murdered. Not content to be a mere vegetarian, she lectured about which specific animals were environmentally acceptable. It was hard to believe that if she had something to tell me, she would hold back. And yet.

"Is this dirt taken?"

Omar Kadeer stood beside me in a black tie and a cobalt-blue tuxedo. Exhausted after the first hour of trying to look interested while talking to no one, I'd made my way down the patio's broad stone steps, past the open-air dance floor, and tucked myself beneath one of the giant oaks.

"Nice seeing you again," I managed, forcing my attention back from Chloe. I indicated the patio where A.J. was posing for photos. "He seems to be behaving, considering there's probably still grass in his teeth."

"His teeth are blindingly white. I assumed that's why you were all the way over here. And he always behaves in public, which is why I like him. Well," he corrected, grinning, "it's one reason I like him."

I calculated the couple hundred million that A.J. had made over the years in contracts, roughly doubled that on endorsements, and took a conservative 10 percent off the top. I just bet Omar liked him.

"It's not easy for him, you know," he said. I looked up, a retort on my lips, but saw that Omar, for once, looked serious. "Getting older."

It probably wasn't—no one wants to feel passed by—but sympathy, I felt, was a bridge too far. "As a woman, I really can't relate to that, since we're famously celebrated for aging. Why are *you* standing all the way over here?"

"Poppy, this place has 'Plantation' in the name. I'm keeping one foot near the exit."

"Fair enough." I held out my glass, and we clinked. A burst of laughter erupted from the group around A.J., and I shook my head. "I don't get it—they scream obscenities at him, and throw water bottles at him, and hope his leg snaps under him when he gets sacked, but then when they see him in person they want a photo."

"Ah, you're one of those," said Omar, and then, when I raised my eyebrows, "a purist."

"I mean, I like plenty of opposing players, but that's because I like them as people. The whole point of him to them is that he's *not* a real person." The wine was like an ice cube trailing along my sticky skin from the inside, the only relief from the muggy night air. It was shocking how the heat could still make itself known down here, at night, in November. At home we had already seen flurries. Resisting the urge to press the glass against my forehead, I swirled it instead and said, "Do you want to take a walk?"

We set off away from the party, around the elaborate grounds and gardens. Crushed stones crunched under our feet, giving me jellylegs in my high heels, and after a minute I pulled them off and left them abandoned on a stone bench near the entrance to an honest-to-God hedge maze.

"Should we?" Omar indicated the opening.

"Oh. I didn't mean—they just hurt."

"I know. But should we?" His eyes narrowed as he smiled playfully, and I laughed in spite of every competing disaster tumbling around my head. Would I take a moonlit stroll with some guy around a definitely haunted plantation under normal circumstances? Of course not. But the nice thing about Omar Kadeer was that he was way too hot for me, we both knew it, and that took all the pressure off. Setting my glass beside the shoes with a light *tink,* I gripped my dress so that it hung above my ankles.

"Okay," I said. "You're on."

It was quiet inside the maze, which rose several feet above our heads in all directions. The earth was soft and cool beneath my toes, and the paths were flooded with moonlight. At the first turn, I chuckled, and then, in response to Omar's raised eyebrow, said, "No—it's stupid. I was just—have you ever seen that Toni Braxton video where she's running in the ball gown?"

His laugh was an easy, full-throated sound. "Our jobs come with a lot of . . . unexpected experiences, don't they? That's what I like about it—never boring."

It was what I liked about it too, and it felt so validating to hear Omar say that. Like this was the kind of job worth devoting your life to. Like it was the kind of job worth sacrificing something precious for. Maybe on another night, as my normal self, I wouldn't have said anything, but traversing a hedge maze with a relative stranger, our hands swishing past each other close enough to make a vibration, it felt like an opportunity to talk to someone who might understand.

"Omar, can I ask you a personal question?"

"Now this is the strategy my ex-girlfriends should have used." He indicated the living walls surrounding us. "Where am I going to go?"

I blushed deeply. "I'm sorry, I wasn't trying to—"

"Poppy, I'm joking. Of course you can."

We turned another corner, met a dead end, and reversed back in the direction we'd come. "I just wondered, with these jobs, and the travel, and no weekends—how do you make it work? Having something outside? I mean, if you do, that is. Obviously we don't know each other that well."

He stopped and faced me, the force of his gaze so powerful it lifted my chin. A skitter of panic crossed my chest—maybe I'd misunderstood. I was suddenly extremely aware of the way my dress plunged at the neck, the salted sweat across my décolletage. There was moonlight caught in Omar's short curls, the shadows of it throwing his cheekbones into sharp relief. His voice was low, and serious. "I'm going to tell you how, but you have to be ready to hear me, because it's not easy. You have to really want it. Okay?"

"Okay."

"This is the secret. Date . . . a twenty-year-old . . . model."

The tension broke so completely that I barked out a very unladylike guffaw and gave him a shove. Omar held up both hands. "It's true! I'm going to tell you why, and you're going to thank me, so you're welcome. They don't eat much—easy to take care of. They stare into their phones all day so you never have to talk to them— surprisingly low-maintenance. And they don't make any demands on your time. We've solved your problem. I'm telling you, a twenty- year-old model is going to be the fix for you. Should we look some up?"

"No," I said, still laughing. "I don't have anywhere near that kind of energy—I need a rescue dog, not a puppy. But thank you for sharing that extremely hard-won wisdom."

"Okay, so tell me who you're seeing that's so great."

I hesitated, but he raised his chin expectantly, so I said, "No one, at the moment. But the previous guy was a surgeon."

"And what are scrubs except the male version of a belly ring? They're both status symbols."

My smile tightened. Suddenly it didn't all seem so funny. "Hey, come on," said Omar, noticing the change, and then, "I'm sorry. That was too far."

"No, no, it's fine. That guy's long gone." My easy tone made it sound like I'd been the one to ditch Peter. It was more bearable that way.

We'd arrived back at the entrance to the maze, where my shoes and wineglass waited. An out-of-season firefly had fallen into the liquid and was now paddling gently around, lightning in a bottle.

*

When I parked in the stadium lot on Monday, I sat in my running car because I didn't want to go inside. Sarah had called on Sunday and, when I didn't answer, left a rambling voicemail apologizing for her comments about Red. "I'm so freaked out, Poppy," she'd said, and I could hear the tears in her voice. "Nisha told me not to tell you, but she's had some weird things going on too. I don't know what to think. But I shouldn't have put that on you. Red's death was not your fault."

It would have meant more coming before we knew that Buster Gibbs's heart attack was just a steak-and-cigarettes special, and it would have helped more if Sarah was right about the second part. Red's death *was* partly my fault, just not in the way she meant.

Once I was in my office I took a long, slow look around. There were awards for leadership and mentorship through the Women in Sports Foundation. The magazine cover featuring "40 Women Under 40 Blowing Apart the Old World Order." A framed photo of me at my alma mater with a group of public relations students. I was proud of what I'd done here. I liked my life, and I was happy in it. Ever since Annika's scandal, since the initial note—really, ever since Red was killed—it felt like it was all being held together with Scotch tape and toothpicks. It felt like the floor could swing open and swallow me at any moment.

The door to the annex clunked but didn't open. An insistent knock that might have been a kick followed, and Chloe rushed to open it. When she did, a pair of crutches swung into view, followed by DeMario.

"*Hi*," I said. "That's new."

DeMario looked like he'd been dipped in foam—his leg from thigh to ankle was wrapped in a hard brace. His usual easy smile was replaced with a grimace, and there were dark circles beneath his eyes. "I need to talk to you," he said, sending my stomach cartwheeling. With a glance at Chloe, he added, "In your office, please."

After I'd closed the door he tried to sit, but the chair was too close to the desk and he didn't have the angle. I hurried to pull it farther out, and he waved me off in frustration.

"You had the surgery?" I asked, and he nodded. Seeing him in front of me looking so diminished drove home that not only had I used him, I'd kicked him when he was down. When he'd needed me the most. How could I have sold him out, my friend, just to cover my own ass? What kind of person would do such a thing?

"Rehab started last week. That's one good thing about not coming back—I don't have to get into football shape, I just have to be able to get out of bed and into my chair."

I winced. "I'm really sorry."

"It is what it is. I've had a good run, you know? My kids are set. Their kids will be set." He hitched forward as much as his bum leg would allow. "I just want to know what shitstain leaked it. Faith found out from *SportsCenter*—she thinks I couldn't tell her. There's no secrets between us, she knows everything about me, and now she's looking at me sideways. I've known you a long time, and you get shit done. I need you, Poppy. How do we find this guy? Because I'm going to fuck him up."

DeMario didn't talk like that. He was becoming a worse version of himself because of me, because of my lies. He and *Faith* were fighting over it? No, I couldn't let that go on. I sighed from my toes and pictured the way his face would twist in shock and betrayal and eventually anger. He was going to hate me, and it would be awful to lose him, to lose them both, because I loved Faith too. This was going to really hurt.

Fuck.

"D—I need to tell you something."

And then my phone buzzed—a call from Sarah in the middle of the workday. I silenced it, folded my hands on my desk, and leaned forward, but it immediately buzzed again.

CHAT ROOM RIGHT NOW 911 SOS.

NOW NOW NOW.

Pulse pounding against the roof of my mouth, I shoved my chair back and swept my phone and laptop into my bag. "I'm so sorry," I told DeMario as I stood, "um, I need to leave right now. I'm sorry. We'll talk about this, okay? Soon. I just—sorry."

I half jogged down the stadium hallway, through the lobby, and opened the front doors into a thick wall of lake-effect snow.

It sucked up sound and color until there was nothing but silence and white. I looked once back down the hallway, cursed under my breath, and went out. In my heels, without a coat, I trudged toward my car, crying out as the snow filled my shoes, forced its way between my toes. The windshield was already covered, and I used the sleeve of my blouse to clear the driver's-side doorframe. Inside, I popped off my heels and flexed my frozen feet. It brought an explosion of pinpricks, but they would be okay, they hadn't been exposed for long. Whatever Sarah needed to tell us so urgently might not be as easily fixed.

I propped my laptop on the dashboard, caught the stadium Wi-Fi, and logged in. Only Sarah was waiting for me.

"What is it?" I said immediately, stabbing at the heat controls. Seat warmer, lower-zone airflow. "Where's everyone else?"

"I can't find Nisha."

"I don't understand what that means, like she's not answering?"

"No, I mean she was supposed to be in Denver yesterday for work and didn't show. Didn't call anyone, didn't say anything. Just wasn't there."

The car was warming now, but I felt chilled to the bone. Taking time off was one thing—though I couldn't imagine Nisha doing that in the middle of the season—but just not showing up was impossible. It meant something was seriously, seriously wrong. I rubbed at the sopping sleeve of my blouse. "So what do we do, call the police? Someone with her team obviously knows she's missing, did they do anything?"

Sarah's curls bounced side to side. "I don't know, I haven't talked to anyone there. Someone at my place was supposed to talk to her for a development story and was complaining in our Slack when she didn't show. I've tried calling and texting, I checked her socials. There's nothing."

I'd lived my entire professional life under stress. I thrived under it and did my best work when the stakes were high. But until that moment, I don't think I'd understood the difference between pressure and danger. Pressure, I could handle, I was built for it, but this was something else. This stress was the fear of monsters in my closet and under my bed, and it was very quickly going to tear me apart.

"What about Dayanna, have you talked to her?"

"She's okay. She's talking about flying out there to check Nisha's apartment, she wants to, like, hug her back to safety. But what happens when she gets to San Francisco and the door's locked? Then what?"

"Okay . . . okay, shit." Nisha was missing. Sarah was in a full panic. Annika was still off-grid, and Dayanna was flying across the country with no plan.

"There's one more thing." Sarah's mouth was a line. "The last time I talked to Nisha was Friday." Three days ago. "She sent this really cryptic message—*Vergangenheitsbewältigung.*"

"What the hell is that?"

A fist hit my window, and I practically went through the roof of the car. I turned to look at the same time I snapped the laptop shut and found Asbel bent at the waist, peering at me.

"You starting a true-crime podcast now?" he said once I'd rolled down the window. He nodded toward the closed laptop with its Bobcats logo on the front.

"Yeah—you want to sponsor it?" I said, still trying to catch my breath. I hadn't seen him coming through the snow-covered windshield. "I had a telehealth appointment. I don't like doing them in my office, and the investigators are in the conference room, so . . . Just needed a little privacy. That's all." I flashed what I hoped was a confident smile, but I could feel my lips trembling.

"You hung up on your doctor?"

"We were finishing up. I actually have to get back inside. First availability in a week, everyone's a little restless."

"Don't forget your coat." Asbel tapped the roof of the car once and then walked off toward his own sleek black vehicle.

*

All afternoon I ran from one crisis to the next. First Rodney shared his "theories" with the detectives, which brought a request for a list of Bobcats wide receivers over the past ten years. Then I fielded a call from a reporter alleging he'd heard our secondary was using bounties to encourage big hits—cash bonuses for violently knocking someone out of the game. Coach Washington had been burned for that once before—not his own initiative, but one of the position coaches who wanted to provide a little extra incentive for his unit. I was sure this was a lazy rumor, but it still had to be dealt with. Chloe flashed me an extra-wide smile every time I saw her—something was not right there—but we were still a professional football team in the middle of the season with work to do and games to play.

What was that word—or phrase, or sentence—Nisha had sent? It sounded Germanic, but I've never been great with languages, and by the time I was done shaking off Asbel I'd forgotten it completely. Sarah and Dayanna said Nisha was about to do something stupid—stupid as far as Nisha was concerned, or stupid for all of us? And what might that be?

I managed to leave work by seven, only to be stranded on Onondaga Lake Parkway because a truck missed the warning sign in the snow and struck the low bridge. I used the time in traffic to repeatedly call both Sarah and Dayanna, but neither picked up. I wanted to scream, but all I could do was inch the car forward, mile by tortured mile, while my mind conjured every conceivable awful scenario. Nisha had found the killer and was outside his house right now in a catsuit, holding a glass cutter in her teeth. Nisha had decided to spill her guts to a reporter in an effort to eliminate the blackmailer's leverage, a tactic that would inevitably blow up in her face. By the time I swiped myself in at the guardhouse outside my townhouse, my nerves were shredded. My stomach felt like it was lined with paper cuts. It was somewhat of a surprise, then, when I pulled into my spot and saw Sarah, Dayanna, Nisha, and Annika waving at me from the next car over.

CHAPTER SEVENTEEN

FIFTEEN YEARS AGO

I couldn't sleep the night before the conference finals. We'd won the division final easily, with the San Diego players near weeping by the end as icicles formed in their facial hair. That felt great for about a day, and then it was straight back into win or go home, because another game was waiting.

I wasn't even the one on the field, and the pressure of it all pinned me to my bed. How did DeMario possibly handle this? How did A.J.? I could never stand there in front of everyone and perform, have the eyes of a whole country on me, the fate of dozens of jobs, the expectations of hundreds of thousands of fans. Didn't it crush them? Didn't it grab hold of their necks and shake?

Wrapping my comforter tightly around me, I got my laptop from the floor and brought it back into bed. I read all the previews, took in all the opinions. Visited fan blogs. Saw the betting lines. It all felt a million miles away from the football I'd grown up with, the one I loved so much. I thought of my dad spending late nights in his home office, the lights out, the game film flickering across the flimsy screen that pulled down from the ceiling. Sometimes I'd wander downstairs in my pajamas and he'd let me join him there, where we'd sit silently, both focused on the figures moving across the screen while he scratched out notes on a yellow legal pad. I thought of all the times our doorbell rang and I'd answered it to find a teenage boy in tears, or looking shifty, or bouncing on his toes, bursting with some recruiting news he couldn't wait to tell his coach. My dad would usher each of them into his office, close the door, and offer them little pieces of himself; and they would walk out a little taller and a little better.

This football was so different. It churned forward, grinding some people up and lifting others to superstardom, and all of it balanced on the flick of a wrist, the path of the wind as it swirled around the stadium. Whether it snowed. Whether fingers managed to grab a fraction of a jersey and clamp down, or if they slipped off the slick fabric and grasped at air, helpless as the receiver disappeared down the field to glory.

"Big day today, kid," said Brent when I walked into the press box.

"The biggest."

But late in the fourth quarter, we were in trouble—behind, with nothing clicking. It was deathly quiet in the press box. No one chatted, there were no little quips. The reality was sinking in for everyone that this could be it. The final minutes of our season.

Brent's face was grim as he held his cell phone to his ear and covered the mouthpiece. "Head down to the field. We have to grab A.J. and Coach for TV, but there's going to be a scrum, so get your elbows ready." He gestured toward the phone. "I have to finish this, then I'll meet you down there."

The sound of the crowd dimmed and then bloomed as I rode the elevator to field level and walked to the tunnel. As I passed through it, the sky grew bigger and bigger until it was a brilliant blue umbrella hanging high above the packed stadium. Every seat was full of rabid fans in Bobcats red, their frozen breath exploding from their mouths like puffs of dragon's fire as they screamed and beat the seat backs and stomped their feet. The noise was deafening, the sun was blinding. Taking it in filled me to my toes with something so big, so powerful that it almost lifted me off my feet.

"Hey!" A voice broke through the crowd—James, wearing a wool dress coat and headset, gestured me toward him. We'd spent the past week eyeing each other flirtatiously, all eyebrow raises and subtle smiles. Abby was the one eating alone now while I joined Mo and James in the café. It was too bad it had to be that way, but she'd done it to herself.

I pressed my hand to my forehead in a salute to block the sun and made my way down the choked sideline to James. He said something I couldn't hear over the tribal drumbeat for defense, and I cupped my hands to my mouth. "What?"

"I said," he yelled, "fancy seeing you here."

"I'm supposed to grab A.J. after, but . . ." I gestured to the crush of people around us—camera operators, sideline reporters, photographers, trainers, equipment guys, ball boys. Giant parab bubbles catching sound for TV.

"Yeah," James yelled. "You're going to need a better seat. Come on."

He took my hand and pulled me toward the team benches, moving aggressively through the clumps of people. I trailed at arm's length as we pushed and squeezed our way through, and offered apologies that were instantly snatched and consumed by the roar of the crowds.

When my toes touched the white paint of the sideline, I pulled back. "I can't be here!"

James turned with a grin that sent a whoosh up my spine. He tapped his badge where it read GM ASST and tightened his fingers around mine. "Sure you can—you're with me."

We were inside the game. If A.J. threw me the ball it would trigger a replay to see whether the pass was in-bounds. Players pushed past us on their way off the field, the heavy odor of cold sweat dripping off them. From behind us came the steady *phwah . . . phwah . . . phwah* of Troy Collins, our kicker, slamming the ball into a practice net in case our entire season came down to his frozen foot.

I looked at the clock—just under two minutes left. Dallas was ahead 34–28 and had the ball on its own thirty-yard line. They let the play clock almost run out, and then on first down ran straight up the middle of the field. It gained only two yards but that wasn't the point—Dallas just wanted to keep the clock running.

"Come on, come on," I muttered, bouncing on my toes.

Second down was another run, this time to the opposite side of the field. Bobcats fell like bowling pins as the fullback's piston legs powered him past midfield and into our territory.

"That high-stepping motherfucker!" said our defensive-line coach. He spit so close to me that I barely moved my foot in time. James's brow was heavy, and I recognized the sinking mix of panic and disbelief moving through me. This couldn't be—it *couldn't*. We hadn't lost a game all season, but that historic run would mean nothing if we couldn't somehow get the ball back and score. The game days, the press conferences, the notes, the clips—all the things that had propelled us through a grinding five months, that incredible churning forward, the feeling of keeping up or being swallowed by something bigger than all of us—it would just . . . end. And we would have to watch another team pile on top of each other on our field, would have to see our fans file out in shocked silence, bitter disappointment written across eighty thousand faces. It was impossible—it was *impossible*. And yet Dallas was almost within field goal range, which would put the game entirely out of reach.

James leaned forward, hands resting on his knees. I bent and twisted my fingers and forced myself to draw deep breaths in and out. The Dallas huddle broke with a unified clap, and they lined up for first down. We were inside a minute left now, but the Bobcats still had all three time-outs, so Dallas was going to have to run a play.

At the same moment the ball was snapped, a blur of red streaked across the line of scrimmage—Chase. He cut through the offensive line like a knife hot from the dishwasher and slammed into the Dallas quarterback just as he'd turned to hand off the ball, hitting him so hard that both bodies flew backward before landing in a pile of meat and pads. Something brown and oblong squirted away from the dazed quarterback's limp hands, and my ears exploded as the sideline shook with people jumping and screaming. *"Fumble fumble fumble fumble!"*

Chase clawed his way over the quarterback's body, but a hand snagged his ankle and the Dallas tight end was bearing down on the football, crouching now as he ran, arms outstretched, about to scoop it up—

BAM. He flew forward and landed chin first on the field. DeMario shot past him and grabbed the ball, tucking it high and tight between his elbow and armpit and then disappeared in a wave of bodies as he flew back down the field, dancing on his tiptoes, feet flirting with the white paint of the sideline at every step. The bench was a teeming, living thing of bodies jumping and pushing, and I couldn't see or hear anything, could barely breathe or keep my footing. I looked to the massive jumbotron above the far end zone and watched DeMario pass the fifty, the forty, the thirty, the twenty, and then fly sideways toward a small girl in a red coat straining to see—

James yanked me hard to the left in time to avoid the full impact, but I still felt the breeze of 285 pounds of muscle soaring past my face. The foot of the Dallas receiver who had finally forced DeMario out of bounds clipped my ankle and sent me sprawling backward, where I landed hard on my tailbone with a teeth-rattling thud. Last week's hot dog costume would have broken my fall nicely, but today I had on only a peacoat. The frenzied crowd writhed and pitched, fists pumping, arms in the air, and a hand appeared above mine, followed by a face.

"Some advice," DeMario yelled as he pulled me to my feet. His eye black was smeared down his cheeks, he was panting hard, and his glove was slick with sweat. "When you see yourself on the jumbotron—*move.*"

After the TV time-out, A.J. and the offense took the field. There were six seconds left, and so this was it—one last play to decide the season. I held my breath, but as soon as A.J. had the ball he dropped back, found a receiver in the back corner of the end zone, and buried it. He'd never hesitated, never checked for a better look. A.J. saw through the crowd and delivered a bullet to a perfect, palm-sized patch of air, just after the clock hit zero. Tie game.

Troy gave one last mighty kick into the practice net before jogging onto the field to attempt the extra point that could win it. James grabbed me by the elbows and screamed something I couldn't hear. I laughed and shook my head in disbelief until Brent put a hand on my shoulder and yelled, "I'll get A.J. You get Coach. He'll do the first on-the-field interview, then bring him through the holding room to the pressroom. Don't wait—as soon as it looks good, get going."

The ball split the uprights, and just like that we were on to the Super Bowl, and I was on the field being lifted off my feet by the crush of photographers all surging toward a Gatorade-soaked Red Guillory pumping his fist. Sparks filled the air from cannons by the tunnels, and a blizzard of confetti caught in my hair, on my clothes, grew slick under my feet. I passed Chase flat on his back making snow angels in it.

I was shoved hard from behind, but if I could take that from DeMario flying out of bounds after scooping up the game-winning turnover, I certainly wasn't going to take it from a middle-aged cameraman. I fought and dragged my way through the crowd until I was standing right next to Coach Guillory. We were the center of the universe, a 360-degree wave of flashing lights ten people deep, beyond that another eighty thousand, all the way out, all the way back to my parents and millions of others watching from home and wishing they could stand where I stood. Wishing they could be a part of it like I was.

Keisha Jacobi, the sideline reporter, was much more experienced than me in fighting for ground, and she and her fur coat forced their way next to Red and under his armpit. With a finger to one ear so she had a hope of hearing, she leaned close and yelled into her microphone, "Congratulations, Coach. What does it mean to you to finally push past Dallas to get this team to the Super Bowl?"

Red's eyes danced. His chest heaved, and no one but me was close enough to notice that his massive hands were shaking. He looked to the sky for a moment before yelling back, "Man, oh man. We're just so proud of our guys—Chaser making an unbelievable play to force the fumble, DeMario getting us that kind of field position, and then A.J. going in there like a sniper . . . This team and their effort are incredible. Just incredible."

Keisha pushed the microphone directly against her lips to force the sound in against the bedlam of the stadium. "Your team is undefeated. You have one game left." She shot him a teasing grin. "Any pressure?"

"Just a bit." Red laughed. "We love it, though, we love it. The great one—Vince Lombardi—said winning isn't a sometimes thing, it's an all-the-time thing. We're trying to make it an all-the-time thing around here, and we're going to keep it going for one more game."

Keisha turned to A.J. next, and Coach and I made our way through the throngs on the field, past the midfield group kneeling in prayer, past Dallas players still sprawled on the Field Turf in defeat. Red stopped to pat one of them on the shoulder before we continued on, all the way off the grass, past the stands of fans hanging dangerously over the railings, their arms outstretched, fingers extended, trying to gain a small touch of greatness, of the man walking beside me.

My entire body buzzed as we walked through a short section of hallway and toward the anteroom off the main pressroom, the cheers from the stadium echoing above us. I'd never felt like this before—my skin crackled. The air was sharp against it. I could jump off a building, I could wrestle a bear. My chest was heaving, my heart straining the skin, and beside me Coach's own rib cage lifted and dropped, lifted and dropped as he huffed out audible breaths. I was flying. We were flying.

The door to the holding room had barely closed when he was on me, a six-foot-four-inch former linebacker's body slamming into mine and forcing me back until I hit the wall, hard. Fingers twisted through my hair and yanked, forcing my face up toward his. Coach's lips mashed mine against my teeth, mixing the taste of copper with the sharp mint of his gum. He wrenched my hair again and I gagged, my neck a mile of exposed, white skin pulled so taut by the impossible angle that I couldn't swallow, couldn't breathe. A gurgle rose in my throat, and a growl came from his. My hands wriggled uselessly against his sandbag body. In response he ground himself into me, all his weight pressing me against that wall as one leg forced itself between mine, prying them apart. My foot slipped, and then I was being held up by my hair until my toes found the concrete floor again. Coach Guillory's shirt was soaked from Gatorade and sweat that leached into my coat, marking and staining me.

My voice was trapped, the air squeezed out—I couldn't call for help, I couldn't yell for him to stop—but the muffled roar of the fans carried through the doors, eighty thousand people doing what I could not.

Screaming.

The door to the hallway opened, and Red shoved me again, this time away from him. My head bounced off the wall, and Red wiped his mouth with the back of his hand as Lexi and the kids followed Brent into the room.

Red pressed his face into Lexi's hair—gently, so gently—while tears bumped against her grin. "You did it! You did it!" she yelped.

"Gol-ly," said Brent, taking in my damp coat and tangled hair. My nose was running, and I could still taste blood. "D'you tussle with an AP photographer out there or what?"

The group moved, laughing and chatting, toward the press-room doors. Red hoisted his daughter onto his shoulders, placed a tender hand on his son's downy head, and stepped through the doorway to face his waiting throng of admirers.

CHAPTER EIGHTEEN

NOW

"Honey—you're home," Nisha said as she climbed out of the car. The others did too, rolling their necks and stretching their legs— clearly, they'd been in there awhile. "I told you guys she'd get here by eight."

"Six," Sarah said tightly. "You said you knew for sure she'd be home by six."

"Your fault for believing that. Who in sports gets home by six?"

Finally I found my voice. "What are you *doing* here?"

"We have some things to discuss," said Nisha.

My mind clunked along trying to process the fact that they were here, all of them, outside my townhouse. "You're okay," I said to her finally, and she snorted.

"For now, but let's get inside. I'm not freezing to death because five smart women were too dumb to open the door."

My little townhouse pulsed with activity. Winter boots were piled around the small vestibule, while the overnight bags covered half the staircase. My Mission-style credenza was buried in a pile of purses, and the line for the bathroom looked like halftime at the stadium. Four guests broke my previous record by at least two, and watching the girls open my fridge and help themselves to glasses from the cupboard and then settle around my white sectional, I felt my chest tighten. "You really came here to . . ."

"Support you, yes," filled in Dayanna. "And for—"

"*Vergangenheitsbewältigung.*" Nisha was digging around in my kitchenette. "Do you have any candles? And what's your pizza place? It looks like Georgio's has the highest rating?"

"Pizza My Heart," I responded automatically, "and can you please tell me what *verg*—whatever is?"

" 'To reckon with bad deeds from the past.' God bless the Germans, they really do have a word for everything."

"Nisha came to see me," said Annika. It was the first thing I'd heard from her since our meetup in Hoboken. Her voice was— broken. Her hair was limp and wilted. Everything about Annika was lesser than it had been, like she'd been used up. Like she'd been rubbed out.

"Well, since you wouldn't answer the *phone,* I needed proof of life," Nisha said, lining up my collection of Diptyque candles down the coffee table. There was a forced lightness to her tone, and she snuck a worried glance at Annika. They've always been a little closer to each other than to the rest of the group. It comes from the ying and yang of Annika's cool, collected demeanor and Nisha's tendency to talk from her neck. With Dayanna and Sarah as the other little unit within a unit, I stand alone. Which is how I've always preferred it anyway.

But now they were here.

"I couldn't get out of bed," Annika said. "It's so much worse than . . ." The four of us were silent, looking at her, Dayanna's face a war between sympathy and disgust. But when a hiccup of a sob escaped, Day's eyes softened. "Nisha came and she just—stayed. Sat in my driveway until Grant let her in, and then sat in the family room until I could stand to see her. Phone off. Missing work."

"It's not like I had much choice once I saw what a mess you were." Nisha straightened and moved her hair out of her face. "Look, I'm not great at this—talking part. But we made this little—

group. Family. Whatever—to help each other out, and at some point it became . . . You're like my . . . Okay, fuck you guys," she said, catching Dayanna's lip-biting attempt not to smile. "Seriously, though, we're here for business. But first we're going to level the playing field a little, because what Anni has to tell us is not easy."

Twenty minutes later the lights were off, and the candles were lit, their combined scents forming a heavy perfume that hung low in the air. An open pizza box sat on a dish towel to protect my rug, and everyone had a wineglass with a pinky finger's worth of empty space at the top. "This," said Sarah from her spot on the floor, "is the weirdest slumber party I've ever been to."

"It's like we're a coven," Dayanna said, passing out coasters. "Witches Against Groping Shitheads."

Once we were served and settled, Nisha took the lead. "All right, focus up. We've talked a lot in this group about other people's bad deeds. Now, at least to each other, it's time to own up to ours. I'm going to start," she said, putting a hand to her chest, "I'll tell you mine. And you don't have to go if you don't want to but—if not, what are we doing? What is this group for if not for this?"

Annika stared at her hands, folded in her lap. Sarah and Dayanna exchanged a glance and nodded slightly to each other. And I felt the anxiety building inside my chest, because that wasn't supposed to be the deal. We complained about *other* people. And ever since that conversation with Chloe, ever since she'd relayed that Red said this season was like that first one, there'd been an itch at the back of my mind. I didn't scratch it, I wouldn't. But it stayed. I took a long gulp of my wine.

"Okay?" Nisha confirmed. "Okay. So—here goes. I can't fall asleep in strange beds, and that's rough because my job is basically to hotel-hop two hundred nights a year, so I use pot to take the edge off."

"That's no big deal," said Sarah.

"Yeah, I didn't think so either, which is why I mentioned it to this other scout who said he has trouble sleeping on the road. I've known him forever, and I honestly didn't think anything of it. But then he pointed out that those hotels are all over the country, including a lot of states where recreational pot isn't legal, *and* I'm transporting it across state lines, which makes it a felony. And he went on to helpfully share that even a first-time offense brings a maximum penalty of five years in prison and a quarter-million-dollar fine. Just your standard tip-of-the-tongue information. But he made it clear that since we're friends—very, *very* close friends—he wouldn't tell my team about my 'substance abuse and trafficking issues.' And then he invited me to his room."

"What did you do?" I asked, dreading the answer.

"I'd like to hear what you guys think—go ahead."

"You slept with him," said Dayanna at the same time Sarah said, "You kept one of his eyeballs." Annika just stared, and I shrugged.

"Wrong all around. I set up a mutually assured destruction scenario. I went to his room, shared my pot—which helpfully *is* quite good for sleep, I swear by it—and took some photos while he was passed out. He's very devout, of course, and the next day I told him that if he didn't blow me up, I wouldn't blow him up to his wife, parents, and pastor. I left his job out of it, because I'm classier than him. But then he got caught cheating with an airport barista and came to Jesus—again—so if the photos ever appear they'll just show what a sinner he used to be and how much he's 'changed.' So that's my big secret. I'm a drug trafficker." She shot Annika a sarcastic smile. "We can share a cell."

She was right, technically they could both face prison. We'd gone from prank to threat to—what? Extortion? But the notes didn't demand anything except for these stories to be made public. And who benefited from that?

"You already know what I did," Dayanna said. "Like thirty percent of relationships start at work, except not in sports, because then people think you're only there to meet guys. Have you ever noticed no one says that about accountants?"

"And it's not like most of the players meet their wives in the office!" Sarah added. "If you really wanted to date one you'd take a shit-ton of Pilates classes and hit the Señor Frog's near spring training. It's the dumbest, dumbest argument."

"Exactly. It was a real relationship—secret, but real—and then we broke up, and it's fine. He's a good guy. But if it ever got out, I'd be reduced to the world's least efficient jersey chaser. No one would remember that we've been a Selig award finalist for the past five years—it's not like that just happens. I *love* community relations, I'm great at it. And I'd never get to do it again."

The warm feeling that came with finding the girls on my doorstep was ebbing away like the light from the candles as they burned through their wicks. In its place was a collection of facts that I'd folded up very neatly fifteen years ago and put in a box on a shelf. I hadn't opened that box. I hadn't even looked at it. But now it was here, coming toward me, forcing me to revisit things that I did not want to know.

I was to Dayanna's left so all eyes swung to me, bringing an instant flop sweat. I wanted to climb inside of my wineglass.

"I'm sorry," Annika broke in. "I know it's Poppy's turn, but if she doesn't mind, I'd like to go next."

"By all means," I croaked.

"It's just—you all know what I did. Or at least some of it, and I can't sit here for another second without at least explaining. And I have something important to tell you, but first, I'd just like to explain." Annika looked like she was going to be sick. Her eggwhite skin had paled even further so that it took on a sickly, bluish tint.

She picked at the polish on her fingernails, making a little *tick tick tick* sound as she chipped it away. "A lot of my job," she gave us an ironic look, "my unofficial job, has been doing some administrative things for Damian. It was nothing illegal." Her chin raised as if it was very important to her to stress that point. "It was just a bit . . . deviant, if that's even the right word to use when you're talking about consenting adults, but he's the face of our franchise, and we have a very family-values-forward fan base. His private life needed to stay private, and so we used NDAs pretty liberally. And as long as I made them very strongly worded and included a sizable cash bonus for their troubles, the young ladies tended to comply without any issues."

"Wait, wait," Sarah broke in. "Why were *you* doing that? Damian has to have his own legal team, right?"

"Our idiot owners. They're control freaks, and they wanted it done in-house. No leaks. So I did it. Then one day the bonus went way up—inflation, right?" Annika gave a frustrated laugh. "I wrote up the document like always, but this time the woman didn't want to sign." Annika looked at her fingers. Only jagged streaks of polish remained. "This time, she claimed it wasn't quite so consensual. Damian said it was. He told me he met this woman on Instagram, that this was what women do nowadays—hook up with athletes so they can make some crazy claims afterward and extort them for money. He showed me messages between the two of them that indicated she might be into this kind of thing. Two other players on the team said they'd slept with her too."

"But that doesn't—" Dayanna started, and Annika held up her hand.

"I know, that shouldn't mean anything, and I'm so ashamed to admit it, but it hit her credibility for me. It shouldn't have. But it did."

A woman who'd been with someone else in the organization was less likely to be believed. And there were messages between the two of them that showed she might be into that kind of thing.

"And this is *Damian,* he's my *friend,*" she went on. "I've known him for almost ten years, for Christ's sake. I wanted to help."

God, I was going to be sick. I was back in that anteroom, my head was throbbing. I couldn't breathe, he was crushing me, I—

"Wait," Nisha interjected, and I gulped for air, trying to bring myself back to my townhouse. Sarah furrowed her brow at me, and I pointed nonsensically to my throat and took another long sip of wine. I was drinking way too fast, I could feel my face going red and tingly from it. "Anni," said Nisha, "what kind of thing are we talking about here?"

"Erotic asphyxiation. Damian said it was a sex game they'd agreed to play. The woman claimed she'd agreed to no such thing and that she thought he was going to kill her. She was terrified, and she wanted to press charges. The entire idea of it was absurd, he would never hurt anyone, let alone . . ." Annika bit both of her lips, bringing them together so fiercely that they disappeared. She cleared her throat. "I redrafted the agreement. The figure went up, she took it, and the whole thing went away. And I got to be the big-shot protective lawyer who'd saved the day. Until the second girl. And by then I'd already done it the first time, and it was easier to believe that they were both lying than to think that I'd . . . that I'd been a part of . . ."

I ached for her. And I feared for me. Because something was shifting inside me, something I couldn't yet understand. A wave was coming to wipe me off my feet and suck me under and away, and I could sense it coming, a scent on the wind that whispered of a storm still buried far beyond the horizon.

Red was my mentor and my friend.

Annika's voice thickened. "But the *third* girl—that was what did it. Not because I'm a good person, because clearly I'm not. Not because it showed a pattern I couldn't ignore anymore." She closed her eyes as if she was in physical pain. "The third girl's name was Joanna."

I felt the word in my gut, the way Annika must have. Or no, not the same way Annika did, because Joanna wasn't my daughter. I didn't have a thousand memories of picnics on sunny days and cold water hitting my face as a tiny body propelled into a pool. I didn't have backpacks and lunches and tutus and the image of a small girl twirling, smiling over her shoulder at me as two braids swung wide in the breeze.

"What if one day some *asshole* did that to her, and some other asshole like me let it happen?"

Several beats passed in silence, and then Dayanna said quietly, "So what did you do?"

"I wrote a letter of resignation. I typed the whole thing up and spent two weeks editing it in my home office. Sometimes it went on for pages, describing exactly why I couldn't work there anymore; sometimes it was just a single sentence. But I wrote it. And I fully,

fully intended to hand it in. I still do, I want to, I *have* to, it's just that . . ."

"What?" Sarah's voice held a note of warning. I realized I was leaning forward, perched on the very edge of the sofa.

"My daughter found it—Carolyn. She needed some financial documents for law school and looked on my computer, and I still had the draft up. The long-form draft. Once she read it, she knew what I'd done, and then she went poking around to see what else was there, and she found our group chat—you know how the texts go to the computer?—so that's how she identified the rest of you. She doesn't actually know anything—there'd be no way for her to, since we never talked about it in any detail before tonight—but she knows who you are and what we do here . . . She sent the letters." Annika hung her head. "I'm so sorry."

It made sense. The delivery of the letters was impressive. Carolyn must have mailed the first set from home and the second, I realized, from JFK during her trip back to school. But now, with the lights on and all the shadows snapped back to their shapes, the rest of it looked like what it was. An unrelated crime. A natural heart attack in a man begging for one. Twitter messages from a creep, because that's what creeps did.

Carolyn was a girl who'd stumbled onto something that shook her to her core and wanted—needed—to feel like she was doing something about it, but had no idea what. So she sent those letters without a plan and then stalled out.

Except that she didn't. I was slower to figure it out than I should have been, but once I did, an aching fatigue overcame me. When I looked at Annika, it was with deep, deep pity. "ESPN. The story . . ."

"She leaked it." Annika wiped savagely at her eyes, determined not to let a single tear escape. "We've always had such a happy home, and we've talked to the girls so much about respect for women, and how to look after themselves. What to demand in their relationships, what to do if they're in trouble." Carolyn was following in Annika's footsteps as an attorney. Joanna was majoring in feminist theory. As if she could read my mind, Annika went on, "She must have felt so *betrayed*. It makes me sick even thinking about it, I don't know how we'll ever . . ."

The four of us sat in stunned silence. Annika's own daughter turned her in. The depth of her betrayal was stronger than the foundation of her love. It was horrible. It was heartbreaking.

"Even that might not have been enough, but apparently Carolyn has this professor this semester who's become very important to her. She didn't know what to do with what she'd found, so she went to talk to her, and the professor was all, *Why are you in law school if you won't stand up for the law.* I don't think—we've talked and talked and talked to the girl, but it was all . . . feminist theory! I don't think it had ever clicked for Caro before that these things really happen, to people she knows. I don't think she truly realized that men are usually bigger than women, and if they want to, they can force them, violently, to do things. It just—hit her, hard. And she didn't know what to do."

Annika turned to me. "Poppy, there's no way she could have done it. She's angry—so angry—but it's directed at me."

"Oh, Anni, I know."

The others spoke softly to Annika, offering words of comfort, but I was lost in my own head. Hearing Annika talk about what a good guy Damian was, how they were friends, it all felt so familiar. Because friends could have a misunderstanding. Friends could accidentally lead each other on, a misread cue, a text meant for someone else. And friends weren't predators. There were more innocent explanations for what they did.

And that made it so much easier to stand.

I dug my nails into my palms and flashed to every time I'd stood with Red over the years, his hand casually on my shoulder as we laughed and chatted. I thought of quiet moments we'd shared on the team plane, late-night flights across the country when the cabin was dim and the players all wore sleep masks. We'd talk—really talk—about our shared love of comedic horror movies, or what college stadiums we dreamed of visiting, or whether lobster rolls should have butter or mayo. We talked about our fathers, both football coaches, and how they'd shaped us, how that made us special. You couldn't hurt someone and then have those kinds of conversations, you wouldn't dare. Everything we'd said and done and been since that one day between the field and the press conference proved that I was wrong, that it couldn't be *that*. And yet when Chloe talked about Red's friendliness, the hairs on the back of my neck had floated up like a spooked cat's fur.

The wine sloshed dangerously in my stomach, it clawed at the bottom of my throat, begging to come up. I was going to be sick. I needed to be sick, I couldn't hold this thought inside my body, it would poison me, it would kill me.

"I promise you—all of you—Carolyn doesn't know anything about you, other than the fact that this group exists. We have a lot to work out together, but as far as the rest of you go, she's done. Your secrets are safe."

But mine wasn't.

Because mine was a secret I'd kept from myself.

And because I'd refused to see, because of what I'd done after, it wasn't just my reputation that was at risk now—it was my freedom.

I was a criminal.

CHAPTER NINETEEN

FIFTEEN YEARS AGO

Sunday morning we gathered at MillionAir to catch the team charter to Miami. There were more than one hundred of us shuffling through the private security screening, but aside from the soft beep of the ticket scanner, it was silent. The players wore headphones, some shifting their weight, some bouncing lightly in place. Several of them twitched their fingers, others looked at the ceiling and blew out slow breaths.

Mo coughed into his elbow, then looked around guiltily. We all moved slowly forward.

"Hey." Brent's voice was barely above a whisper as he nudged me with his hip. He indicated the players. "You look worse than them. You okay?"

I read once about Giles Corey, the only man killed in the Salem witch trials. They laid a board on his chest and added boulders one at a time until he was pressed to death, and the only thing Corey said as they told him to confess his sins was "more weight." That was what this season felt like. From the outside, the Bobcats were at the top of the football world. We were it—the likely champions, the ones everyone wanted a shot at and everyone wanted to be. But the reality was crushing. The pressure was crushing. And we were all failing to handle it in our own way.

"Yeah," I managed. "I'm fine."

And I was. I was never unsafe, not really, with Brent and Lexi and everyone else about to walk through the door. This was someone I *knew,* and I wasn't drunk, and there was no knife to my throat, and my clothes were on the entire time. I didn't bite him, I didn't push him off. Right afterward, surrounded by people, I didn't say anything. I celebrated our win. And so this wasn't that—it was a humiliating misunderstanding.

I couldn't believe I'd fucked up so thoroughly between the text messages and all my extra-bright smiles to make Coach Guillory think I was flirting with him. It was cell-shreddingly mortifying. On Monday I'd inched toward his office, feet sticking to the carpet, but he'd given me the same friendly smile as always, with nothing behind it, like a teller at a bank, and it was so good of him, so gracious that I almost wept. In fact, most of the week I'd found myself near the edge of tears, which underlined just how unbearable the pressures of this season had become.

I watched the back of James's head disappear into the jet bridge and felt a guilty pang in my stomach. He'd been seduced by Abby, but here I was the seducer. I'd led on a grown man and then been shocked that he wanted to do something about it. And *Abby.* Girls like Abby, who muddied the waters between the personal and the professional, were the reason mistakes like this happened.

I was determined to make up for my screwups by working even harder. I was in by five fifty, diligently snipping away at the papers. GUILLORY ANSWERS PRAYERS, read one headline. RED ALERT— COACH GUILLORY GETS THE BOBCATS TO FIRST SUPER BOWL IN 30 YEARS, read another. I methodically copied, pasted, and formatted article after article, over and over, about the wonders of Red Guillory. About what he had done for this team and for football and for this city. About how much everyone loved him.

*

People worked their entire lives and never made it to the Super Bowl, and at twenty-two I was here. Our team hotel was a quiet zone, with no media allowed, but it did nothing to create an oasis. We were overtuned guitar strings, all pulsing with a tension so strong it was amazing the lightbulbs didn't shatter. Richard, Brent, and I worked around the clock in a ballroom set up as a makeshift office. I ate, sometimes, slept, occasionally, and otherwise just alternated between interviews, transcripts, and game notes.

On Friday I finished up Saturday's media call sheet, then yawned and stretched my arms, which was of course the moment that Richard approached my desk.

"Tired?" he said as I hastily reset my posture. "It's okay, I know these hours have been tough. That's why," he dug into his pocket, "I have a thank-you. Congratulations, Cinderella, you're going to the ball."

"The Commissioner's party?"

Brent let out a low whistle. "That is one hot ticket."

"What is it?"

"Well, if everything else you've seen this week is the career fair, that party is the prom."

"And the game is the . . . ?"

"Don't strain the metaphor. Last year's was in an airplane hangar in the middle of the Arizona desert. This time it's on some little island that the guy from Seattle described to me as 'that place in *Pinocchio,* before the shit hit the fan.'"

"Wow. Thank you." I held the ticket back out to Richard. "Don't you want it?"

"No, no—youth is for the young. Go have fun."

*

On the advice of my mother, I'd brought one fancy outfit with me— a strapless, carbon-colored bubble dress that made me look ghostly pale. I already stood out against the deep tans of South Beach, and so I might as well lean into it. Giving myself a last look in the mirror, I decided I looked young and pretty. I looked happy.

The shuttle was mostly empty, with coaches and the front office getting ready for tomorrow. I took a seat near the back and pressed my face against the window to watch the Miami skyline slip by. The sun sinking into the water drenched the buildings in citrus oranges and pinks, the whole city lit like a nightclub. By the time we got through the Super Bowl weekend traffic and crossed a small bridge to the island, the last bits of light were gone. The air was hot and sticky, sweat already forming as I followed the few others from the shuttle to a torch-lined path. It disappeared into a tunnel of vines, twisting and winding its way through the darkness. After a claustrophobic minute it opened to a clearing surrounded by a lush man-made jungle. Strings of lights crisscrossed overhead, a supplement to the star-filled sky. White-shirted waiters balanced silver trays of champagne flutes, and a bouncy, brassy salsa drifted from a quartet.

"Pretty amazing, huh?" Bernie appeared in light khakis and a Hawaiian shirt that should have been charged with assault. He held a glass of champagne in one hand and three pigs in blankets in the other. He was trying to maneuver one into his mouth without dropping the other two. "Take this," he said, thrusting the champagne at me in defeat. "It's brand-new, I haven't touched it."

I sipped gratefully as he bit into the first pig. "I've never been anywhere like this before. I'm from Ohio and I live in Syracuse."

"This is just the cocktail area. That path you walked in on loops around the whole island." He pointed to the left, where the opening to the next tunnel gaped like a missing tooth. "You have to try it all before you go."

Brian and Steven, two other beat writers, came through the tunnel and joined us. Brian had replaced his usual band T-shirt with a polo and a porkpie hat, while Steven kept his trademark blazer but wore a white V-neck T-shirt underneath. Steven clapped Bernie on the back. "You having some people over for the Weekend in that shirt, Bern?"

"Poppy's too young for that reference, and I'll have you know my wife bought me this shirt."

Brian pointed toward the hors d'oeuvres. "I'm glad you found some food. Don't want you wasting away in Margaritaville."

"I will not be mocked by a man in that hat," Bernie shot back.

"Hey, have you guys seen—anyone from the office?" I finished the champagne, and a waiter appeared at my elbow to swap the flute out for a full one.

Bernie shook his head. "We'll walk with you, if you want to take the path."

The four of us wandered to a second clearing, this one filled with buffet tables. Chefs waited, knife tips in the air, behind mammoth hunks of meat at the carving stations, while the smell of ice and brine rose from a bed-sized raw bar. A table groaned under the weight of every type of fruit imaginable, grapes plump to bursting dangling over the sides and pineapple leaves stretching toward the night sky.

"I love my job," breathed Steven, heading for the raw bar. I picked up a small plate and browsed a surfboard on planks serving as a charcuterie platter, loading up on prosciutto and little dollops of seashell-shaped cheese.

I had just popped one of the seashells into my mouth when a warm hand pressed against my shoulder. I turned to see James at the same moment I gagged the shell into a napkin. "I thought that was cheese but it was butter," I managed.

He laughed and moved the hand to my lower back. Instinctively, I danced away. James probably didn't know these were our writers, and with most of the Bobcats staff huddled over their desks at the hotel, they were some of the only people we knew here. I washed the butter taste away with a swig of champagne and nodded toward the tunnel. "Do you want to take a walk?"

The clearings were spaced farther apart now, and James and I had several minutes alone in the tunnel as we walked. "You look good in women's clothes," he joked, a reference to the enormous team gear I often wore. His hand found mine and squeezed, and I met his eye in the light of the torches.

He was crushing me, I couldn't breathe, my neck didn't bend that way, my hair hurt, it would come out in his hands . . .

I licked at the spot on the inside of my lip where I'd bled. It had just about healed.

We heard the next space before we saw it, a live band, a dance floor of flashing lights, and a smoke machine. "You want to give it a try?" James asked, and I laughingly pulled him back onto the path. The night was clear and calm. Most people had stayed closer to the bars and food, and so it was quiet as the fading sounds of the band gave way to insects and birds. The path got sandier and sandier until it opened out onto a small beach. The water lapped against the shore beneath a paper moon, and the whole thing felt like a set from a play just waiting for us to take our places. I kicked off my sandals and let them dangle from my fingers as I followed James to a tree swing that faced the water. I sat and he pushed, cool palms against my hot skin. I let my toes trail through the sand as the swing rocked gently back and forth in time to the waves.

"Not bad for a corporate event," he said.

"I'm starting to see why they don't hold Super Bowls in Green Bay."

James grabbed the ropes and held them steady. My pulse roared in my ears like the inside of a shell as he leaned down. My head turned, because my body remembered what to do even if my mind was broken, and then soft lips met mine. The salty scent of the ocean mixed with hot breath, a sea breeze lifted my hair as James tucked it behind my ear, and now the swing was still, and it was the world around that swayed.

It didn't hurt and I wasn't afraid.

We rode the shuttle back to the hotel, shoulder to shoulder. To the other staff we looked tired, professional, but in the darkness of the back seat our hands were clasped, James's thumb rubbing gently against my palm. I ached to lay my head on his shoulder. "You should go up alone," he whispered as the shuttle pulled back onto hotel property. "I don't want to start any rumors."

I nodded and gave him a last smile before hurrying across the lobby and into a waiting elevator. As the door glided shut I leaned back against the rail with a happy little sigh. There were good things waiting for me—parties and drinks and cool sand and warm kisses. Someday soon, when this crushing season was over, my life wouldn't be only about football. There would be room for a relationship, hopefully with James. During the off-season we could go out to dinner, spend lazy weekends at his apartment, lying on the couch together under a blanket and making each other watch our favorite movies. We'd find a show that was just for us and binge it. In the summer, maybe we could take a trip, somewhere warm and sandy to re-create that island beach. Nothing would ever compare to tonight. But we could chase it, I thought, as I padded down the quiet hallway toward my room. We could have fun falling short. For the first time in a long time, there were things to look forward to.

When I slipped my key into the digital lock, the flash of red was like a warning light, and it hit me—I'd never dropped off the call sheet. *Shit.* I turned on my heel and raced back toward the elevator, cursing and jabbing at the buttons. The coaches needed that sheet for the morning, the *day before the Super Bowl.*

I bounced on my heels as I waited, and then forced myself through the doors before they'd slid all the way open. I held down the button for the second floor, where our workspace was, and leaned on it as if that would make the elevator move faster, praying that Richard had left the office unlocked.

When the door opened I took off my sandals again—this time not to wander a moonlit beach, but so I could half run down the hallway. Thankfully the knob turned, and I snatched the call sheet from where I'd left it on my desk. The coaches were on the lower level, and I didn't want to take the elevator for fear it would stop back at the lobby and admit someone who would see me holding the call sheet I should have delivered hours ago, and so I followed the signs to a stairwell instead and scurried down two flights. I pushed open the door to find a canyon of empty ballrooms and dark conference spaces. All the lobby's hustle and bustle was muted down here, where the walls had been built to absorb sound. Most of the lights were off, but dimmed sconces dotted the walls every few doorways, casting shadows that spilled up the cream-colored wallpaper.

My heart filled my throat as the hotel carpet curled around my toes. I couldn't believe I'd forgotten something so important.

It was inexcusable. Absolutely inexcusable. I took a wrong turn, found myself at the end of a small hallway, and let out a grunt of frustration.

I retraced my steps, tried another hallway. Not one pen could be out of place when the coaches reached for it tomorrow. I wasn't here to attend parties, I was here so that every ounce of their focus could stay on the game, the game, the game.

I turned the corner and gasped as I collided with someone so hard that it knocked my teeth together. "*Ooof!*" My tongue throbbed where I'd bitten it, the taste of blood now back. I swallowed and struggled to catch my breath. The call sheet lay on the carpet beside the other person's left foot, and my eyes traveled from the paper up a set of bare legs and past a crooked skirt.

Abby.

Her normally peachy cheeks were streaked an angry red, and her mascara was badly smeared around one eye. Her chest heaved beneath a missing button on her blouse, and as our eyes met she raised a trembling hand against my open mouth.

Don't.

She pushed past me and into a stairwell. I heard her feet pounding like the echo of my heart. And then the door swung shut and I was alone.

Not alone.

Because when I peered down the hallway that Abby had come from, every door was shut but one. It was at the very end, tunnel-visioned to a focal point. The lights in the room were off, but there was a lurking, hulking shadow, a smear of black among the gray.

I pressed myself against the wall, but I couldn't turn, I couldn't leave. I squinted toward the shape. It was the profile of a person, their face lost to the darkness. Hands reached for something at waist level—a belt?—and threaded one side through the other.

I knew whose office that was. I knew the shape of those shoulders, the rough power of those hands. And as I stood there, barely breathing, begging my feet to move, the shadow stretched, a hand reached out, and the door was quietly but firmly closed.

CHAPTER TWENTY

NOW

I tossed and turned, sharing my bed with Annika while Dayanna and Sarah used the guest room and Nisha took the couch. Exhausted, Annika dropped off to sleep, her brow smooth, but I couldn't get comfortable. I gripped the sheets and stared at the ceiling, not wanting to bother her but unable to stand the feel of my skin.

I'd told Chloe twice now to come to me if anyone was inappropriate, and had asked her specifically about Red. When she said everything was fine, I had no reason not to believe her, because Chloe hadn't grown up in the world that I did, where assault meant gags and zip ties, and good girls didn't flaunt their bodies in front of men who couldn't be expected to keep control. In college, I'd read about a woman raped at knifepoint in a park and realized that the park in question was twenty feet outside my freshman dorm. She later passed her rapist outside a bar that my friends and I liked to go to on Thursday nights and had a panic attack right there on the sidewalk. *That* was assault. It meant dirt in your hair and a grubby hand over your mouth. It meant fear for your life, and years afterward spent jumping at shadows. It meant being shattered.

If none of those things had happened, I'd thought then, I

couldn't have been assaulted. It'd be self-aggrandizing to even put myself in the same category as women who'd suffered such pain and fear. Besides, it was right there in our text messages—I'd led Red on, the beloved coach who'd just brought his team to the Super Bowl. I was at fault. I had to be. Or that's what I'd always believed.

In today's world, of course, women knew that all kinds of things qualified as assault. An entire spectrum of behavior was inappropriate. My memories of what happened in that anteroom formed when I was very young. Over time my beliefs evolved, but the memories didn't. They'd locked in, become unimpeachable, until tonight forced me to go back and look again with the eyes of an almost forty-year-old woman. And I saw something completely different.

The simple truth was, if any of the other WAGS had told that story, there would be no doubt in my mind that they were describing an assault. It couldn't be otherwise just because Red was someone dear to me. And now he was dead, and I had no idea what to do with this new perspective. I couldn't confront him. I couldn't tell anyone—how could I do that to his widow, Lexi? What would be the point?

Annika sighed in her sleep and pulled the covers toward herself. I let her have them.

It would have been bad enough if it had stopped there, but it hadn't. Because my mistake—my stupid, youthful lack of understanding—had wrought serious consequences, and now I had to live with the fact that I wasn't just a victim of Red's criminal behavior.

I was an enabler.

*

In the morning the WAGS headed back to their own cities. As the others maneuvered their laptops and overnight bags into the trunks of the rental car, Sarah bumped my hip. "I noticed you didn't share anything," she said quietly.

"I noticed you didn't either."

"Isn't it obvious?" When I raised my eyebrows to indicate that no, it wasn't, Sarah went on, "My deep, dark secret is all of you. Knowing all the stuff we talk about happens and not writing it because it would make life harder for my friends."

I was still thinking about that at the end of the day while staring at a cost sheet of vendors for Red Guillory Day. This wasn't my job, we had people for this, but they wouldn't do it as well as I would. A detail would be missed, some problem not spotted. When I looked up and saw that the lights outside my office were off, I stretched and looked at my phone—almost eight thirty. Without realizing it, I'd been sitting here for the past three hours while the rest of the staff quietly left for the day. There was nothing waiting for me at home but an empty townhouse and my own thoughts, but I turned off my heating pad, gathered my coat and bag, and forced myself to head out.

My phone buzzed—a text from Annika to the group.

Today was the first day since it happened that I had any appetite. I'm so grateful for you girls, and I want to reiterate again that your secrets are safe. Thank you for sharing them. <3

Another light was still on, and I followed it to Asbel's office. To my surprise, he was sitting at his desk behind not a computer screen, but a mostly empty bottle of Macallan whiskey. His tie was undone, and he was holding a bottom-heavy glass, tilting it this way and that to make the amber liquid sway. I'd been avoiding him, to the extent one can avoid their boss, since I learned about Red's second call the night of the murder, that Asbel also lacked an alibi. But after last night, I needed to talk to someone who knew Red the way that I did. Or maybe, someone who knew him better than I did, who saw him clearly in a way that I could not.

"Everything okay, boss?"

If Asbel was startled, he didn't show it. He just gestured toward a chair and reached, long and slow, under his desk for a second glass. His movements were thick, and I suspected the bottle hadn't been quite so empty an hour ago.

"Cheers," he said, handing over my drink. I inclined the glass toward him, then took a sip. "That's an eight-hundred-dollar bottle."

"Meh. Tastes like five."

He snorted.

"Are we celebrating?"

"Not celebrating. Honoring, I guess. Red gave me this."

"That was nice of him. After one of the Super Bowls?"

"No, I confiscated it when he showed up here drunk as a skunk before minicamp."

We sipped in silence. The whiskey was rich and soothing, like a hot bath from the inside out, and I fought not to close my eyes and sigh. It felt good, being there with Asbel, drinking Red's whiskey. Missing him together, not as the canonical figure he'd become to the football world at large, but as ours, fucked up though he might have been. Because I couldn't just throw that away. The way I felt about him now didn't take the place of how I'd felt before; it sat beside it. They existed together. He was a mentor and a monster. And I didn't want to let him go.

"You know," Asbel said, splitting the remainder of the bottle between our glasses, "I really miss that fucker."

"Yeah?"

"Well, I miss winning, that's for damn sure." He sipped, exhaled. "Red was . . . complicated. There was a lot to him that people didn't know."

I got the sense what Asbel really meant was that there was a lot to *himself* that people didn't know. Football could be lonely. It wasn't easy breaking apart a pretty good team for the moonshot of building a great one, and not many people could understand the validation, the vengeance, when it paid off in the biggest way possible. Asbel and Red were bonded together, and that had shown in Asbel's refusal to give up on him the last few seasons, in the way he'd defended him from what was becoming a deafening roar of detractors.

"He called me, you know. That night."

I looked at Asbel carefully. "He called me too. I didn't pick up."

"Me either."

Without the whiskey, maybe I wouldn't have said it. Maybe I wouldn't have been able to stand the answer. I sighed deeply, and watched Asbel with eyes so heavy and sad I could barely hold them open. I needed to know. I just needed to hear him say it. "Where were you?"

The silence stretched. It was just Asbel, me, and Red in the room. The stadium was dark and deserted, and I gripped the arm of my chair, because if Asbel was involved in this, I needed to hear him say it. He was always three steps ahead—maybe he'd seen a darkness in Red that I hadn't. Maybe I didn't care so much anymore who killed Red, because he wasn't such an innocent victim. But I needed to know.

"I was here."

"At midnight?"

Asbel sat back and stared out the window. It was dark and the office light was on, so there was nothing to see there but his own reflection. "You know, it's not my job to be Red's friend. It's my job to look out for the team, to make the best decisions for everyone. Not one man."

There was a defensive edge to his voice, and I didn't understand it, because as usual I was behind him.

But then I caught up.

"You were interviewing coaches."

"Coach, not coaches. Just Craig. It was preliminary, but I couldn't just keep throwing money into a pit. I couldn't pretend we weren't losing and going to keep losing while A.J. got older and Red kept trotting out his playbook from the early Obama years. So I did my due diligence. I brought him in."

An in-person meeting with our biggest rival, traveling from Texas to Syracuse, didn't sound preliminary to me. The midnight part, on the other hand, made sense. Asbel wouldn't have wanted anyone else to see.

"I was going to tell him no," he said with a very unfamiliar note of pleading in his voice. "I was going to say thanks but no thanks, we're sticking with Red. But no one would believe that now that Craig's feet are up on Red's desk. Red's dead, and I don't want the last impression of him to be that he died right before he got fired."

I nodded, pretending not to notice the tears gathering at the corners of Asbel's eyes. I squeezed the arm of the chair. It was the closest I could come to touching him, to offering some comfort. "I won't say anything."

"I know."

I spent the drive home thinking about legacy. What it meant. Who decided it. If it could or should be changed. Media relations is about facilitating access, but it's more than that. I once read that diplomacy is the art of telling someone to go to hell and making them feel flattered by the invitation and excited to get there. *That's* media relations. I was very, very good at it, and that meant I'd been as big a factor in crafting Red's legacy as anyone. I'd built him up into the figure he was today.

I owned this mess.

Asbel didn't want anyone to know he'd given up on Red, and so he wouldn't tell the police what he'd been up to that night—unless it ever got past this stage and they wanted to charge him with something. He wasn't going to prison over a memory. But the odds were it never would go that far, and for now there were whispers around the building. Whispers were sticky. They had a way of hanging around a person forever, no matter what answers and explanations came later, because once you've heard something enough times, it becomes true. Asbel was destroying his own legacy to protect Red's.

And what about me? For what noble purpose was I protecting my secret alibi?

On the night that Red was murdered I was sitting in my car on a quiet suburban street. The heat and headlights were off so I couldn't be seen, and my breath had puffed out in little clouds across the dash. Across the street, past a broad, sweeping lawn flanked by oaks, was a neat white Victorian.

I'd been there for hours, watching the lights move through the house. First the whole lower level was lit, then just the family room, and then a bedroom upstairs. Now the house was dark. Inside, I imagined, two people slept wrapped around each other, his chin to her hair. An overflowing folder of notes and vendors and guest lists and church fees sat on the nightstand, where they would pick it up again tomorrow. There was so much to do, because she was young and they were in love and their wedding, I'd learned by cracking the password on their website, would be in the spring.

She smiled as she slept.

His name was Peter.

I'd driven by their house before—lots of times, if I was being honest. I knew it well because Peter had shown me the listing before our last big fight. He'd wanted to buy it together. To make a life there.

And I'd said no.

Peter swore it wouldn't mean giving up my job, but of course it would. He was already so frustrated when I wasn't available, when I didn't have weekends or holidays or summer vacation the way normal people did. What would happen once we added kids to the mix? It was inevitable, an explosion waiting to happen, and I wasn't going to feel guilty over the career I'd spent my life building, the one that was just as important to me as Peter's was to him.

Now I was outside the house with the detritus of a Big Mac and fries on the passenger seat. The ice in my Coke had long since melted, but I lifted the cup and took a deep slurp. Peter was getting married. It was going to be another losing season. I was thirty-seven.

At that moment, Red Guillory called.

I didn't answer. I was feeling sorry for myself and angry at him for something he'd had nothing to do with. I was sick over what my job had cost me, sick over my choices and choking on regrets. I silenced the call.

And by the morning, Red was dead.

*

Practice was closed all week—very unusual, but Coach Washington was entitled to do things his own way. I was much more worried about the players coming into the cafeteria afterward with hung heads and headphones in. No one talked or joked around. The training-room line stretched down the hall, and it looked like almost everyone had a bag of ice strapped somewhere on their body.

A.J. pushed his way into my office after practice on Wednesday. He wore white Bobcats slides, light-gray jogger-style sweats, and a long-sleeved navy T-shirt. His hair was wet from a shower. "We need to talk."

"Sure." I indicated a chair, but he paced back and forth in front of my desk, and I stood so that he wasn't above me. I folded my arms. "Something on your mind?"

He stopped, pointed at me. "I am *not* holding a poodle."

"I'm sorry?"

"The rescue dogs shoot. Drea has me holding a fucking poodle named Noodles, and I'm not doing it."

Sweet Drea. My dear, dear friend in Community Relations. I picked up a notepad and pen and looked at him with the most serious face I could muster. "What kind of dog were you hoping to hold, A.J.?"

"A golden! A white lab! A bulldog! Something you'd see in a Ralph Lauren ad."

"Well, that might be tricky because these are rescue dogs, not purebreds. Noodles is probably a whole mix of things."

"Then get a different dog."

It stopped being funny. I put down the pad. "You'd like me to find you a fake rescue dog to hold in this campaign. And then what happens when someone wants to adopt it?"

"Find a breeder for purebred goldens—no, a lab. Purebred white labs. I'll hold it in the photos, and then—whatever, it can go to the shelter with the others. It's like a donation, someone will be thrilled to get that dog for cheap. And get a receipt, I can write that off." He shook his head. "This shit comes so naturally to me, I don't know why I pay you and Omar."

"You don't actually *pay*—"

"Text me when it's done." He left.

For this, I gave up Peter.

For this, I'd sold my soul.

Rodney poked his head in after A.J. left. "Was that what I think it was?"

"That stays here." I walked out of my office and held up a finger to Chloe and Edward. "Everyone got it?" They nodded, and I rubbed the spot between my brows. "Chloe, can you please research breeders? And do any of you want a dog?"

*

On Sunday afternoon when I looked out at the mostly empty stadium before kickoff, Chloe was at the opposite end of the press box handing out roster cards. She wore a black bodysuit and wide-legged black pants, and her ash-blond hair was twisted at the top of her head. My clothes felt ill fitting and unflattering. My skin itched.

"Chloe?" I called, and she looked up, a half smile on her face. "Sorry, would you mind just—could you grab me coffee? With milk. Thanks, I don't want to miss . . ."

As she left the press box I straightened my laptop so that its edges were flush with the desktop and stretched my spine as far as it would go.

"Oh, we're doing this again." Rodney sighed when he saw the first formation. As expected, A.J. handed the ball off to Alec, who managed to squirm a yard or two downfield before being tackled. Second down was a short pass that picked up two more, and then we were facing third-and-seven.

"That was quick," I muttered. A.J. dropped back, the pocket collapsed around him, and he scrambled around the field looking for someone to throw to. A hulking defenseman broke through and came at him, arms raised, a wall of clay, and A.J., instead of leaning in to protect himself or throwing the ball out-of-bounds, heaved it downfield.

An instant after the ball left A.J.'s hands, the defender leveled him with a bone-crunching thud. The outraged fans cheered as yellow flags bloomed—the hit was clearly late—as the ball continued its long, slow arc toward Raj streaking up the slot. I felt the familiar bubble rise through my chest and into my throat as a safety picked up coverage and fell into step with him. The ball hit its peak and began to fall, gracefully, beautifully, toward two sets of outstretched hands. Raj and the safety were locked together, stride for stride, each face twisted back and up, directly into the sun, as the ball came closer, more floating than falling, until at last it landed nestled against a jersey of Bobcats red.

"YES!" The press box exploded, the staffers with cheers, the press in surprise, as Raj tumbled to the ground at the twenty-yard line.

"Holy shit!" Rodney said, yanking me back and forth by the shoulder. "Holy shit!"

My reply caught in my throat when I saw Deon and the training staff jogging onto the field. A.J. was still down, curled onto his side and clutching his shoulder. "Oh no." The writers clicked away, tweeting out updates as Deon went down on one knee next to A.J. and leaned in. A pause, and then A.J. shook his head. Deon asked him something else, and the head shook again. Deon nodded, once, firmly, then signaled something to the sideline.

When the clock stops for an injured player, he has to come out for at least one down. But A.J. didn't go to the bench or the trainer's area. Instead, head down and clutching his shoulder, he went straight off to the locker room.

Chloe appeared, my coffee in hand. "Just the way you wanted it," she said. She meant the coffee, but I looked at the field and felt sick.

Will Campbell, the backup, jogged off the sideline looking impossibly small. He was bigger than A.J., bulkier, but he took up the space only of a person, not a legend. "*Jeeeeesus,*" breathed the AP writer as we watched our left tackle grab Will's face mask and pull their helmets together. Will nodded, the helmets shook, and then he nodded again, more forcefully.

"Anything, Poppy?" Bernie asked, twisting around from his seat in the front row.

"Rodney's heading down now." I signaled Rodney with my eyes to go to field level and get an injury update, although I could have told him right now it would say *upper-body injury, out.*

The tackle whacked the side of Will's helmet and released him. Will clapped his hands together with all the force of a butterfly's wings and sent the team to the line of scrimmage.

"This should go well," I muttered. Beside me, Chloe drummed her nails on the desktop. Unlike A.J., Will was lined up under center, which made sense because red zone or not, these first few plays were to shake off the dust, and Cleveland had poor run defense. All Will had to do was hand the ball off to Alec and get out of the way.

Instead, he dropped back and looked toward the end zone. "What the hell . . . ?" Without thinking, I grabbed Chloe's arm. The defense was sucked forward like air toward a black hole, collapsing in on Will. "Oh, fuck. His brain is broken." The press box froze. There was no sound. Every mouth was open, every eye trained on the speck of a person on the field who was about to become a crumb.

But then Will tucked the ball and took off. A path emerged, a tunnel through the bodies held back by blockers, and Will pounded through it. This wasn't the tight, compact speed of a running back, it was a powerful, destructive force. He shook off one linebacker, then made a balletic spin move to juke past another. A safety reached for him, connected, grabbed, and they fell together to the earth, a tangle of bodies and helmets and cleats that made an audible *thud* as they landed impossibly hard with the tiny, pointed, protruding end of the football just past the goal line.

And we *won.* Two-and-seven had never brought such joy. Will showed up to the press conference with his hair pushed back and dripping champagne, having been nearly waterboarded with the stuff in the locker room. Coach Craig was pleased but measured, saying he was proud of their progress but concerned about A.J.

"Did you actually draw that up?" I asked him afterward, while we walked back toward the locker room.

He grasped the door handle, pulled it up, and gestured me courteously inside. A broad grin split his face.

"Hell, no."

*

We won again the next week, and we did it without A.J. Caufield. His shoulder wasn't as bad as it had seemed—a few hours in a cold tub helped—and Deon told Mo, who told me that there was no reason not to start him. Except that A.J. had looked grim and determined out there, a weathered soldier clinging to the smoldering end of his last cigarette, determined to guard that bridge if it killed him, and Will looked like a kid at Dave and Buster's. He could take a hit, and his mobility cracked open Coach Craig's offense, which was predicated on forcing opponents to defend the entire field at once—spreading them out. "*Can I kick it?*" blasted out of the post-game locker room, the entire team chanting back, "*Yes, you can!*" loud enough to shake the walls, and I was just allowing myself a moment's shoulder shimmy when Bernie approached, looking serious.

"Can this wait, Bern? I just want to bask a little longer. Just until Monday. Then you can ruin my day."

"I don't think you want me to do that. I got a note."

My blood froze. The music, the room—everything drained away except the muffled high-pitched ringing of a sonic vacuum after a bomb.

CHAPTER TWENTY-ONE

FIFTEEN YEARS AGO

That was the last time I saw Abby.

She wasn't there when we won the game—of course we did, has anything ever been more predestined?—and she wasn't there when Red Guillory was named Coach of the Year.

She wasn't at the airfield back in Syracuse when we deplaned through the darkness to a crowd of thousands waiting in the snow, under floodlights, cheering louder and louder as each person appeared at the top of the mobile stairs until A.J. finally emerged carrying the League MVP trophy in one hand and the Lombardi trophy in the other and sent them into the stratosphere.

She wasn't at the parade through downtown, the coldest day my body has ever experienced, when the city leaned into its snowy identity and used sleds as floats down unplowed streets, pulled by horses from a local farm in brilliant coats of Bobcats red.

She was just—gone.

"What do you think happened to her?" I asked Mo and James. Now that the celebrations were done we were settling into the languor of the off-season. The players were home, wherever that was for them, which meant staff could have lunch at any time. Until the draft, there wasn't much to do in Media Relations except work on next year's media guide and finally get some rest.

"I called her a few times," Mo offered. "Straight to voicemail. She probably just moved on, though. She really wasn't that into football."

"She wasn't a great fit," said James. His voice was flat. "You know, you can't do the stuff she did and hang on with a team very long. Once everyone knows about it, it's pretty much over."

I took a tiny bite of my sandwich and chewed it into dust. My postseason dream had been slow to start, but James and I were supposed to go to Francesca's tonight, a popular restaurant on the North Side with brick walls, tea lights, and meatballs the size of bocces. I wondered if James saw the irony in his comments, since he was one of the men Abby had hooked up with and was going out with me later. He winked at me over the top of his cup and changed the subject to snowboarding.

*

"Mm-hmm. Mm-hmm. Okay, right on. Poppy?"

Brent hung up the phone. I'd been staring dully at the empty Word document on my screen, watching the cursor blink, but when I heard my name I swung my chair around and raised my eyebrows. "Richard wants you. Not there," he said, noticing my glance toward Richard's empty office. "He's with the big boss. They're calling you in, kid."

My hands shook as I swiped myself out of the annex, because if they wanted to talk to me together, it could be about only one thing. So much time had passed—it felt like years—since the conference finals that I'd almost convinced myself no one would ever know. But there were text messages and security videos, and what would I say if they confronted me with those now? What *could* I say?

My Bobcats badge flapped against my waist where it was clipped. Once, I'd imagined wearing it outside this building, a literal badge of honor. I never thought it would be ripped off and thrown into the trash. How was I supposed to explain that to my family? How could I tell my dad that I'd been fired—and why?

James smiled at me as I walked past his desk, but I couldn't bring myself to do more than lift my fingers in a half wave.

The door to Asbel's office was open, but Richard was standing with one hand on the knob, and as soon as I walked in he pulled it shut.

"S'down," said Asbel by way of greeting. His face was unreadable. I looked to Richard, leaning against the wall. His hands were clasped in front of him, thumbs fidgeting. His eyes were on the carpet.

Lowering myself onto one of the chairs across from Asbel's desk, I tucked my legs tightly together and ran my palms down my pants, trying to subtly wipe off the sweat gathering there.

Asbel put his elbows on the desk and looked at me like he could see under my skin. "Poppy. Is there anything you need to tell us?"

My heartbeat turned to horse's hooves. This was it. I'd probably never see my desk again, they'd escort me out from here. Later someone would send a pitiful cardboard box of my belongings to my apartment, where Dave and Flossie would throw it away because I'd already moved home to Ohio. An endless pause stretched between us, lengthened, filled the room. I could hear my own breaths.

"We've received a complaint," Asbel said finally, never taking his eyes off of me, "but there are some conflicting reports."

"Oh?"

Richard picked up the thread. "Someone made a complaint about—a senior member of staff. Now, as a father of daughters, believe me, that makes me sick. But as Asbel said, there might be more going on in this case."

It wasn't about me. My mind raced through knee-deep mud, trying to catch up. "Abby?"

Richard tried unsuccessfully to exchange a glance with Asbel, who was still locked on me. "What makes you say that?"

I knew that there were going to be moments in my life that

decided everything afterward, but they didn't come when I'd expected. Choosing a college, a job. Making promises in church with the man I'd build my family with. Those were big, but you got to prepare for them, to think, and consult, and consider. The real defining moments were the ones that crept up on you on a quiet off-season Tuesday, when you had to answer fast, from your gut, and find out what your guts were made of. For just a moment, we were suspended in the intake of a breath. The air whistled past us like the breeze through a canyon, a deafening roar that filled my ears, nose, throat, lungs. The three of us sat, tipped at the very precipice of my life.

And then the moment was cleaved in two.

"It's just that she had kind of a reputation. I don't want to spread rumors, but she's been with a few guys on staff, and there were some alcohol issues, too. So it doesn't surprise me. Unfortunately."

Abby didn't even want to be here. She didn't care about football, about the Bobcats. Maybe she'd left a little early, but she was always going to go. I, on the other hand, belonged here. I'd proven that, I'd earned it.

"Good," Asbel said finally, slowly. "That's good to know, thank you, Poppy."

"I'm glad to help." The meeting was ending, but there was more to say. There was more to take. Five minutes ago I'd thought I was about to be escorted out of here, and the threat of it made me want to fight. I wasn't ever going to be bounced back to the outside. I wanted to be here. And I realized now—this was the game, it wasn't changing, and I could either complain about it or start playing. "I think I could help more," I said.

Richard's eyebrows brushed the ceiling. Asbel just raised his chin, indicating that I should go on. My pulse was pounding in my ears, but I forced myself to stay steady. I forced my voice to be strong. "It sounds like nothing has been made public, which is great. But if it did . . . I just don't see how anyone could believe something like that about a team hiring women to prominent front-office positions. Do you?"

*

Abby never went public with her claims, and shortly after the draft, Brent announced he was moving on to join the staff at Miami.

"I'll finally be able to get a real tan," he cracked.

"I didn't know you were job hunting," said our admin, Julie. She was standing in the doorway to her office with her arms folded and the corners of her mouth turned down.

"I wasn't! They called me out of the blue—scouted! I met the director there during the Super Bowl, and I guess he liked what he saw."

I wouldn't be delivering papers and clips anymore. Now that I was the media relations manager, that job would fall to someone else. But first there was one last day of it.

I took my time and saved the coach's papers for last. The coaches' wing was quiet. Coach Guillory's admin was off somewhere, as she so often was in the mornings. He was at his desk, drinking a refillable water bottle full of electric-green juice. "Mmm," he said, holding up a finger as he swallowed and wiped his mouth with the back of his hand. "Hey there, Pop Tart."

I smiled sweetly.

"Hey, Red."

PART III

CHAPTER TWENTY-TWO

NOW

I climbed out of bed before dawn and pressed my feet to the freezing floor. The winter darkness was thick and deep as a mud puddle, and I shivered. I pulled on a bathrobe and slipped my phone into the pocket, then padded out to the kitchen. Coffee wouldn't fix things, but it never hurt, and I started my expensive machine and rummaged in the fridge for some fruit. It wasn't that I had any appetite—although my last solid food was yesterday's lunch. But I needed the sensation of crushing something, of biting down and feeling it burst between my teeth.

I found an orange on the counter and peeled it. Its sharp, citrus scent hit my nose at the same time as the coffee, and together they snapped me into focus. I popped the first wedge in and game-planned.

Bernie's face had been a mix of confusion, apology, and suspicion. When he suggested we step into the hallway, I'd followed, although everything in me was screaming to run, that if I didn't hear this, it wouldn't actually be happening.

Carolyn had sent the letters. She'd admitted it, and it was over. But when Bernie dropped his voice, looked at me hard, and said, "It was a tip," I knew that it wasn't. "You're friendly with that lawyer for the Blizzard, right? The one who—"

"Yes. Good friends, actually. She's a great person. You can quote me on that. Seems a little outside your jurisdiction, though."

"It is . . . but you're not."

One of the equipment guys came through the doorway pushing a giant bin of laundry, and we stepped apart to let him pass, then came together again. "What are you talking about?"

Bernie scratched the back of his head. His shirt pulled untucked on that side. "I don't like having these conversations—and with you . . . You're like a daughter to me. I've known you since you were this high." He hovered his hand above the floor. "You know, career-wise."

"Tell me."

"I got a tip that there's a similar story around you to the one involving your friend. I can't picture it, Poppy, honestly, I know that's not you. I wasn't going to say anything. But, you know, thirty-eight years of journalism, I can't just shake it off, I have a responsibility. So I thought I'd come here, look you in the eye, ask you, and we can be done with it."

Here was my chance. If I was sorry—now that I'd come to terms, now that I knew what I'd really done—I could stand here and tell the truth. I could dump out to Bernie, my friend, what Red did to me and what I did in turn to Abby. I couldn't fix it, ever. I'd have to live with what I'd done. But I could be honest. I could let myself be called to account.

"Bernie . . ."

His eyes were pleading. His hand was on my arm. I was suddenly aware of the ache in the balls of my feet, screaming after twelve hours in heels. My neck was stiff. I felt tired, and old. "I am so hurt that you would even ask me that."

*

Now I texted Annika, outside of the group chat. *I'm sure things are still really tough at home, but I need you to get Carolyn some therapy or anger management or* whatever. *I want to help, but this can't keep happening.*

It was just after six here, which meant just after five in Wisconsin, but the text changed to "Read," and almost instantly my phone rang. "What are you talking about?" I quickly filled Annika in, and just as quickly she said, "It's not Carolyn."

"I know you—"

"*No.* Believe me, I understand she's capable of it." That shut me up. "But it can't be her. Grant took her to the cabin for the week. It was too much here, we couldn't . . . Anyway, there's no service. Or very limited. And she doesn't have her phone. The doctor recommended it."

It was the third week in November, which should have been the beginning of finals crunch for a first-year law student. Instead, Carolyn was back in Wisconsin undergoing a tech detox on the suggestion of a doctor. The Jensen family of highfliers had been torn apart, obliterated, and my cold heart ached for Annika.

"Anni, what Bernie said." My head throbbed. "It's true. And I'm sorry I didn't tell you when things broke apart. It just . . . There's a lot more to the story."

"There always is."

After we hung up, I stared hard at the counter thinking through my options. Someone knew more than I wanted them to about my past. Okay, then—why the dance? Why not just tell Bernie instead of being cryptic? In Carolyn's case, I suspected it was because she'd wanted there to be another answer. Deep down, she'd wanted to believe that her mother was good, that there'd been some kind of mistake. For Bernie's source, I had a more cynical explanation— whoever it was didn't actually know the details, at least not yet. And I wasn't going to just sit here until they found out.

I was sick of this—sick of these little surprises threatening everything I'd built. Yes, I'd hurt someone, badly, when I was young and stupid and naïve. Yes, there were things I'd give anything to redo now that I knew so much better. But if I was wrong, Red had been *more wrong,* and I wasn't about to be held more accountable for not preventing his bad deeds than he was for committing them.

Damian Jokiak would be welcomed back someday. Mike Tyson served six years in prison as a convicted rapist, and now most people knew him for his fun celebrity cameo in *The Hangover.* Look at the guest list on his podcast. You could build a Pro Bowl roster out of NFL players who'd been accused of sexual assault, up to and including a multi-Super-Bowl-winning quarterback. Accusations were not convictions, but in one case the league felt strongly enough to suspend the player for six games and require that he undergo a league-mandated "professional behavior evaluation." He won the Super Bowl again the following year, confetti raining down around him as he kissed the Lombardi trophy.

So while Damian would be back, Annika would not. And that was bullshit.

It was time to go on the offensive, and the most logical starting point was with Red because the only thing I knew for sure was that everything tracked back to him. The first note came on the day after his death, and all this started when he'd assaulted me in that anteroom. He was the key, and if I couldn't go talk to him, I'd have to settle for the next best thing. Because like DeMario said, there were no real secrets between husbands and wives.

*

Lexi Guillory looked better one month after the death of her husband than I had on headshots day. That's not to say she wasn't suffering, because when she opened the door her eyes were sunken from too many tears and not enough sleep. Her hair—a long wavy mix of real and tasteful extensions, balayage blond—was scraped back into a greasy ponytail, and for the first time I could remember, she wasn't in heels but fuzzy beige slides.

"You're the first person from the team who's come," she said, bending down the four inches between us to wrap me in a hug. "I've had texts and calls, but no one else has actually been here. We're selling the house, obviously." It clicked that I was now in the place where Red was murdered.

My phone buzzed—a call from my brother Jeff. I hit Ignore and followed Lexi down a blond wood hallway and into a living room roughly the size of my townhouse. It had a soaring two-story ceiling and oversized windows with trendy black square frames. The sofas were white and cloudlike with no support, and as soon as I sat on the one across from Lexi I knew it would take an act of God to get me back on my feet.

"Do you want water or something? We have still, Perrier, San Pell . . . ?"

"I'm fine, thanks." What do you say to a woman whose husband was murdered? What if you were in the process of understanding things about him that made you want to shatter the windows, to scream so loud that the house came tumbling down around you? I've never been married, and so I don't claim to understand the dynamic between husband and wife, the extent to which one becomes the other. But when I imagine two people linked the way they were, I don't picture them laughing or walking into a black-tie event or having sex. I picture them sleeping, the hours each night spent defenseless and vulnerable, trading breaths, sharing the air. It seemed to me that during those hours everything in each of them tumbled into the narrow slip of bed between and swirled around, hitting one body, bouncing back to the middle, swirling again until it reached the other. Maybe that little world existed only while they slept and once their eyes opened it was gone, but I thought something must stay behind. Some essence of Red must have seeped into his wife's bones, because she couldn't spend so many years creating that nightly symbiosis with someone and not have an idea of who he really was.

The sound of Lexi's sniffle pulled me back. "It's awful," she was saying, "but since we knew, you know, it was going to happen one way or another at least we'd had some conversations. And I don't know, maybe it's better this way. I don't think he would have handled the treatments very well."

I blinked. "I'm sorry, Lexi—I don't know what you mean."

"He didn't tell you. Of course he didn't." She shook her hands in the way only a spouse can, that mix of frustration and "isn't that just like him"–ness, and for a moment Red was alive again for Lexi. "Well, there's no point in keeping it secret now—Red was dying."

My pulse skidded. How did he keep doing this? Even after he was gone, Red Guillory could still wrong-foot me. He could still take everything I thought I knew and shake it. I could almost see his knowing smirk.

"Prostate cancer," Lexi went on. She dabbed at her undereye with the tips of her ring fingers. "His dad died from it when Red was a kid, so he has this genetic predisposition, and that selfish asshole *still* didn't take it seriously. He thought he was above it, like the cancer wouldn't dare. Which is, you know," she barked out a caustic laugh, "*not* how it works."

"I'm sorry," I murmured. I looked around the living room at the family photos lining the walls, shots of Lexi and Red with their kids, now almost grown. What an arrogant ass Red was, to not have taken better care for them.

"He was going to have this big blood panel done the day after . . . it happened. I can't get over that, you know? Like, this guy who fought me tooth and nail to go see a doctor was at least going to do this one thing, *finally,* and the night before . . ."

Red was killed when he was already dying, which meant nothing practically speaking because the killer wouldn't have known, but cosmically, it felt . . . almost *just* now. Red wasn't going to be allowed to slip away. He was taken, violently. The thought stirred up a confusing tangle of emotions as it flew by, like a dust cloud in the wake of an old pickup truck.

"I was like, 'You are not drinking today, you are not taking anything today. *One day.* We need *clean blood.*' We had this huge fight about it because he seriously needed that stuff, especially at night. You know."

I nodded, because I did.

Lexi pressed perfectly manicured hands against her perfectly unlined face. "I told Asbel, I told Coach Nate, because I thought they could convince my stubborn ass of a husband, and then Red was pissed that I'd told them. And you know what Asbel said? He told me it wasn't Red's fault, the drinking, that I couldn't understand. He said to be in that business, to, like, devote hours and hours to training and working out and drills takes an addictive personality, and that everyone in sports is an addict; the lucky ones just get addicted to the right thing. I mean, how fucked up is that?"

Asbel defended Red's worst habits, and even after Red was dead he'd kept his secrets. There was a loyalty between them that I hadn't understood and couldn't touch.

"Anyway, Red and I had a huge fight, I said he was being stupid and selfish by not taking care of himself. I locked up and went upstairs to bed. And then in the morning . . ."

She found him.

"Later, from the toxicology, I learned he actually did it. He didn't take a single thing all day, and I was so *proud* of him. You want to know the most insane thing, too? I was almost happy to hear he was attacked, because until then I thought it was my fault. I said he had to keep clean, which he clearly could *not* handle. It gave him the shakes, and he'd *sweat* like . . ." She trailed off, hands waving from her armpits down her trunk. "So if he lost his balance, if he fell, that was on me. But someone came into my home while my kids and I were sleeping and murdered my dying husband, and I'm *happy* about it because it means it wasn't my fault."

"Lexi . . ."

I don't comfort people. I don't know how, and I certainly wasn't equipped to comfort *this* person over *this* particular loss. Lexi and I had barely spoken beyond normal pleasantries in the entire fifteen years I'd known her, and that distance seemed to let her open up, to unload on someone not really in her life but not out of it, who knew Red not through Lexi's lens, but my own. I let her vent about his stubbornness and his bad habits—the ones you could mention in polite company, anyway—wondering why I'd really come here and what I hoped to get out of this. She was hurting. She was a widow. I was disgusting.

"So then," she said, winding up a long story about Red's medical history, "they sent him the results of the first test, which," she held up her index finger, "*I think* must have been what made him understand that he couldn't drink his way through it. They were all messed up or something. He knew he'd fucked up too, because he wouldn't let me see it, and I was like, 'Babe! It's right there, I can see the envelope, Waverly Ave. Specialists Group. Or no, Group Specialists, I guess, it was abbreviated, but like, obviously that's the medical center right across from University Hospital, so—"

"Sorry, Lexi," I broke in. My exhausted mind was playing tricks on me. "What did you say? About the letter?"

"It was the results of the first one, I think, because—"

"No, sorry." I swallowed. There was an inordinate amount of saliva in my mouth, I couldn't keep up with it. "The group. Waverly Ave. . . ."

"Specialists Group, or Group Specialists, I don't know which. Inc. It definitely had 'Inc.' on the end."

WAGS, Inc.?

What. The. Fuck.

Did Red get a letter from someone posing as us? It wasn't Carolyn, because we'd already closed that door. But whatever was in that envelope was serious enough to make Red stay sober for a night, and during that night, someone killed him. Someone tall. Someone strong. Not Asbel. Who? The same person who sent Bernie that note? But that meant they'd have to know about the WAGS *and* the other notes. Who did that leave?

I had to go—immediately. I struggled to my feet from the overly soft couch and grabbed my purse from the floor. "I should get back." My voice didn't sound like me. There was too much air in it.

"I still think it had to do with that shit he was always taking," Lexi said as she walked me out. The hallway felt twice as long now, the ceilings twice as low. "The doctors said it wasn't connected, but how could it not be? You load up on testosterone, your prostate gets fucked up."

I stopped by the front door. "Testosterone?"

"Oh, Red's been on a shitload of testosterone supplements ever since . . . God, since right after we were married. As soon as he finished playing and switched to coaching, it was like he couldn't function without it." She gave me a knowing look. "I mean, he could *function* just fine, believe me, it was never about that. I think it just killed him that he couldn't play anymore. At the beginning some of those players were his age, it just ripped him apart. And then he chose this job where there were all these young, jacked players coming through, year after year. He couldn't keep up. I think some testosterone is supposed to be fine, a lot of guys do that, but he was . . . I don't want to say abusing it, but he was taking a lot. Pills. Subcutaneous placements. Patches. It was like he couldn't get enough. And then, you know. Prostate cancer."

"I'm so sorry."

"Poppy, thank you so much for coming," said Lexi, surprising me by pulling me into a tight hug. She sniffled near my ear. "It means a lot. Red always liked you. I think he had a soft spot because you were both new during that first season—the undefeated one. God, he was under pressure."

I put my hand on the doorknob. "We all were." How stupid that must sound to her, an intern equating herself with the head coach. But Lexi wasn't listening enough to take offense. She was lost in her memories of that long-ago season.

"He used to tell me how it was crushing him, the weight of this entire," she flicked her fingers out from her thumb, "thing. By the time he made the Super Bowl he was just guzzling antacids. Honestly, the only other time I'd seen him like that was this fall. You know, the losing was hard for him. And the medical stuff. It takes a toll."

I swallowed hard. "Take care, Lexi."

I drove until I found a gas station and pulled into a spot. The winter sun was blinding, reflecting off the snow. It was frigid, around ten degrees, and I'd started shivering on the walk to my car and never stopped. My hands gripped the wheel.

I didn't *care* why Red did what he did. I didn't care if he was hav-

ing a midlife crisis or hopped up on aggression juice or just felt entitled to anything and anyone around him. He took what he wanted
without any thought for anyone else, and being sad about his knee
didn't make that okay.

I opened the group chat, where Annika's message was still the
most recent one.

Today was the first day since it happened that I had an appetite.

I closed the chat. It wasn't all of us this time. It couldn't be.
Dayanna's dating life, Nisha standing up to a jerk, Sarah passing on
some stories—none of that was a dead body. None of it was a sexual
assault cover-up. The only one on the same level was Annika, and
she was going through enough right now. I needed to let her be.

Jeff called me again, and again I silenced it. Did he not watch
the news? Could he not tell that I was busy right now with things a
little more important than Mom's fucking birthday cruise?

Someone had possibly sent Red a note from WAGS, Inc.

Someone had definitely killed Red.

Someone fed Bernie breadcrumbs about what happened that
first year.

Was it three different people? Or two?

Or one.

My phone pinged, announcing a voicemail, and I gave a cry of
frustration. "Jesus, Jeff," I muttered, bringing the phone to my ear.
What? What could possibly be so important?

His voice on the message was hard and cold.

*Poppy, I know you're way too busy to think about anyone other than
yourself, but you might actually have to answer your phone once in a while.
We need you home. Dad had a heart attack.*

CHAPTER TWENTY-THREE

NOW

Asbel was unimpressed when I called him as I drove over the state line from Pennsylvania into Ohio. Maybe he regretted his moments of candor earlier in the week, or maybe he'd snapped out of whatever it was that had made him introspective, but he was back to full form. "It's a family emergency," I repeated for what felt like the fifth time. "I have never once asked for unexpected time off, which should underline how important this is."

"Is your dad dead? Because Red is dead. I need you here."

"That's not fair, Asbel."

"And this isn't playtime, Poppy. We're in the middle of the season. That fucking puppy calendar shoot is today, and A.J. wants to know if you got his special dog? I don't even want to know what that means. Oh, and—the police are using conference room three to interview my staff about the murder of *our* friend."

"I'll be back by Friday," I said, gunning the accelerator. "Okay?"

"Tomorrow."

"Fine, tomorrow. I'll see you then." I hung up and threw my cell phone against the passenger window.

*

I can't stand when people say they don't like hospitals. *Oh, really? What's your stance on beestings?* No one likes hospitals, but when someone you love gets sucked into one, the last thing that matters is whether you hate the smell or are scared of the machines, or whatever other stupid issues people bring up in the face of much bigger problems.

Dad was on the far side of a shared room, and I ducked my head as I hurried past his roommate's area. A young woman—I guessed his daughter—was propped up in one of those uncomfortable visitor's chairs holding an open magazine without reading it, and we exchanged a look of mutual understanding at the mix of pain and privilege that is watching your parents age.

I found him dozing. He had the white gown with little blue flowers, the too-thin scratchy blanket, the fuzzy socks with grips on the bottom. That bed shrank him. It took my giant of a father and brought him right back down to the size of a normal person, and of everything that had happened over the past month—the death of our coach, the trauma of the notes, and my earth-shattering revelations about Red—it was that that finally made me cry.

"Hey, kiddo." His voice was weak and scratchy.

I wiped my eyes quickly. "Hey Dad."

"Pretty stupid, huh?"

"*So* stupid."

I pulled a chair next to the bed, cringing at the scream of its legs against the rubberized floor. Although his roommate couldn't see me, I mouthed *sorry* at the curtain. "You know you scared the shit out of me."

He chuckled, which made him wheeze. "It wasn't great for me either. It's okay, though, babe. I'm good."

"You *look* good." I was trying for a joking tone, but my voice broke and then so did I. Dad reached out his hand. With an IV strapped to the back and a line tethering it to a pole, it looked like it belonged to some other, weaker man, but he cupped it at the back of my head and I closed my eyes at its familiarity, its tenderness. My dad. He was still my dad.

I wished I was still young enough for my dad to make things okay. How long had it been since I could really come to him, since I could tell him—truthfully—what was wrong and have him fix it? Not since that first season. Not since, I now realized, what Red did. Maybe a part of me knew that my dad would see the stain of it on me. He would know something was wrong even where I didn't, and we would have to talk about it, and I would have to face it. I would have to leave. It was better to bury it, to keep going, to pretend that I was the one who'd had agency in the situation. Red didn't assault me—*I* led him on. Because otherwise, the enormity of it would knock me to my knees.

Dad clapped his hands together, a sound no louder than fluff coming off a dandelion. "The upside is, your mom and I can come to some of your games next season. Got a good source for tickets?"

I picked at the blanket. "You're free on weekends now, huh?"

"It's okay, babe. I'm okay with it."

I wasn't—not even close. It was so cruelly, viciously unfair. There were all these bad people in the world. They were allowed to just crumple people up in their hands, drop them to the floor, and keep moving, and here was a good and decent man who had only ever wanted to help, and he couldn't do it anymore. The unfairness of it made me want to spit. How could his heart keep him from coaching when without it his heart would break?

Even that short conversation had worn Dad out, and so I made up an excuse about needing the bathroom because as long as I was there he would keep pretending to be stronger than he was.

I was halfway through the door when I collided with someone walking in. "Oof! Mom?"

"Oh, Poppy. You came." My mother wrapped me in a hug that squeezed the air out of me, and after several beats I realized I was effectively holding her up.

"Let's not go back in there just yet," I said, shuffling her into the hallway. "Come on—we'll get coffee."

It was midafternoon, and so the hospital café was mostly empty. A few tired-looking people in blue scrubs or white nursing smocks pushed their trays along the steel rails, and I had the strange sensation of being back at the stadium cafeteria.

My mother perched at the edge of her chair, eyes bright and alert. She was wearing a delicate silk blouse under a cashmere cardigan, and it irked me that she would bother to dress up at a time like this.

"I'm so glad you came," she said again, reaching across the table to grab my hand. I forced myself to let her.

"Why does everyone in this family act like I don't care? I come home when I can. I can't help it that the big holidays are during my season."

"I know that, we understand."

"Jeff doesn't."

"I'm just happy to see you."

"That's a strange thing to say, given why we're here."

"Poppy, why are you so angry with me?"

The question came flying out so fast that I wondered how long she'd been holding it behind her teeth. Years? A decade? I pulled my hand away. I take my coffee with almond milk and collagen powder, but I picked up two Sweet 'N Low packets from the tray and took my time emptying them one by one into my cup. "I'm not angry with you."

"Then why don't you call me? Why don't you tell me things? I don't know anything about your life, I barely know you."

"This isn't the time for this."

"There's *never* been a time for this—"

"It's because you don't like me." The answer surprised us both. "Not the way I am. You wanted me to be something different, something more like you, I guess, and I just felt that *all* the *time*. I know you don't like my job. I know you don't like my choices, but I do. I'm happy."

Am I? In all the times I'd run through this little speech in my mind, it had never, ever occurred to me that it was anything less than true.

We sat in silence, watching people in scrubs move in and out of the cafeteria. At a nearby table, a man sat by himself with his head in his hands. "How can you think," my mother said finally, "that I don't like you? You are my sunshine."

She used to sing me that when I was little, a throwaway song I hadn't thought about in years. But now, watching her face, I realized it wasn't a throwaway to her, and that the nickname "Sunshine" wasn't what I'd thought either. It wasn't her tongue-in-cheek way of reminding me to smile once in a while, it wasn't her forcing her aspirations for a perfect daughter on me. It was from that song. *You'll never know, dear* . . .

I shifted in my seat. "Thank you. I mean, that's nice to hear, Mom, and I love you, but it doesn't take away the rest of it. We're just—not close. We never have been."

"Poppy, your father had an affair."

The world tilted. A thousand images flashed behind my eyes— my dad in his windbreaker, clapping chapped hands together on a November sideline, yelling out plays across a field at night. My dad lifting me up onto his shoulder after a Sectionals win. His shirt was still wet from where his players had dumped a Gatorade cooler all over him, and it soaked through my dress and made my leg sticky. My parents at the end of their driveway as I drove away for my first day at the Bobcats, Dad's strong arm around Mom as she hid her face in his chest.

Red had assaulted me, and my father had an affair.

I swallowed. "What?"

"I can't believe this is where I'm telling you. I wasn't planning on ever telling you, I know how much you worship your father, the last thing I want to do is take that away from you. But I'm so tired. I'm *so tired* of being the second favorite, I'm tired of covering for him. It was a teacher at the school—a little English teacher, with pencil skirts and big doe eyes, who carried around books about poetry. Like your father's ever read a goddamned poem. I found out when Luke forgot his lunch. There was construction on the main road, so I went in the back way, by the soccer fields. Your father's car was parked there, half in the woods. And I saw them."

My mind was reeling. This didn't make sense. It was like she was telling me he'd blown up the moon.

"It happens, and we got through it. But our whole lives spun around him, and *his* job and *his* football, and when it became your favorite thing I just . . . saw red. It wasn't fair. He didn't get to have you, too. I tried making special little traditions for just you and me—remember how we'd make Thanksgiving dinner together, the two of us? But I was forcing it, and you could tell." She offered a wobbly smile. "You were always too smart by half."

I wanted to calcify myself. I wanted to harden each inch of my skin, cell by cell, until I was safe behind a protective shell. I didn't want to know this about my father. I didn't want to have to understand my mother. Everything—*everything*—I'd believed to be true about my family life was wrong. It was more than I could handle.

I wasn't about to be held more accountable for his bad deeds than he was for committing them. Like mother, like daughter.

"What am I supposed to do with this?" I said. "Dad's upstairs with a stent in his heart. Am I supposed to go yell at him for cheating on you thirty years ago? Am I supposed to *not* yell at him, knowing he cheated on you? What—tell me what to do?"

"I don't *know.*" This time it was her hand that slammed on the table, causing my coffee to slosh out of its cup. Seeing her mimic my exact gesture—realizing that, actually, I was probably mimicking hers—shocked me as much as anything else had that day. My mother was practically a stranger to me. How could I carry her gestures in my hands?

"Parents are just people, Poppy, we mess up. Haven't you ever wished you could take something back?"

Abby.

She sounded as exhausted as I felt. I was, as it turned out, too tired to keep holding this grudge. There were other mistakes I would have to carry forever, but this—this one I could put down.

I walked my fingers back and forth across the tabletop. "Could we . . . start small? We don't have to do, like, a spa weekend, do we?"

Her lip trembled, then stretched into a smile. She gestured toward the table. "How about a cup of coffee?"

*

I'd booked a hotel, but my mom insisted I stay with her for the night. "No funny business," she promised, "I won't make you look at photo albums with me or anything. It's just a place to lay your head."

We had a quiet dinner of creamed tuna fish, a gelatinous mass of fish in cream sauce served over biscuits that instantly transported me back to my childhood. The kitchen was still the same—white Formica countertops, hard wooden chairs—and if I closed my eyes while I ate, I could imagine that I was twelve years old again, wolfing down dinner between ballet class and Jeff's practice.

"It's nice to see you eating," Mom said.

"I eat."

"I meant—it's nice to see you eating here. Maybe you could stay for the holiday? I'm sure you have to work, but—"

My phone buzzed.

I thought I'd see you today. Are you out of detention?

Omar Kadeer. He must be in town for that blessed rescue dog calendar. I stared at the text for a minute and realized I was disappointed to miss a visit. *Back tomorrow,* I replied. He liked the text.

I let Mom's question go unanswered, and she knew not to follow up. We chewed in silence for a few minutes, and then I asked, "So what happens now, with Dad not coaching anymore?"

Mom got up to refill her water glass and gestured toward mine, mostly empty. I waved her off. "I guess he'll have time for some hobbies now," she said from behind the refrigerator door. "Maybe he'll start coming to tennis with me. Although, maybe not. I don't know if he'd be able to manage those swings with his heart. It takes a lot of power." She returned to the table.

"What did you say?"

"The swing?" She mimed hitting a ball. "It kind of pulls across your chest, you know, like this? I don't know if he'd be able to do that for a while."

Tennis. A powerful swing. It didn't make sense, though, because of the height . . .

"Poppy?" Mom rapped her knuckle on the table. "Are you okay?"

"Fine." I wiped my face with a napkin. "I should really leave tonight, Mom, I told my boss I'd be back in the office tomorrow." Her face fell, but she recovered quickly and smoothed the front of her cardigan. "Things are still pretty tough after what happened with Coach," I added apologetically.

"No, of course. I understand. It was so good of you to drive all the way out here."

I scraped the remains of my dinner into the garbage and put my plate in the sink. Then I walked back to the table, hesitated, and bent to peck her on the cheek.

CHAPTER TWENTY-FOUR

FIFTEEN YEARS AGO

Sarah and I were meeting for dinner.

We were both in Indianapolis for the Scouting Combine in March, which meant I'd been in my new job a little more than a month. By that time I'd stopped heading for the intern desk by habit and moved confidently toward Brent's old office—*my* office—in the mornings. Like magic, once I transitioned from intern to staff, Neil from accounting stopped knocking me into walls. The other day in the break room I'd heard him tut-tutting over a story about an NHL executive who had exposed himself to female staffers in the elevator. I was sure old Neil felt that story affirmed that he fell safely in the land of office high jinks, because he didn't do *that,* he'd never do that.

The steakhouse was only a few blocks from my hotel near the Convention Center, and so I decided to walk there. There was no snow, but the ground was frozen. Even the sidewalks somehow felt harder beneath my feet, and I walked with my hands shoved into my pockets, where I felt my cell phone vibrate. It was my mother.

"What's up, Mom, I'm on my way to dinner." I hated the way

my voice automatically got short when I spoke to her, but she had such a knack for inserting herself. I was on my way to meet a work colleague. I didn't want to be mothered just then.

"Oh, a team dinner?"

"No, with this woman I know who's here too."

Now her voice was the one to change. "It's just the two of you? You're taking a cab?"

"I'm walking, Mom. It isn't far."

"Honey, I wish you wouldn't do that. Dad and I will pay for cabs, you're a young girl, and you shouldn't be by y—"

"I'm not a girl, Mom! I'm an adult. With a job. I can pay for my own cabs, and I can decide if I want to walk. I don't need you hovering over me all the time. You think all these bad things are going to happen and they're *not*. I'm not helpless, I'm not stupid. Just *stop*."

For a full block after I hung up, my feet slammed against the sidewalk. Throwing a fit was not the way to show my mother I was older than she thought, but she was always, *always* talking down to me, especially when it came to anything that had to do with football. I knew what I was doing. I knew how to take care of myself. The restaurant's awning came into view, and I drew deep, full breaths to calm myself.

Sarah was waiting outside, her hood up against the chill, and as we hugged I said, "There are more steakhouses in this neighborhood than trees." I forced my mind past the conversation with my mom. This had nothing to do with her. She didn't understand this.

"Basketball and beef," Sarah said. "Hoosiers love 'em."

Inside was dark and clubby, with red velvet booths deep enough to be stagecoaches. The black-paneled walls held a collection of photos, mostly black-and-white horses, and oil portraits of what looked like nineteenth-century oil barons. The restaurant was packed with football people, and as we followed the hostess we passed a group of scouts I recognized sitting with a young woman I didn't. She raised her fingers in a tiny wave, and Sarah nodded back.

"Who was that?" I asked once we were seated. My feet didn't touch the floor.

"Nisha Khatri. Seattle just hired her."

"As an admin?"

Sarah smirked. "As a scout."

"No way!" I couldn't name a single female scout in the league, and that woman looked young, about our age. "How . . . ?"

"Because she's fucking good," Sarah answered. "I introduced myself when I saw her in a press box earlier this year. She's from L.A. Kind of mean. You'd like her."

"I want to meet her." I leaned out of the booth to look again and caught her looking back at me. I colored and gave an embarrassed little nod, then turned back to Sarah. "So you're on a beat. Congratulations."

"Thank you, thank you. I'm moving to Philly next month, so it's closer to home, which is cool, but it means breaking up with the guy I've been seeing." She spread butter on a roll. "Whatever. It's not like I was going to marry him. There're guys in Philly."

"Good for you."

The waiter arrived with our drinks, and I took a long sip of my whiskey, then coughed into my hand as it burned. Sarah was right—there were guys all over, and if they saw us as interchangeable, we might as well take the same approach.

Two weeks ago, I'd asked James if we could talk.

"Yeah," he'd said, kissing my neck. We were on the sofa at his apartment with college basketball on in the background. "I love talking."

I'd gently pushed him back and sat up. I was wearing the black sheath dress I'd bought with my first official paycheck, which I was convinced made me look like Addison from *Grey's Anatomy*. The week before, James and Mo had helped me move out of my creepy little apartment and into a proper starter unit with a roommate I was learning to tolerate. My hair had been recently cut, my nails were done, and I felt like the adult woman I was, with a job, an apartment, and hopefully . . .

"I think we should, you know. Make things official. This." I'd moved my hand back and forth. "Us."

James had run a hand through his hair, which was un-mussable. He'd looked like I'd asked him to solve a particularly complicated math problem in his head. "I mean, yeah. Like, we are." He'd laughed. "I don't really know what you're asking here, Pop."

"Well, okay." I'd shifted to face him. "So right now, if we go out to dinner, we both feel kind of stressed that we might run into someone from the team. And I just feel like, if we were a *known thing,* that wouldn't be the case. Like it might be . . . just easier."

Please understand what I'm saying, I'd thought. If we were just hooking up, it meant I was sleeping my way through the office. But a relationship, a proper one that happened in front of people like we weren't trying to hide anything, would have the opposite effect. There's no credibility for a young female professional like being in a relationship, because then you're neutralized. You are no longer a threat.

He'd leaned toward me and kissed me slowly. I'd closed my eyes and sighed in relief. And then, an inch from my mouth, he'd whispered, "Don't you think the secret is kind of what makes it hot?"

So that was that. James, apparently not very heartbroken, had moved on almost immediately to a ticket office intern who came in Tuesdays and Thursdays while finishing her senior year of college. They weren't subtle about it, and he and I hadn't spoken since.

"You know," I told Sarah now, "thank you for the heads-up on that guy James. What an asshole."

"Totally. He's such a skank."

She'd tried to tell me, and I hadn't wanted to listen because it was new and exciting, and I didn't want to believe it. But a lot had happened since then, and I could see the value of having someone to watch your back. Of helping watch someone else's.

"Can we . . ." I hesitated, not sure how to say what I was thinking. "Can we do this? Have dinners and talk and stuff? There just aren't that many women, especially our age—"

"Oh my gosh, I know. Honestly, I was so happy to run into you that day. Like, mentors are great, so I love meeting older women in sports, but especially with the Creep Defense Initiative, it's just not the same. Guys do not take the same kinds of liberties."

"Cool. So let's do it. And maybe Nisha . . ."

"I'll ask her." Sarah held up her glass.

We clinked.

CHAPTER TWENTY-FIVE

NOW

My townhouse was cold, the smart thermostat having reset itself—again—to sixty-five. I climbed into bed without washing my face and stared at the ceiling. Since the last time I'd been here, my entire sense of self had changed.

I was chilled by the proximity to tragedy. If my father had died today, would my mother have ever told me the truth? Maybe she'd also realized how close Dad had come to being gone, and maybe she knew that once he was she'd have to carry her secret forever. I wondered how she was sleeping tonight, alone in her bed for the first time in forty-five years, but no longer carrying the weight of our disconnect.

I tried box breathing to slow my heart rate, to try to rest after driving ten hours in one day, but my head felt pinched. My dad had almost died today. It was the kind of near miss that made you question everything. Were you living your life or just letting it pass? Had you built something, left a mark, and was it the kind of legacy you could be proud of? What would remain of you after you were gone?

I didn't like the answers. And I didn't know what to do about it.

With a sigh, I threw back the covers and ran downstairs to pull my laptop from its bag by the front door. I brought it back up to my room, climbed back into bed, and typed in Abby's name. In all the years since I'd last seen her, I'd never searched her out on a social networking site, I'd never Googled her name. I was too afraid of what I might find. I was too afraid of what I'd done, and of what I might have caused, and that was when I'd been so sure that I made the right call. Now nothing was certain. I didn't know how to trust my own memories.

I paused. Cringed. Hit Return.

The top result was an attorney with a white-shoe law firm. I would have scrolled right past it, except for the image preview. It showed an attractive blond woman in a white blouse and black suit. Her arms were crossed in front of her in a power stance, and she was flashing every tooth she had in a broad, confident smile.

It was her. According to Abby's bio, she'd started law school less than a year after she'd left the Bobcats. Her résumé was a dizzying collection of academic articles and professional accolades. She was, apparently, a "clear future leader in the field of intellectual property rights" with "oral advocacy skills that far outpaced most of her peers." She was an adjunct professor. She was married, with two kids and a dog named Barkley. I went back out into the search results, found her husband's name, matched it to a voter registration record, and found their address. I typed it into Zillow and saw a stunning white colonial with five bathrooms, a three-car garage, and lush landscaping.

I closed the laptop. Abby was *killing* it. Her life was going great. And mine?

I picked up my phone, opened the text chain with Omar. *I'm sorry I missed you,* I typed, then deleted the first part.

I missed you.

But in the end, I wrote, *Are you up for breakfast?*

*

"The All Night Eggplant." Omar examined his menu. "I don't think I've ever had breakfast in a short story before. And we're sure there's no hyphen in that?"

"You are about to experience a Syracuse institution." It was seven o'clock on Tuesday morning, two days before Thanksgiving. In the past day I'd driven ten hours and slept for none, and this no-frills, unironically eighties diner was exactly what I needed. Everything from the paneled walls to the tables and chairs was wood, and everything not wood was orange. A stack of seven high-chairs sat ready to service the restaurant's fifteen or so tables, which at this hour held a collection of blue- and white-collar workers.

I hadn't really expected Omar to say yes—or maybe I did, I was too tired to turn around and examine my own motives. All I knew was the world was spinning and chunky monkey pancakes would help.

When the waitress filled my coffee cup from an orange-topped industrial pot, Omar put his hand over hers. "Oh, regular for me, please."

She gave him a look that would have spoiled fruit. "It's all regular, hon." I kicked him under the table and tried not to laugh. "Alrighty—today's special is two eggs, two pieces of sausage or bacon, and two pancakes or French toast for six dollars."

"It's kind of nice, isn't it?" I said once we'd ordered. "Syracuse gets a bad rap, but where else can you get a breakfast like that in a city?"

"Is that why you're still here?"

"What do you mean?"

Omar crossed his leg, resting one foot on the opposite knee, a position the space between the tables could barely accommodate. "You've been director for how long now—six years?"

"Seven."

He spread one hand. "So, what's next? You've climbed as high as you can here. I assume you're not holding out to be GM."

"Over Asbel's dead body."

The line hovered in midair, and then we both laughed. It was weird to feel so comfortable with someone I'd spoken to only a handful of times, but Omar and I just got each other. It was like sitting next to a stranger on an airplane and pulling out the same book.

"Seriously, though, what's your plan?"

"I executed the plan. This *is* the plan—I did it."

"And that's it?"

I raised an eyebrow. "It's not enough?"

"For you? Nah."

I hadn't even thought about a life *beyond* the Bobcats. Becoming media relations director was the pinnacle, and it claimed every bit of me. Omar was the first person I'd ever spoken to who suggested it might be too small.

I pivoted. "What about you? What comes after agenting?"

"That is a good question. Being an agent is strange because you start out trying to get as many clients as possible, and then if you're good at it you end up representing as few guys as possible—the top tier. That's where I am now."

"Maybe next you could be God's agent."

"Maybe I could."

We ate and chatted, and for just an hour I pretended that my father wasn't in the hospital, that Red wasn't dead and hadn't assaulted me, and that I hadn't in turn dismissed his assault of Abby. I pretended to have slept, and that I hadn't shamed a good friend for asking me about something true. I ignored it all and ate pancakes with Omar while we talked about how to keep climbing.

CHAPTER TWENTY-SIX

NOW

I didn't know how long I'd been staring into space when Edward's voice broke in. "Hey, man. She's expecting you."

My mind had been churning since breakfast because the conversation with Omar went back to everything I'd been thinking about what remains when a person is gone. *Have you built something, left a mark? Was it the kind of legacy you could be proud of?*

I wanted to climb, yes. I wanted to build something big and dominate it and have my name on it in big fucking lights. But that was only half of a legacy, and that second part needed some work. That was why I'd left a message for DeMario to please meet me in my office.

He plant-swung his way in on the crutches. This time, I had the chair already pulled out so that the injured leg would fit, and once he was settled he let his head hang back and sighed. The simple act of sitting had completely wiped him out.

I leaned forward, intertwined hands resting on my desktop. "Thanks for coming. I'm sure it's not comfortable."

"No, but I'd meet you up on the roof to hear what your man Kurt dug up. What's the deal, Pop?"

My stomach turned to lead. My face hurt. A thousand skin-saving excuses rushed toward my tongue. *We're still working on that, but he thinks he's getting close* or *Kurt found a lead—it looks like someone from your doctor's office may have leaked your record* or *look over there and whatever you do don't blame me.*

I took a deep breath.

Jumped.

"I owe you an apology. I'm the one who told Bernie."

DeMario blinked slowly. He frowned and tilted his head back. "What?"

"I didn't mean to, initially, it was a misfire. But I also didn't correct it when I had the chance. And then obviously, I lied to you about it. I'm so sorry. I'll talk to Faith too, I . . ."

I trailed off, pained, because he was struggling to his feet but couldn't quite get there, the angle of the chair was too low. "Can I . . . ?" I half stood and hovered behind my desk. The chair tipped onto two legs because it couldn't handle DeMario's braced weight against one side as he pushed upward. He got himself up, but it toppled to the floor. I flinched.

DeMario never said a word. He just gave me a long, piercing look, and then made his way slowly, painfully out of the office. The annex door closed quietly behind him.

Rodney, Chloe, and Edward all stood open-mouthed in the annex. I raised my chin but felt it wobble and softly closed the door to my own office. Inside, I drank an entire bottle of water. I walked to the window and pressed my cheek against it, leaching off the cold to fight against the flames across my face and neck.

Back at my computer, I searched for Abby again. Her bio had an email address and a phone number, but this wasn't something that could be done remotely. I needed to see her face-to-face. I doubted her firm was the kind of place where I could just drop by, and I wasn't about to show up in her posh neighborhood and ring the bell.

Scanning her bio, I noticed something near the bottom and froze. Reread it. Cursed.

I'd skimmed over the fact that in addition to her legal work, Abby was also an adjunct professor. It hadn't pinged for me the last time because I was so taken aback by the life that she'd built for herself, the totality of all that wealth, power, happiness, and prestige. Now, however, it pinged in a big way.

Because Abby wasn't just any old adjunct professor.

She was an adjunct at Annika's daughter's law school.

CHAPTER TWENTY-SEVEN

NOW

I blew off work on Wednesday—didn't call, didn't let anyone know. I'd started the week traveling west in this car, making the trip home to Ohio. Now I raced to the east, to the extent that racing was possible on the busiest travel day of the year. The Thruway was a snarl of SUVs with luggage pods snapped to their roofs and college-era sedans stuffed with suitcases and laundry bags. When the GPS flashed a last-minute alternate route, a windy little road through the mountains, I cut in front of a Peter Pan bus to make the exit. I was determined to reach the Berkshires in time for Abby's office hours even though I didn't know what to say. I just needed to be in the same room and to hope that, unlike me, Abby knew exactly what she'd want to say if we ever came back together.

Rodney called me at ten. "Where are you?" he asked urgently. "I was worried this was a fall-in-the-bathtub situation. Asbel is completely losing his shit."

"I had an emergency appointment with my gynecologist," I said, relishing the look of abject horror I knew would be crossing Rodney's face. "Really bad, it couldn't wait. Asbel should know about it, though—he saw me on a telehealth call with her a few weeks ago." When Asbel himself called as I passed Albany, I sent him straight to voicemail.

Winston College was a small liberal arts school nestled on the Massachusetts border. With its brick walkways and hundred-year-old buildings, it was so beautiful it was almost boring. Students with leather backpacks gathered in little clusters on benches and beneath trees. The air was laced with a trace of chimney smoke, and in the distance church bells rang. I found Abby's building at the far end of the quad. It was a Gothic gray-stoned monster smothered in ivy. A young woman in a plaid blazer held the door open for me with a glance at my black slacks and sweater.

Inside, the hallways were dark and cool. Everything was stone, and the heavy latticing on the windows didn't let in much light. Abby's office—a shared space for adjuncts to cycle in and out of—was located in the basement, and I shuddered at the parallel to our Super Bowl hotel. Every step I took down the narrow staircase brought me closer back to that memory, to that dimly lit hallway, to Abby's crooked skirt and Red's silent silhouette closing the door. By the time I reached the bottom I could barely breathe.

What if I'm wrong?

It was lighter down here, because without windows the hall relied on proper fixtures. The numbering outside each office told me that Abby's would be the last one on the right. I could see its door propped open. I'd barely made it, her office hours were just ending, and as I reached the end of the hall, a tall, thin boy walked out and called back over his shoulder, "So much for a summary determination of infringement and no validity!" He saw me as he turned and stepped aside. "Sorry."

When I stepped into the doorway she was standing, papers half stacked as she packed up. She froze with her chin and eyebrows lifted, a soft smile on her face that drained away like an ebbing tide as she took me in.

Abby wore a taupe fisherman's sweater and white jeans, her honey-blond hair loose around her shoulders. While I'd fought my damnedest against aging, Abby had allowed it to pass over her gently, so she looked like a warmed-clay version of herself.

We squared off, her Hamptons neutrals set against my all-black ensemble. I wondered briefly if she would hit me. Instead, Abby straightened her last stack of papers, turned them neatly over so the blank backs showed, and gestured toward a chair. "Why don't you sit?"

Once she was settled in at her desk, hands under her chin, a diamond the size of a Golden Graham caught the light and sparkled from her fourth finger. I folded my own hands in my lap, covering the left with the right.

"I take it you don't have a question about IP."

What could I say? How could I start? I was here to apologize, but also to accuse. Finally I said, "It's about Red," and figured in one way or another that covered everything.

Abby let the words hang in the air for a few beats before saying, "I heard about that."

"How do you feel about it?"

"I don't think I'd like to get into that with you."

She said it simply, without vitriol, but it was the first acknowledgment that there was something between us, something massive. I wanted to get out of her office, race back to Syracuse, and leave Abby in the distant past where she belonged.

But then I thought of Lexi, coming downstairs in the morning after realizing that Red had never come to bed. She'd probably checked the kitchen, the patio, looked to see if his car was in the garage. After that she would have padded around their eight-thousand-square-foot home, maybe calling his name but maybe not, so she wouldn't wake the kids. Eventually, she would have made her way to the office. She would have opened the door, cautiously, wary of finding Red passed out at his desk drunk or high, and trying to figure out what that meant for the blood panel and the treatment she so desperately wanted him to get.

Instead Lexi would have seen a puddle of red soaking the carpet beside the desk. Rushing over to it, she would have found Red's body, and here it was hard for me to go on because I didn't know whether she dropped to her knees and frantically tried to revive him or if the head wound was such that she knew it would be no use.

I crossed my legs. Cracked a knuckle.

"That's fair enough," I said, "I can understand that. There are a few other things I wanted to talk to you about. Do you know a Carolyn Jensen?"

"Sure—Carolyn's a very bright young lady. We've had a lot of meaningful discussions about law, and life. I think it's so important for young girls that age to have female mentors, don't you?" Abby's eyebrow quirked up. "I know you've done quite a bit of mentorship yourself."

"That's important to me, yes. Because otherwise girls can find themselves in situations they don't know how to handle. If no one ever prepares them, they might not realize what something is when it happens to them. They might not have the words to name it."

Abby was quiet for a moment, thinking. When she looked up, she said, "Am I supposed to feel sorry for you?"

"I didn't realize—" I cleared my throat. My heart was hammering away in my chest, and there were stars behind my eyes. "My framing of the situation was wrong. When it came to me. When it came to Red and me. And then when it was you, I thought . . . because of . . . James, and some other things, I thought that you . . ."

I could hear how futile it all sounded, how tepid. But it was the truth. I had nothing to offer her but the truth.

Abby stared at her desk. Her cheeks grew bright red and then faded slowly back to their normal shade as she drew even breaths in and out. When she'd recovered herself, she looked directly at me. "Red Guillory raped me, and you helped cover it up."

Something essential inside of me, some tension rod that kept me upright, snapped. I think somewhere deep down I'd thought that even if Abby wasn't having an affair with Red, even if Red had done to Abby what he'd done to me, she should have been able to get over it, like I had. Except, of course, that I never did get over it. I'd just learned to live with it, like a hole in the roof that drips water directly onto your face while you're sleeping. I was shaking. My teeth chattered.

I looked down at my hands. Supposedly the totality of cells

in a body are replaced every seven years, which meant I'd had two full cycles to shed what he touched, but I could still feel it. It was like nothing of me had stayed through that regeneration but the bits of him he forced into places they weren't allowed remained, so that now I was more him than me. I carried him, I hated him. It was such a relief to realize that, finally, after all this time. I *hated* him.

Fifteen years clicked by like cards in a shuffled deck. I thought of all the times I'd helped him, covered for him. The times I'd eviscerated a reporter for being too tough on him, or spoken glowingly of him to media outlets, politicians, community groups, my family. Red's wins and his enormous personality spoke for themselves, they were the clay, but I'd been the one molding it. So much of who he was now was a result of my work. Our legacies were inextricably linked, and so hating Red necessarily meant that I also hated myself.

"I'm so sorry," I whispered.

Abby, who'd had fifteen years to deal with this truth, was more agile on her feet. She drew her lips into a tight line, sat back in her seat, and crossed her arms. "I'm a Kant, you know that?"

"Excuse me?"

She snorted. "Not that—you've got it covered if we're talking about that. I mean Immanuel Kant, the guy who developed moral philosophy. It's a theory that it's never moral to lie for any reason, even if the lie does more good than the truth. A friend asks you if you like her hideous dress, you have to say no. When I teach my students, we use the mnemonic 'you Kant lie.'"

"That wasn't my understanding of 'intellectual' property law."

"It's a bit outside the syllabus, yes. But Poppy," she gave me a pitying look, "who wants their whole life to be about only one thing?"

I deserve this. The least I could do was to sit here and take whatever insults she wanted to throw at me—the very least. But it was amazing how all this time and that trauma and her success later, Abby was still Abby. She was someone who always wanted to be more than she was. Already a lawyer and professor, she also fancied herself a master of philosophy. Ranked as the hottest woman in the office, she also needed to steal the man I liked right out from under my nose. It was never enough for her, just like me coming here and apologizing was never going to be enough, although on that point I happened to agree with her. But there was also the issue of the other reason I'd come.

"I know Carolyn came to you to talk about her mother. Annika is a good friend of mine."

"That tracks."

I ignored the dig. "I know what Carolyn did afterward, but I want to talk about *you,* because I think that conversation brought up a few things you'd buried. And once that happened, I don't think you knew how to shove them away again."

"You should leave." The record scratch of Abby's chair legs against the stone floor echoed through the tiny office. She stood and began gathering her papers, tapping them vertically against the desktop until their edges were flush.

"Do you still play tennis?"

She tried to hide the hitch in her movements, but it was there—barely. Then she recovered herself and loaded the papers into a leather satchel. "I'm a wealthy middle-aged woman who lives in suburbia—of course I play tennis."

"I was just wondering, because a former Miss Junior Vermont Tennis Association Champion must have a pretty powerful swing."

Our eyes met. A jolt passed through my lower abdomen and straight to my spine. I watched her eyes flick once to a bookcase behind me but forced myself not to turn.

"You, Poppy," she said quietly, "are a utilitarian. You believe the most ethical thing is whatever yields the greatest good for the greatest number of people, no matter what it does to an individual. So if five homeless orphans needed organ transplants and one healthy man walked into the OR, you'd gut him like a fish and divvy his insides up, and call yourself a saint for doing it. You think that by being where you are now, you can help so many women, right?

You can hire them, you can drive team policy on acceptable behavior. Poppy Benjamin, champion of women in sports, and who cares what you covered up to get there? You said, 'Red and me' earlier. That's interesting, don't you think? It almost sounds like you knew even more than I thought about what he was capable of."

I forced myself to stand, but not to run. I dug my heels into the rubberized floor and set my shoulders.

"Which philosopher says to murder the people who've wronged you, Abby? Which one says to bypass the police and kill a man in his own home while his kids are sleeping upstairs, and then leave him there for his wife to find in the morning? He was dying, by the way. He had cancer—prostate cancer, so the same stupid thing he let lead him around ruining lives was in the process of taking his. You split your soul for nothing."

"I didn't *mean* for—" She caught herself, too late. "I didn't kill him, and that wasn't why I went there that night."

"What was?"

"I needed to talk to him, because you're right—it's not something I'd examined for a very long time. My husband doesn't even know, I just stuffed it down."

We could have been each other's strongest ally—the two girls who'd stared down Neil from accounting and made him back away, now grown into a fierce tandem of self-possessed women—if I hadn't betrayed her for a job. For a boy. For revenge.

"But when Carolyn told me about her mom—another powerful woman in sports who could have stood up and said no, who could have made a *difference*—choosing instead to cover it up and make it go away—make *them* go away . . ."

The non-disclosure agreements. The payouts. "Abby, is that what happened with you?"

"Of course it's what happened to me—I was a girl with known 'relationships' with multiple men in the office. I don't agree that I had a drinking problem, especially not in the context of that workplace, but I came in hungover one morning and from that moment on, I was an alcoholic. Red had just won that team its first Super

Bowl, and my only witness"—she looked at me pointedly—"said I was a slut. I signed the paper and took the money, and I used it to put myself through law school. But now everything is supposed to be all Me Too, and this shit is Still. Happening. I think I could almost process that if it was men being horrible, because you and I know more than anyone that men can be horrible. Give them an inch, give them a space where that's okay, and they'll hip check you on your way to the bathroom. But it's the *women*. It's the women helping them I just—cannot—"

"I am so s—"

"*Don't.*"

Abby's hands had formed claws, and she shook them hard against the empty air. She looked down, noticed them, and let them fall.

"The letter," I said quietly.

"Yeah, well. When Carolyn told me about your little group, I thought, this is what you all *should* be doing. Not pathetically complaining to each other in bars, but actually *using* your power to *do something*. I figured you wouldn't mind if I borrowed the name. You did owe me a favor." Abby's face twisted. Her lip trembled for just a moment before she pulled it back in with a flare of her nostrils. She huffed out a dismissive laugh. "When did all that WAGS stuff start anyway?"

"Right afterward." Weeks afterward, it wasn't even a month. There'd been a hairsbreadth between when I ruined Abby and joined a sisterhood, and although she tried to hide it I could see the painful thought written in the tightness of her jaw—*Why wasn't that us?*

I had no answer.

"Anyway, we'd planned to meet at his house," Abby said, falling back into her story, "so it would be private—it's not like he could go anywhere in Syracuse without being recognized. I *just* . . . needed him to say it. I needed him to look at me, now, like this," she gestured to herself, a poised, successful, powerful woman, "and admit what he did. And I wanted him to see who I am now. That I got past it and over it and that he didn't ruin me. He didn't get to do that. But there was something wrong with him, he was high or something."

He wasn't, and that was the problem. Lexi had said when Red was off his substances he sweated. She said he shook, and he was unsteady on his feet. Abby's eyes darted again to the bookshelf, and again I fought the urge to turn.

"He started walking toward me, and I told him to stop. He said he wanted to *explain,* like there was anything in the world he could tell me that would make me think, 'Oh, I understand now. Thank you for that context, Red. Thanks for that backstory that allows me to see why you did what you did, it's fine now. I'm so glad we had this talk.' I didn't want to hear it! I didn't want to hear whatever bullshit he was peddling to make himself feel better and me feel wrong about my own rape."

A tear escaped, making its way past the delicate, thinning skin of her undereye and down those peachy cheeks, less full than they once were, until it nestled into the smile line at the edge of her mouth. My own eyes watered too. *Rape,* he had *raped* her. "He lunged for me, or I—I thought he did. I realized after he might have been falling, he was so out of it, just so heavy on his feet—and I panicked. And I hit him."

With the force of her tennis champion's swing. From above, not because the killer was taller than Red, but because Red was falling.

"I didn't mean to hurt him, but when I saw him coming at me, again, it just brought everything back. It sent everything white, I couldn't see, I couldn't breathe, I just . . ."

"What did you use?" I asked. We were standing on opposite sides of her desk, a hunk of wood and fifteen years between us. She glanced again at the bookcase, and this time I turned. It looked like the one in my office, with its vast collection of awards and honors. Abby had Super Lawyer plaques and framed diplomas with ornate script and thick gold seals. She had a glass pillar with a black base and various heavy rectangular stone awards engraved with her accomplishments. And on the bottom shelf, on the left, she had a bronze statuette of Lady Justice holding her scales, supported by a heavy, thick base. Brain-bashingly thick.

"I wanted to show him who I am now," she said. "I brought it like a kid with a book report to show he wasn't the only one who won trophies. He wasn't the only one to succeed."

"You kept it? You brought a murder weapon back here and put it on your bookshelf?"

"It was self-defense, and I didn't kill him! I told you—he was hurt, but I know he was alive because he tried to apologize." She laughed bitterly. "Can you fucking imagine? Once he was bleeding on the floor he wanted to say he was sorry? No. Too late by fifteen years. But I took his cell phone off the desk and put it nearby so he could call someone for help—to come clean up another one of his messes. He was alive when I left."

A whimper escaped my lips, because Red did call for help. He'd called two someones, and neither of us picked up. I could have saved him, and didn't, and that meant I'd contributed actively to Red's death. It was going to take a long time to figure out whether that made me feel better or worse.

"But how did you think he was going to explain being attacked?"

"Not my problem. He wouldn't bring me into it, because that would beg the question of a motive."

She wore white and I wore black, and together we made gray. Fifteen years ago I hadn't believed her. I'd made a choice at twenty-two that was coming home to roost now, when I knew better but couldn't change what I'd done. We own the consequences of our actions long after the person who made that choice no longer exists. And here, on some level, was a second chance. I could choose now to believe her.

But.

"He was behind the desk," I said quietly.

"What?"

"You said you hit him because he came at you and you panicked, but Lexi found him behind the desk. Almost as if he wasn't coming after you at all. Almost as if he was walking away."

CHAPTER TWENTY-EIGHT

NOW

The detectives packed their things and left. They'd uncovered no motives beyond the usual office politics, maybe a bit heightened in a workplace that involved tackling. They had no murder weapon, because it was sitting on Abby's bookcase. I was sure that some drawn-out process would continue behind closed doors, but as far as the general public was concerned, the saga of Red Guillory's death was over.

We won two more games, improving to 5–8. It wouldn't be enough for the playoffs, but the future in Syracuse looked extremely bright. All that was left now was Red Guillory Day. At our last home game Lexi would wave to the crowd and accept a framed jersey with her dead husband's name on the back, and then a highlight reel of his glory days would play on the Jumbotron. Every time I finalized another part of the celebration, vomit bubbled at the base of my throat.

By mid-December the city was a snow globe. Every day the sky hung low, the color and density of conditioner, before darkness set in by three thirty. The stadium club lounge looked like a Dickens pub when we gathered there for the team holiday party.

We were each given a long, stadium-style Bobcats scarf at the door, and they dangled from necks and shoulders like crimson tinsel. The wide windows showcased the wind and snow swirling around the stadium bowl, while inside two types of bars—open and hot chocolate—kept celebrants warm and happy.

The secondary, in personalized Santa hats, arms slung around each other's shoulders, rapped along to *Christmas in Compton*. A group of kids sat listening to Deon read *Peppa's Christmas* in his trademark aviators and felt reindeer antlers. The music, the bursts of laughter punching through the din from this group or that—all of it served as a reminder that for most of these people football was work and real life was something else, and that those things can and should be separated.

"This is the best food of the year," said Mohammad as he snagged a slab of toasted baguette from a passing caterer's tray. We'd staked out a relatively quiet corner with Mo's husband, Sal, who gave me a knowing smile. "Look," Mo said, angling its marbled white topping toward me. "Ricotta and artichoke hearts with black pepper."

"Looks amazing." I sipped around the lemon slice in my hot toddy and wished I'd ordered something stronger.

"Computers and canapés," said Sal. "That's my man." He was gangly to Mo's stoutness, and soft-spoken to his bombast. They met ten years ago in a walk-to-run group and got married on the *Maid of the Mist* below Niagara Falls.

A waiter appeared at my elbow with a tray of sliders, a single tot speared atop each like a jaunty little hat. I turned to reach for one and froze. Past the waiter, by the acrylic-sock skating rink set up near the back corner, DeMario sat next to Faith. His injured leg was straight out in front, but they'd pulled chairs up to the edge of the rink and were throwing fluffy fake snowballs at their three kids. A pile of the snowballs sat in DeMario's lap, where he and Faith held hands.

We hadn't talked since that day in my office. It hurt, but I would rather have him be furious with me over the truth than friendly through a lie.

"It's nice that he's here," said Sal, following my gaze. "Do you think he'll end up working in the front office?"

"I could totally see him in player development," said Mo. "Don't you think?" And then, when I didn't answer, "Pop?"

I snapped out of it. "Sorry—yeah, he'd be great. In fact, I should mention that to Asbel." I'd been avoiding him ever since my meeting with Abby, because when he told me Abby had made a "complaint," he'd chosen that word carefully. He'd kept the word *rape* for himself. Would I have reacted differently if he'd made that fact available? I wanted to think so, but then, looking again at DeMario, I wasn't so sure. Putting in a good word was the literal least I could do. I quickly scanned the room. "Where *is* Asbel?"

Mo shrugged. "Haven't seen him since the tree was lit."

"Hmm." Something nagged at me, some piece I'd overlooked. "Hey, Mo—does anyone get access to our text messages? From our work phones?"

He shook his head. "Emails are fair game—those live on our system—but no one here would be able to see texts even if they wanted to. They're not in our cloud." I was just about to go find myself another drink when he corrected himself. "Well . . ."

"What?"

"It's just—one thing about those shitty ancient phones is that facial recognition isn't great. If someone had physical access to your phone and a really good-quality photo of you, they might be able to unlock it." He scanned the room. "Why, were you texting about someone? Who do we hate?"

A good-quality photo. Like the staff headshots.

Suddenly the room felt overfull, and stale. "Sorry," I said. "Be back in a minute."

The hallway connecting the stadium and our offices was cold and empty with the staff enjoying the party. I drew in great breaths, but the air was brackish and caught on the way down, choking me on my own secrets.

The lights were off in the coaches' wing—everyone would leave from the club lounge. My nose caught the familiar corporate smell of toner and old coffee.

251

And then, a light spilling out of Asbel's office. Remembering the time we sat together drinking Red's whiskey, I quickened my pace. I'd thought we were two of a kind. I thought we understood each other. But he knew who Red was all along.

I opened my mouth as I rounded the corner, a slick remark from my reserve collection ready to fire, when I came to the doorway and froze. Something thick forced its way to the base of my throat. My spine turned to oak, my blood burst from its veins, splashing and spilling inside me. I tried to scream, but nothing came out, just the stabbed-in-the-stomach guttural push of air out and away and then nothing.

As I'd thought, Asbel was in his office. But he wasn't alone.

Because there, under his arm, bodies touching from shoulder to hip, beaming up at him with a familiarity that grabbed my stomach and yanked, was Chloe.

CHAPTER TWENTY-NINE

NOW

"*No!*"

My body propelled itself forward before I knew what I was doing. I didn't remember crossing the room, I didn't remember raising my arms. As soon as I saw them together everything went white, I could hardly see. And then I was rushing past a shocked Chloe, and the fabric of Asbel's shirt was in my hand, and I was yanking him down toward me while my other hand closed to a fist and drew back—

"Don't!" Chloe's voice was far away, she was yelling from underwater. And then my fist connected with stubbled skin, and my knee raised sharply between Asbel's legs. He pitched forward in pain and Chloe was still screaming and I wanted to hit him again and again, but in the end he was bigger and stronger than me, and when I wound up for a second punch Asbel caught my fist in his palm and forced it down.

"Poppy, *stop.*" I stared disbelieving at the corner of his lip. There was blood there—I'd done that, I'd never hit a person before in my life, but seeing him touching her had brought out something animalistic in me, had switched off any reason or logic or propriety.

My fingers ached, but I longed to hit him again. And again and again and again. *That was what Abby said.* When she saw Red that night in his office, everything had gone white for her. Did she know what she was doing when she bashed his brains in, or had she come to afterward, gasping, and been horrified to see what she'd done? What condition would Asbel be in right now if I'd been holding something heavy in my hands? There is a point where a person who has been pushed so long for so hard and held it together, and smiled, and held it together, and swallowed it down, simply cannot take it anymore. And in that moment, anyone can snap.

Tears filled my eyes and turned everything to blurred shapes until I blinked and they sharpened into focus. The two of them were standing there, Chloe several paces behind Asbel, whose arm was stretched out protectively, holding her back.

"*You* stop," I managed. "All of you, *just stop.* Can't you control yourselves? Don't you have any sense of—"

"She's my niece."

"What?" He'd spoken in shapes, I couldn't make sense of it.

"My sister's daughter." Asbel gave Chloe a look I couldn't see that must have told her to stay put, because she hung back as he advanced slowly, his open palms in front of him patting the air. "We didn't tell anyone because I've always been such an asshole about nepotism hires."

I was still struggling to put it together. "But you're— She's only—"

"Michaela is my half sister, from my father's second marriage. She's fifteen years younger than me, and Belgian. Does that help? Chloe's postgraduate internship fell through, and she needed something else. I made it happen."

My heart was slowing to a sustainable pace, my limbs were responding properly again. But it still didn't make sense. There was too much going on, I was too tired, and my fucking hand hurt. I struggled through the fog and came upon a vital truth, something I couldn't have known that tied it all together. Chloe. Red. Abby.

Asbel.

"Something *did* happen with Red," I said finally. I raised my chin toward Chloe. "Didn't it?"

Chloe's eyes flicked back and forth between Asbel and me, her mouth dropped open into an O. "It was only— He didn't—" she began, but Asbel cut her off with another chop of his palm through the air.

He didn't rape her, she meant. It was *only,* I guessed, something like what happened to me. I hurt so badly for her, and I wanted to tell her to never use that word—*only*—again.

"And then she went to you instead of me because you're family . . . and you believed her."

It was the crux of it all. When Abby told Asbel—when Asbel in turn told me—what Red had done, we'd made our choices. I'd had my reasons and Asbel had his, but we'd both determined that Abby either could or would not be right about him. Because of her dating history. Because I was angry about James. Because of who Red was and what he'd done for this team and this city and our careers and what would happen if we blew that open and how much easier it would all be to just . . . let her slide away.

Twin seasons. One a struggle to stay undefeated and the other the pain of a crumbling legacy. Now they were alike in another way. Did we believe Chloe because times had changed? Because of all the stories that had broken in the past fifteen years showing how very capable powerful men were of this kind of behavior?

Or was it because when Chloe came to Asbel, she came not as a young female intern, but as his niece. His sister's child. It made her more precious, yes, but also more *real.* She was real, and what Red had done was real, the way the death of a friend's parent brought sympathetic murmurs, but the death of your own brought protestations. *No, but you don't understand . . .*

As if he could read my thoughts, Asbel said, "We made a mistake, Poppy. With Abby—we did the wrong thing."

"I know that."

Once, a long time ago, I'd compared the pressures of an undefeated season to the rocks used to crush a man during the Salem witch trials. It felt so stupid now—what did it matter who won or lost? It was just football. It was only a game.

But there was something else I remembered about Salem. The best defense against being called a witch was to name one yourself. I'd dated someone in the office. I'd been seen, several times, coming out of the coach's office after conversations that lingered longer than they should have. The text messages. I'd named a witch. I'd pointed the finger at someone else before it could be aimed at me.

"*I* did the wrong thing," Asbel insisted. "I was the adult. I knew all the facts. It was my fault. And I would have defended him forever. Losing seasons, rabid fans, all that shit. I would have kept him on until we went down together. But after Chloe . . ." He looked at his niece, whose arms were folded tightly in front of her. She looked shocked, stunned. Young. "I was always planning to bring Craig in. I was going to fire Red, not because it was best for the team, but because I couldn't stand his fucking face knowing what he'd done. If Red died instead, then fine, I'd leave him there. Either way, he deserved it."

I'd leave him there . . .

I looked back to Asbel. "But you weren't there. You didn't kill him." I was struggling to tease it out. *Abby* killed him, she'd told me she hit him, because he'd attacked her, but it wasn't true . . .

"You didn't?" Chloe turned to her uncle, looking troubled, but I was sifting through facts. Abby left Red his cell phone, and he'd called both of us. Not Lexi, right upstairs, because how would he have explained who Abby was or why she was in their home at midnight? Or why she'd hit him?

It was the cruelest and most just irony of all—if Red had called his wife, he probably would have made it. She was so close, she could have gotten help. Instead, Red went to the ones who'd protected him for years. Just like Sandra at Looky Lou's had called me when Alec needed to leave in a hurry. Just like dozens of players had come to us when they had a "light" DUI that needed reclassifying or had trashed a hotel room.

"What do you mean?" Asbel said to Chloe, his face twisted in confusion. "How could *I* . . . ?"

I was also struggling. "I don't understand. If you didn't pick up . . ." And then it clicked. "He left you a voicemail, didn't he?"

"It wasn't much." Asbel's jaw was tight with the strain of keeping his own tears in check. "It just said, 'The girl . . .' I found him on the floor. There was blood everywhere, it might have been too late anyway."

"No, it wasn't."

"I didn't kill him. I just didn't save him."

Now I understood.

Fifteen years ago, when Red needed Asbel's help, Asbel had cleaned up his mess. He'd made Abby go away. But not this time. This time, he'd left Red, the life seeping out of him and onto the floor. He'd backed away. Because when Red said, "the girl," he meant Abby. Of course Red would call a forty-year-old woman that, and of course he didn't even remember her fucking name. But when *Asbel* heard that, he thought "the girl" was Chloe. He thought it was Chloe who'd been there that night, Chloe who'd struck him for what he did to her. And he was willing to let Red die to protect her.

And as for Bernie's tip . . . I glanced at Chloe, still bodily behind her uncle. All those times that I'd asked, *Are you sure there's nothing you want to tell me? Nothing about Red?*—she'd been bursting with it. It must have destroyed her keeping that quiet, watching me plan Red Guillory Day. I'd even assigned her tasks to help. But she thought that her uncle killed Red because of what she'd confided to him. And she wouldn't risk getting Asbel in trouble.

I'd been almost right, thinking that she might know something because she delivered the mail. She put that envelope on my desk, and when I got it, it fell open, like it wasn't properly sealed. Since she was carrying her own secrets about Red, when she saw that return address—Truth or Consequences—she needed to know what was inside because maybe there was another way to make sure Red didn't get away with it. He was dead, but his legacy was alive and well. And that couldn't stand.

When weeks passed and nothing happened, she'd bluffed. I left my phone on my desk all the time when I ran to the bathroom or had meetings with Asbel. All she had to do was hold up my head-shot to unlock it. And then she could have read the group chat.

Her eyes were pleading, and I responded with a barely perceptible nod. I wouldn't tell him. All season, even after whatever happened with Red, she'd walked so tall. I'd thought it was over-confidence, but really, it was defiance. Gen Z with social justice tendencies, it must have been ripping her to pieces not to scream out loud who Red really was. But she and her uncle had stayed silent, each thinking they were saving the other.

CHAPTER THIRTY

NOW

"Hey, boss." Rodney ducked his head into my office late Friday afternoon, one week after the party. "I'm heading downstairs for availability. You wanna come? Take a break from your desk?"

"No thanks."

"Come on—I'll let you push the elevator button."

My dad was still sleeping in the ground-floor guest room, unable to navigate the stairs. DeMario wasn't speaking to me. And I lived every day knowing I'd enabled a rapist, that as much as I'd been hurt by this endlessly shitty game of blame the victim, I'd also benefited. I'd used it to my advantage. I didn't deserve this desk, I shouldn't even be sitting here, and so it wasn't the sweet concern behind Rodney's invitation but a disgust at myself and what I was that made me say, "Okay."

Downstairs a TV crew had staked out an unused room to do interviews for a special piece on the Bobcats' resurgence. Alec came out of the other elevator wearing gray jeans and a black Bobcats half zip.

"Thanks for being on time, buddy," Rodney said.

"If you're on time, you're late," said Alec in a military cadence over his shoulder as he walked into the interview room. "Early is on time."

"He seems to be handling everything well," I said. Ever since Coach Washington took over, Alec's game had exploded. The system, with its giant rushing lanes, favored him, but without A.J. on the field he also just seemed looser. More comfortable.

"Well, as my neighbor Mrs. Keller says, it's nice when nice happens to nice." Rodney sent a text, then tooled idly around on his phone until he opened Twitter, when his face went slack as if it was melting. "Oh, fuck . . ."

My stomach dropped. "What?" Wordlessly, he handed me his phone.

It was Alec—pictures of him inside Looky Lou's. On the dance floor, pressed behind a man and whispering in his ear. In the roped-off VIP area with the same man, kissing him tenderly.

"It's everywhere," said Rodney. "Everyone has it."

"Come on . . ." I shook my head in disbelief as I skimmed. A gossip page had shared the photos of Alec with the caption "Bobcats RB Alec Burgos's impressive chemistry with new QB Will Campbell might be down to more than just reps. The duo are regulars at Syracuse gay bar Looky Lou's, where they enjoy private rooms, top-shelf bottle service, and exclusive rights to the back door."

In tandem, we looked toward the interview room. Alec was in there now, on camera, and maybe the broadcasters hadn't seen this, since it just broke, but maybe they had. Either way, it wouldn't be long.

Reading my mind, Rodney said, "You want me to grab him?"

"No—if you parachute in there and pull him out, it's going to look like we think this is worst thing that could happen."

"Yeah, but if we don't, they could blindside him with it."

I spun around once, found what I was looking for by the bathrooms. Then I walked calmly over to the little red box, opened its front, and pulled the fire alarm.

*

"That is . . . fucked up."

Alec and I were in my office while the rest of the building waited outside for the fire department. I'd grabbed him in the lobby and circled back here so that I could tell him, over the scream of the sirens, that his private life was now very public.

"Listen," I said, furious. "We'll talk to Kurt, he's incredibly good at this kind of thing. He can go full Liam Neeson mode, and you'll be wearing that guy's fingernails as a necklace. And as for Will, that's no—I mean, obviously it's not a problem, that's great, and we're just here to support you however you need."

"*Eh-hah.*" Alec's chortled laugh stopped my rambling. "Oh man, a white lady's upset, I'm saved. You gonna post a rainbow square for me? You got a stash of poster board and some markers behind your desk? I don't think we need Kurt in here to crack the code. I've been going to Lou's for years, and no one's ever leaked a photo. It's not about me—it's about Will. He's not gay, but who do you think benefits by getting in his head?"

I blanched. "A.J.'s an ass, but I don't think he'd—"

"Then you don't know him that well." Alec's voice was hard, his smile gone. For three beats there was nothing but the bleat of the sirens. Then he hopped onto the edge of my desk, weight balanced in his flat palms, and gave me a wry look. "You really pulled the fire alarm for me? Let me see your hand—do you have ink on your hand?"

"That's only for schools." I sat next to him. Alec's toes just barely touched the floor; mine dangled. "I'm sorry."

"I mean, it wasn't a secret, it was just private. I don't want to be giving speeches, you know?"

"I know."

He nudged me with his shoulder. "I still appreciate you."

*

My next call was to Omar, who I could tell from the sounds of wind and grinding truck gears was outside. "If it isn't my favorite media mastermind."

"We need to talk. You've seen it?"

Omar coughed. "I've seen it."

"We're not letting this slide. It's against the player code of conduct, and I've already talked to Asbel," I bluffed. "We're filing a formal complaint."

"Wait, wait." There was a pause when Omar must have ducked inside somewhere, because when he spoke again the background noise was gone. "First of all, what makes you think A.J.'s responsible?"

"I'm telling you as a courtesy. It's getting filed before Sunday. I don't want him dressing." Sunday was the last home game. Red Guillory Day.

"Poppy, come on. I know you have this personal thing against him, that's . . . you've worked together a long time. And he's not the easiest person to get along with, I'll grant you that. But you're too smart to blow up your own team's superstar. It's symbiotic—he helps you too."

"Not anymore he doesn't."

Omar was trying to maintain his silky-smooth voice, but I could hear frustration building around the edges of the syllables. "Think about this—he was in a public place, no one invaded his privacy. Sandra will be thrilled with the publicity, and in this day and age, why should Alec feel like he has to hide? A.J. is ready to put his full, superstar public support behind him. This is a *good* thing. Everybody wins."

I interlaced my fingers and squeezed as hard as I could because I'd really, really wanted to be wrong. "How do *you* know Sandra?"

I heard Omar's breaths through the phone, closed my eyes, and imagined that I could feel them on my cheek.

"Come on, Poppy," he said finally, his voice low. Pleading. "We understand each other, you and me."

"No."

"We do the hard stuff that other people don't have the stomach for. We see an advantage and we *take* it. We're doers, Poppy, both of us. It's why we have this . . . thing. Don't—you know. Don't throw it away. Over this."

A tear bumped against my lips, pressed so hard together that they nearly disappeared. I opened my drawer and looked at my note. *Slow. Confident. Calm.*

But since there wasn't actually anything to say, I disconnected the call without saying anything at all.

CHAPTER THIRTY-ONE

NOW

Friday afternoon, late enough that I could credibly hope she wouldn't pick up, I dialed the number for Abby's firm. Her direct line rang three times before she picked up with a stiff "What, Poppy?"

"I need to talk to you. I know you didn't kill—"

"Are you out of your fucking mind?" she hissed. "Not that I have any idea who or what you're talking about, but I'll call you on my cell. Give me twenty minutes."

I was back in the club lounge, cleared of the holiday decorations and ready for the last game of the season. Rows of empty silver steam trays, their domed lids gaping open like fish mouths, lined the walls. While I waited for Abby's call, I leaned against the oversized windows and took in the stadium. It was so cold the grass looked gray, and the goalposts trembled against the wind.

"I find it curious," Abby said briskly when I picked up her return call, "that you now say you *know* I didn't kill Red, since I told you that the last time we spoke. It almost sounds to me like you didn't believe me, Poppy."

"I have a lot to apologize for. I don't even know how to begin to do it—"

"I don't want your apologies."

"I know." The line crackled in silence, and then I went on. "I have a friend—a reporter. I know she'd love to tell your story. I'm ready to own up to everything in my part of it—all of it. On the record. We could release it tomorrow, right when the ceremony starts. We could make sure everyone knows exactly who he was."

I was practically panting, a mix of nerves and excitement. I'd have to quit my job, if I was even allowed to do that before I was fired. Everything I'd cherished about my life would be gone. But it would be worth it to prove that no, I wasn't like Omar. Or Asbel. I didn't just take and manipulate and step on. I could be better.

"No."

I blinked. "What?"

"No, I don't want that. I have a husband, I have kids. I don't want it out there."

"But—"

"You don't get to *fix* this, Poppy. You missed your chance for that. I have a life now, and I don't want to reduce myself to a trending topic. I don't want weirdos outside my house or hate mail sent to work. I don't want my students looking at me and wondering how fuckable I was when I was twenty-five. I don't want any of it. Red's dead, that's good enough for me, and you're going to have to just sit with this."

I'd imagined it all so clearly: Red's video would reach its crescendo, soaring music over pulsing shots of Super Bowl after Super Bowl, trophies hoisted, confetti, and parades, and end on a close-up shot of Red, eyes blazing into the distance . . . with no one watching. Instead, almost every fan would have their phone out.

But Abby didn't want that. And it wasn't my story, it was hers.

"Abby," I said desperately, "I'm trying to help. I want to own up to what I did."

"You don't get to."

*

Everything within me wanted to burst out screaming until my voice was gone and my lips were chapped, and the entire world knew exactly who and what Red Guillory really was. Maybe then I could sleep again. Maybe then I wouldn't have to spend the rest of my life avoiding mirrors. But with Abby, Asbel, and Chloe all locked up tight by their own motivations, there was no way to do it. There was no place to go with what I knew.

Except, I finally realized, for one.

*

It took almost twenty minutes to tell the whole story over Zoom, but the WAGS sat there, listening. Faces drooped and heads were in hands, but no one signed off in disgust, and when I was done, they were still there.

"Holy shit," Nisha said after a minute of silence. "That's like a real murder."

"Why didn't you tell us about Bernie's note?" Dayanna said. Her hands hovered like she wanted to reach through the screen to hug me or throttle me or both. "Why would you deal with that alone?"

Annika shook her head. "I get why. Oh, Poppy."

Sarah said nothing for a moment, just pressed her lips together hard. Then she leaned forward. "I've covered a lot of these, and I've talked to a lot of victims. You know it wasn't your fault."

"No, I know," I scoffed. "He was totally unjustified."

"No, Pop, I mean what happened with Abby. What you did. That wasn't your fault."

I squirmed in my seat. "I don't know about—"

"It's a thing, with victims. They, like, reclassify it as a way to protect themselves, so that it's not the worst thing to ever happen to them. It's how they manage to keep getting out of bed in the morning. *That would be unsurvivable, and so this wasn't that. I'm good. I'm okay.* And then when it happens to someone else, that transfers—

266

come on, it wasn't that bad—or else the whole thing comes tumbling down. And Poppy," her voice got softer, "a *lot* of victims stay close with their attackers, for the same reason. There's nothing wrong with you."

"Yeah, for sure." I blinked furiously. There would be a time, later, to consider what she'd said more carefully, but right now I could not. Right now I needed to stay upright. I cleared my throat, and then cleared it again, harder. "So I guess it's just going to stay this way. Red's dead and everyone still loves him. Abby goes back to her life, Asbel and Chloe figure out how they're going to deal with things, and I . . ."

I had no idea. I had *no* fucking idea.

"And what about everything else, with Alec?" Nisha asked.

The story was huge when it came out. The idea that two NFL players on the same team were dating broke the brains of a lot of fans who had no idea that even though *this* pairing wasn't real, it would hardly have been unprecedented. I mean, come on. The usual people said the usual dumb things, and then a second wave of people said the usual how-dare-theys in response, and then the cycle wore itself out when something else happened. And A.J. skated past, as usual.

"Do you know," I huffed, "that he made me get him a fake dog?" I explained the saga around Noodles, which left the others shaking their heads.

"I mean . . ." Nisha trailed off.

"What?"

She waved a hand at the screen. "Whatever—forget it."

"*What?*"

"It's just . . . not his first time with that."

I had no idea what she was talking about. "Can you just say it? I don't think I can deal with anything else cryptic at this point."

Nisha tucked her hair behind her ears. "Okay, well, you know when he and Roxanna broke up." We nodded. A.J.'s long-term relationship with an early-aughts pop star who also happened to be the most beautiful woman I'd ever seen in real life had ended publicly and messily a few years before. "Do any of you know why?"

"He cheated on her, right?" said Dayanna.

"That was the rumor," Nisha said, "and his team didn't refute it because no one cares if he cheated on her, but a *lot* of people would care about the real story. So while Roxanna was on that big arena tour, her dog stayed with A.J. During the European leg, she was papped at a beach club with that guy from Real Madrid."

"Oh, I remember that," said Annika. "He was rubbing sunscreen on her, right?"

Dayanna snorted. "Something like that."

"Wait," Sarah said, "how do *you* know all this?"

"My cousin is a celebrity assistant, and her friend worked for Roxanna once, and she'd kept in touch with the next assistant. You know how those chains go. Anyway, so . . . I have to get this out, it's horrible. I'm warning you guys now."

I'd just gotten through a murder in my backyard and hadn't felt this anxious.

Nisha went on, "A.J. saw the photos and got mad, so he told his supplements guy to dump the dog at a shelter—it's not like he could do it himself, because he'd be recognized. I don't know the details about this next part, whether it was on purpose or the assistant is an idiot—"

"He is," I put in.

"Well, regardless, when A.J. cooled down and sent him back there a few days later, the dog was gone. *Hopefully* it got adopted out, but it was a kill shelter and they just . . . don't know. They don't actually know what happened to it."

All our hands flew to our faces. This was sick beyond sick. It was unthinkable. I didn't have any words for it beyond that.

"But why didn't Roxanna tell people?" asked Dayanna. "Why didn't she tell *everyone*?"

"Because he told her on the first night that he'd donated her dog like a fucking sweater, and she didn't come home. She finished the tour."

"She'd be eviscerated." Annika shook her head. "It's much better for her—especially after those photos—if people think he cheated."

"But how could you not tell *me*?" I asked.

"He's your quarterback!" Nisha practically yelled. "What was I supposed to do? It's rumors, first of all, and second, what would you have done if I had told you?" She paused. "Also, don't take this the wrong way, but . . . I thought maybe you already knew."

That hurt, but what could I say when ten minutes ago I'd told them about the rape I'd helped cover up?

"*God,* I am so sick of this!" I slammed my hands on my coffee table. "I am so tired of bad people getting away with whatever they want because they're too valuable to take down."

We sat in silence, five women scattered around the country, alone but together. If anyone asked, I would have said these were the most competent people I knew, that if someone needed something done, properly, now, these were the women to call. So . . . why couldn't I be the one asking?

"What if . . ." The plan formed slowly as I clicked through the implications. Personal. Professional.

Legacy.

Red was dead. He was untouchable. But this—this I could do.

"What if we didn't let him get away with it this time?"

Nisha made a face. "What does that mean?"

"Well, Sarah, you said you don't report these kinds of stories because we're friends. What if I gave you the go-ahead?"

"A three-year-old story based on multiple levels of hearsay?" She looked doubtful.

"Okay, but," I warmed up, "now it's not hearsay, because you'd have a named source on the fake rescue dog."

"Who?"

I raised an eyebrow.

"Poppy," Annika said, "I don't know about that. Didn't you direct your intern to get the dog in the first place? You're going to be the one to take the hit."

"I know. I can handle it."

"But you shouldn't have to!" Now Dayanna was the one who was frustrated.

"I don't think it has to be anything that formal," said Nisha. "We are living in the golden age of unsubstantiated rumors—all we have to do is each throw a little piece out there and let the Internet do its thing."

*

If the world was a fair place, Red Guillory Day would have been dark and wet and freezing. He deserved to have an anemic crowd sheltering in the concourse until the moment of kickoff, his hype video playing to a stadium of empty seats echoing back nothing but silence. But the weather was unseasonably warm, with traitorous December sunshine that drew winter-weary Syracusans outside. Hours before kickoff, the lots were jammed with fans in sweatshirts and sunglasses cracking open their first beers at ten o'clock in the morning. Red was dead, and that was going to have to be good enough.

It had been years since I'd taken a walk among the tailgaters, but I did that day. In my red power suit, I walked past open hatchbacks with full buffets, past sizzling grills and outstretched hands offering me a coney, a Styrofoam bowl of chicken riggies cooked over a hot plate. I remembered selling packets of M&Ms in the parking lot at my father's games for a dollar apiece, the way my mother would slip four quarters into the cash box and let me choose what I thought was the fattest bag.

"Heads up!" A beanbag landed at my feet, and I tossed it back to a group playing cornhole. The boards had been painted so that the target was Red's open mouth.

Usually at kickoff I was in the press box, but today, because of the ceremony, I was at field level. At fifteen minutes to go, the stadium was packed. The teams were tucked up in their tunnels, ready to run out as soon as the ceremony concluded, and without them the field felt strangely empty. I glanced once at my watch—it should be soon.

You're sure? came the text.

"Ladies and gentlemen," said the public address announcer now. *"Please rise as we honor legendary Bobcats head coach . . . Reeeeeeeeeeeeeeeed Guillory!"*

The video started with clips of Red in his playing days, first at college and then briefly in the NFL. The footage was intentionally low-res to make him seem like a ghost from a beloved bygone era, a nostalgia bomb, and the crowd loved it. All calls for Red Guillory to be fired were long gone, lost to the forgotten history of last September.

But as the video played on, a funny thing happened. Instead of keeping their eyes locked on the Jumbotron, the fans started checking their phones. They leaned over the rows in front of them to peek toward the tunnel. They looked at the time. *They're bored.* They'd already moved on, to Alec and Craig Washington and the new, exciting chapter that was unfolding. Red was yesterday's hero. And it was almost kickoff.

Red's secrets would stay with him. He wouldn't be outed as the weak and abusive man that Abby, Chloe, and I knew him to be, but he *would* be forgotten. He would be left behind. And that, I realized, looking around with an amazed smile, more than anything else, would have killed him.

I'm ready, I wrote to the group chat. And five phones hit Send on five carefully crafted messages, each one containing a piece of the puzzle about A.J.'s behavior, past and present—just enough to raise some questions and pique curiosity. They would stumble their way toward each other across the Internet, picking up speed and attention like snowballs down a hillside until they met in the middle with a mighty crash that would take out an icon forever.

I looked toward the tunnel, now clogged with the team jumping in place and ready to run onto the field. Bobcats football would go on without Red. It would go on without A.J., it would go on without Asbel if he ever retired, and if I walked out of here today and never came back it would certainly go on without me.

The difference was that now I knew I would go on without it, too. There was more to me than this team, and this job, and there were things I wasn't willing to hide anymore in order to protect them. As the team burst out of the tunnel and onto the field, the fans lowered their phones and cheered.

Acknowledgments

Sue Edson and Pete Moore at Syracuse University Athletic Communications made me fall in love with working in sports. Special thanks to Susie Mehringer, Marlene Ouderkirk, and Joyce Hergenhan, three women I admire who helped me immeasurably.

I am extremely grateful for the experiences I had working in the NFL, which were some of the most enjoyable times of my life. Pat Hanlon, Peter John-Baptiste, and Avis Roper at the New York Giants hired female PR interns when that was not a common practice and went out of their way to find opportunities for me. They set a standard in 2006 that would still be a high bar today. Thank you to Mike Eisen for always correcting my stats math. Stacey James, Jeff Cournoyer, and Casey O'Connell at the New England Patriots brought me on a PR master class through an undefeated regular season, culminating in "my" two teams facing off in the greatest Super Bowl of all time. Scott Barboza and Christy Huggins helped me recall the details, a fun and triggering walk down memory lane. Interning for the Patriots during that particular season was our Real World—a bonding experience that no one else will ever fully understand.

Thank you to the coaches, staff, and players of the 2007 Frankfurt Galaxy.

ACKNOWLEDGMENTS

This book made its way to you because Andrea Somberg read an early draft and gently suggested that I add a plot. She's an incredible agent—kind, professional, and so very good at what she does. Thank you to Rich Green for handling the TV/film side of things so adeptly.

Ellie Pritchett's smart and insightful edits focused this story and made it so much stronger. I was also very touched by the amount of support she offered throughout the publication process. I'm incredibly grateful to the entire Doubleday team. Thank you to Jessica Deitcher, Kayla Steinorth, Michael Goldsmith, Nora Reichard, Soonyoung Kwon, Chris Zucker, Kristen Bearse, Maddie Partner, and Rosalie Wieder.

Thank you to Sara Herchenroether, Ashley Tate, Georgia Howard, and the 2024 debut group for being the best. My husband and agent unknowingly thank you, too, for intercepting so many freak-outs before they made their way up the ladder.

Katie Strang has been encouraging my writing since my first, terrible book twelve years ago, and to have the support of someone who does what she does at the level she does it is a gift. Hayley Levine solved many a plot hole while hiking with me, and sometimes we even remembered the details by the time we got back to the car.

I have, quite simply, the best parents in the world, and the older I get, the more I realize what a gift that is. When I told them I'd sold my book they cheered but didn't blink, because they'd always believed I would. My sister Stephanie is my first and best friend. Steph, I enjoy being sisters with you. Nanci Staple and Mike Hadjistavrou, I love you for many reasons, but I'm particularly grateful we can share and talk about books together. My grandmother Carolyn Long is one of the most important people in my life. When she sees articles about this book, she will cut them out and save them in her Grandchild Filing System, under B for Beth.

It's all peaks, no pits with Elliot, Annie, and Rosie. I'm so thankful for those three.

Every day is better with Arthur in it. He is the funniest, most interesting person I know, and I love him.

ABOUT THE AUTHOR

Elizabeth Staple is an attorney. Prior to law school, she worked in media relations for the New York Giants, the New England Patriots, Frankfurt Galaxy, and Syracuse University Athletic Communications. She was a member of the NFL media relations staff at three Super Bowls and has also worked in events for Madison Square Garden, the PGA, and the NCAA Men's March Madness tournament. She lives in Connecticut with her husband and three children.